fatso

Born in Norway in 1974, award-winning
Lars Ramslie has published four other
novels: *Biopsi*, *Mikrokakos*, *Destroyer* and
Ugly Bugly. *Fatso* is his first novel to be
translated into English and is soon to be
made into a feature film.

Deborah Dawkin and Erik Skuggevik have
worked as a team on a variety of literary
translations. Deborah trained as an actress
and worked in theatre for ten years. As well
as working as a director and teacher, she
has written creatively and dramatised for
the stage. Erik lectures in Translation
Studies at the Universities of Surrey and
Westminster and is currently working on a
PhD in Translation and Culture.

fatso

LARS RAMSLIE

Translated from the Norwegian by
DEBORAH DAWKIN AND ERIK SKUGGEVIK

NEW
ISLAND

Original text copyright © 2003 Lars Ramslie

Translation © 2006 Deborah Dawkin and Erik Skuggevik

Fatso
First published 2006
by New Island
2 Brookside
Dundrum Road
Dublin 14

www.newisland.ie

Original edition published by Forlaget Oktober AS 2003

The moral right of the author has been asserted.

isbn 1 905494 12 2

This translation has been published with the financial support of NORLA.

The publisher acknowledges the financial assistance of Ireland Literature Exchange (Translation Fund), Dublin, Ireland. www.irelandliterature.com, info@irelandliterature.com

Quotation from *On the Road* by Jack Kerouac (Copyright © Jack Kerouac 1955, 1957) is reproduced by kind permission of A. M. Heath & Co. Ltd.

Quotation from 'Full Tank' by Raga Rockers is reproduced by kind permission of Michael Krohn.

British Library Cataloguing in Publication Data.
A CIP catalogue record for this book is available from the British Library.

Book design by Fidelma Slattery @ New Island
Printed in the UK by Mackays

10 9 8 7 6 5 4 3 2 1

If it's dreams you want, go to the movies
If it's cash you're after, go to the bank
But if you're searching for love, go no further,
I've got what you need, full tank.

                                    Michael Krohn

Offer them what they secretly want and they of course
immediately become panic-stricken.

                        Jack Kerouac, *On the Road*

I would have screwed you so fucking hard. It would have been the greatest fuck of your life.

I would have pinned you down in front of me and pounded and pounded you as you slid up and down. Pinned down.

Deep fucked you in your throat, and at the same time thrust my tongue way up inside you and licked your wet pussy till it ran over your thighs. Wrenched you round, grabbed your hair and pounded into you from behind till your brains blew. Cleaved your ass apart. Pounded till you screamed. Rammed in your pussy, jacked my rod in your throat. Then tossed you round and screwed you, and screwed you again.

Then I'd have squirted you so chockful of cum that you'd be forced to swallow it down to stop yourself drowning.

And my cream would flow and flow from you.

For days.

If you'd only let me try. But of course you're not about to. And never in the world could I do those things. You see, more than anything I want to *give* something of myself. From deep within. If only I had the chance, for one short moment. If things weren't so shallow, then I could prove how caring I can be, and how totally devoted. Perhaps, one day, if you could just see beyond everything else, see what's inside me, and if I could find the courage and just ask you. If, for example, I just said: *'Hi. I like you'* or *'You know what? You're...cute. Would you like to...'*

Because I reckon I could really love someone.

For real.

I think I could have had a girlfriend. It shouldn't really be so hard. If only I had the opportunity to show there's more to me. If I could show that I'm a good person. Reliable and good. That I can be kind and thoughtful. If only I could just get to know someone. If only someone would take the time to get to know me.

I need somebody to love.

But I'll never be allowed to even get close to experiencing anything of the sort. No one's going to want to waste their time on someone like me. It's a million miles off. Light years.

Single

Fatso

Because. I'm fat. I'm dull. Just fat and dull. One desperately, pathetically dull man. That's all I am. People stare at me, heads leaning into one another. It's plain to see from way off: there goes one fat, tiresome misfit. I press a pale, short, stubby and sweaty finger into the release button for the gate and a buzzing noise issues from the lock. On my way to the gate I dump a bag of rubbish; plastic and cardboard takeaway boxes, empty crisp packets, wank wipes and some old stuck-together pages torn from *Men Only* that I'd barely remembered having, but which I found lying there in my basement storeroom when I was hunting for a pair of tracksuit bottoms last night.

The iron gate hums open and this one boring, fat individual exits, swinging out of the courtyard and making his way down Thorvald Meyer's Street. The café terraces have already been serving for a while. From up in my flat I can only watch as far as the first table. That's as close as I ever get. I had plans of setting myself up with a pair of binoculars or a telescope just so I could *see* down there. Truth is, I've not once actually considered sitting there. For almost ten years now I've been content just to watch.

It's difficult to say what comes first: whether I'm a misfit because I'm fat, or fat because I've always been an outsider. And I can't understand why I'm expected to be so particular about how I dress, just because I'm fat. I've never spent much money on clothes. My glasses are the same ones I've worn since sixth form. My father bought them with a view to nothing but their practicality.

As I pass people and places along the street it's like I'm being exposed to radiation. It's like my body is passing through the field of some strange electric force. I never lift my gaze: I'm not permitted to stare, failures are never permitted to stare. *What the fuck are you staring at?* they all think. People and places become shapeless splodges or shadows of movement on the edge of my horizon.

But then it's as if something clicks, and I look up and I can't get my eyes off her midriff, her buttocks, the curve of her back, the cleft of her crotch, her neck or her breasts. But I can never imagine having any of this for myself, because I'm fat and ugly, aren't I. The only eyes I ever meet when I finally do look up examine me as though I'm something the park keeper overlooked. Something that ought not to exist. Fat people are only allowed to be attractive when their skin is smooth and brown all over, when their teeth are white and they're forever happy.

No one's looking at me. I pass unnoticed. My sole experience is one of rejection. People see me, but at the same time they don't see me.

My skin's like a hog's, white as skimmed milk with reddish, almost golden hair, beard and eyebrows. I'm not even really fat enough: I'm overweight, but not enough; not so my features are round and soft so you'd want to cuddle me. Instead my fat is grotesquely firm, like I've smeared silicon or something all over my body.

I could carry on for hours. Go on and on about my enormous nose and grey-coloured eyes under my puffy eyelids, but I oughtn't. I know it's irksome. Which is why I keep my mouth shut when I'm invited to parties. But then again, I don't get invited to parties. To get invited to parties, you have to know people, you have to have a social life. Something I don't have because I never say anything, because nobody wants to get to know me. I'd have nothing to say anyway. The only thing I'm moderately good at is my job, it's my only interest: and my job is the dullest thing about me. If I were to open my mouth more than was strictly necessary, everybody would think what I said was dull. Perhaps not if I was good-looking, but I know what everybody thinks. I've heard them say it; at school, in sixth form, at college, when friends back then tried to persuade me to go to parties, when people thought I couldn't hear – *he's just such a bore*.

Company parties are the only ones I go to. But everyone's at least ten years older than me there. And there's only one female member of staff. It's an insignificant, meaningless job. The only advantage of my job is that I don't have to go in more than two days a week. I work from home most of the time. My dad owns the flat where I live. My mum died when I was nine.

I am thirty-four and what have I achieved?

Nothing.

There are people outside Bar Boca. A lady with blue trousers cut low on her hips jumps up and down two or three times to stay warm, or from happiness or impatience. I gaze over at her; she must be frozen. She has two nice dimples in the small of her back. Then I notice the look I'm getting from the bloke beside her. I know: don't look, don't touch. He swivels round and signals to his mate, who looks across at me.

But his glance isn't aggressive; it's utterly indifferent. Fat-Rino has been caught ogling again. Nothing more. Like some old mongrel staring up at her.

Chicken

It's as if the parcel's transparent. My fingers are stained blue from the queuing ticket at the post office. But the wimp at the counter cocks his head to one side, and on his way back from the post room he turns the parcel this way and that, before pulling himself up sharply and opening the flap. Lying inside the parcel are two DVDs from blackgirlweb.com. I've put off their collection until I got the reminder. It's always the same. When I put an order in I generally put an additional one in for a family film or something. Just to have an alibi ready.

'What's that written there?' asks the clerk, pointing at my signature.

I lean over the form.

'Rino Hanssen,' I answer. 'With two esses.'

Truth be known, it says Mickey Mouse in one long scrawl.

'Right. OK.' He gives a toss of the head, shoves the parcel towards me and shuts the flap.

With the parcel in both hands I wait for him to buzz for the next in the queue. Then I quickly walk out of the post office, across Olaf Rye's Square and nip into Mega for a six-pack of beer, a pack of toilet paper, a pack of kitchen rolls and two packs of frozen chicken.

In the queue I find myself accidentally ogling the checkout girl's breasts. Which of course she registers with an irritated glance before turning to the customer she's serving.

8

But my point is this: if it had been any other man sneaking a look at her breasts, it would scarcely have bothered her. But it was me staring. Naturally, it had to be that repulsive fat-ass at the end of the queue watching her.

And what does he have in that discreetly wrapped parcel of his? You guessed it: porn.

And he loves it.

He loves watching naked women. He's nothing but a peeping Tom, a voyeur who watches every woman with his pig-cunt eyes. Yeah, go ahead. Get pissed off that that fatso's ogling your tits. Let me be the one to ruin your day. Feel the pang, that little pang of anxiety in your heart, that little voice that tells you what league you might suddenly be relegated to. Let me be the mark for how attractive you are. Nobody looks at you any longer, the only blokes you attract these days are fatsos and nutters: from now on we're all that's available to you. Times are gone when those cute guys drove you away from your high-rise suburbia in their new-fitted cars. You can't pick and choose at the disco any more. If it finishes between you and your fella, that's all that's in store. You'll be sitting here, day in and day out, shoving frozen goods down the conveyor belt and thinking: *Keep your eyes to yourself, fatty!*

Fucking hell, you think to yourself, work would have been reasonably all right, if it wasn't for those repulsive fatsos that want to gawp at my tits the whole time. That repulsive fatso, fucking *loser*...peeping Tom. Why do *I* have to go attracting blokes like that?

Because you really are worth a whole lot more, aren't you?

'D'you know what happened at work today...' you start the minute you come home to the boyfriend, grocery bags in both hands ('cos yeah, that's the way things are these days, he doesn't come to pick you up from work like he used to when you were first in love: you get the tram and change to a bus after waiting forever at the snowed-under stop, carry the bags up the stairs wearing your keys on a string round your neck). 'Shit,' you start. But you get no further. Because you know what?

Your boyfriend has a friend visiting. A special friend. Someone you don't see very often. Some guy you both met in Spain. He is lying stretched out on the sofa in front of the telly, while your boyfriend sits in the armchair with his feet up on the footstool, remote control in one hand and beer in the other. They're watching the football. A friend you don't see very often, and you know why he's here, you know what it means, what he's come for, why he's been invited. You smile all over your face.

You are gonna get dick.

No introductory niceties, you don't need asking, you just glance over at your boyfriend, then step across the floor. Creases still in the palm of your hand from the plastic carriers, you open his mate's flies, the two of you don't even kiss, you open his flies and shove the already very stiff dick into your mouth. Your boyfriend swivels his armchair round towards this performance on the sofa. You, still wearing your shop uniform, a little plastic badge with your name, Catherine, on it, your fingers still smelling of the plastic off the frozen carrots.

You stretch out towards your boyfriend. They lick you all over.

It's like their dicks bury the experience, the memory of that fatso, deep inside you; like it never happened, you're pure. They cum all over your hair, your uniform, your breasts, your face. And the day is saved. There's no way you're boring any more after that. It's the weekend. You're going out. You can gossip with your best friend about it in secret. Or brag about it in the toilets. There are rumours going round about you. You're a lucky bitch. You're desirable. There's always something bigger and better out there for you.

You are *modern*. Which means you're liberated, right? Because the magazines you read tell you nothing else. You live like the celebrities. Life's not over for you. You may be a checkout girl, but that's only provisional, because you have hidden talents: a great singing voice, a poet in your guts, an acting talent to be discovered, sex appeal to be awakened.

And gorgeous, gorgeous tits.

If nothing else, you can always go back to college.

I would have fucked you. So bloody hard. It would have been…wild.

You'd have been crammed to bursting.

Disney

She runs my goods across the scanner with her face turned out towards the shop, staring past me before reading off the total. She's not about to give anything away. I take out my card and hold it up in front of me.

'Cash back?' She scratches her neck disinterestedly, her voice totally mechanical.

I shake my head. Put my card in.

'Excuse me?' she continues after a momentary silence, studying her clasped hands.

'No, thanks,' I say.

'Pin and enter, please.' She throws a bag to the end of the conveyor belt.

But you're damned well not going to sit in judgment on me. Don't you come pointing the finger at me. Don't bloody well come here and moralise about my life. You think I'm so repulsive.

Because you're the beautiful one. You can do anything you want. You can stand about outside cafés with your tight-fitting clothes, posing at parties, at discos and clubs with a dummy in your mouth. You can go about with your bare midriff and take drugs. Go to the gym. You can dress in filthy clothes, use foul language and wade in shit up to your ankles without it mattering. You are the liberated one. If you're beautiful you can permit yourself absolutely anything. You can even be a checkout girl.

You're gorgeous when you wank. You're gorgeous when you take a shit. Your juices are gorgeous. You're gorgeous when your teeth are unbrushed, your feet smell and your armpits are unwashed. You can have group sex, anal sex, buddy sex, sex in public. You can wear latex and leather, you can be perverted for a night. Each day is new. You're an eternal virgin. Eaten is eaten. Forgotten is forgotten. You can travel the world, go to the Mediterranean, join the tourist merry-go-round: play on the beach, enter the competitions at the lock-in discos where they offer you drinks prizes to get your kit off, boozy games of doctors and nurses, you're gorgeous when you puke and your mate holds your hair back on your neck. You can walk through life naked and no one will dare do a thing, you can live off it, you can post it on the net (and you do, I see you. I see you; you're everywhere), this is your industry. Smooth-shaven Disneyland. You have the monopoly over everything.

This is your orgy. Not mine. It's not me who's mad.

I am not repulsive. I am not sick. I am lonely. I am totally alone. I want what you have. But when I want what you have, I become disgusting. I'm obliged to steal from you. Because you also want to have command over who gets to look, who gets to peep.

I want someone to go to bed with.

I want someone to love.

'I've got you on video.' It pops out of me suddenly as I move to the end of the counter. My voice is kind of gruff, since I've scarcely spoken all week. I've just been on my own at home, in and out of bed, working at the computer, watching videos. Fortunately my words fade into a mumble.

'Pardon?' she asks.

I place the frozen chicken in the bag. Rather than politeness, there's nothing but irritable scepticism to be seen in her face.

'Could I have the receipt, please?' I ask, relieved at finding such an obvious means of covering my tracks. I lean towards her. Without answering she rips off the receipt and sends it to the end of the conveyor belt.

I take the stairs in five strides and I'm out.

Perfume on a Pig

I hurry home with my parcel. The sweat pours off me. I want to be in, back home, on my own. I don't want to see another human being for days. Just want to be on my own, open my parcel and be alone. Completely alone. Behind lowered blinds.

The point is this. I can't redefine myself: I'm trapped inside this body, this life. I can't go moving to a new city, a new country, walk into some place and pretend that I'm a new me and make out I'm cool. And I've tried it before; I've lived in loads of places, worked with all sorts of people, studied, lived in student halls. There's not one social scene, not one network where I can feel at ease. Open up. Everyone's always going to think *What the fuck's the matter with that fatso*, or *Who is that jerk?* I can't make pretences, think of things to say. I don't have anything to talk about. What could that possibly be?

I'm on my own with this and that's it. There's nobody there to help me, to support me. I'm sharp enough to see the choices and moves that would have brought me attention, I just lack the advantages to utilise that attention.

On the other hand, perhaps I'm just scared.

But then, I'm so totally alone. Friendless.

These are my best years and things can only get worse.

The Wank Room

The moment I have my parcel over the threshold, I relax. All the anxiety attached to it is replaced by tingling excitement: home, in here I'm safe, I'm alone here, nobody can see me, nobody can peek in, it's dangerous out there, but in here I'm safe. In here I can do what I like without anyone judging me. I can sit for days in front of the screen just feeding new films into the player. The sweat pours off me. I piss for what seems an eternity. And after I've put the oven on I really need a shit.

The living room comprises a table, a corner sofa with matching armchair, a bookshelf filled with work-related reading materials, a rug over the parquet. Two of the windows have curtains, which are pulled to. Behind the curtains, Venetian blinds. The flat is on the top floor, set on a corner overlooking the park and with an L-shaped balcony that follows the living room the whole way round. The white plastic garden furniture has dark stains from the traffic. I hardly go out there.

A double bed. White wardrobes with an extra set of sheets. My clothes. This is the bedroom.

Two greasy, dust-covered dumbbells under the kitchen table. I hardly use the dishwasher. Mouldy dregs in empty beer bottles below the sink and by the fridge. A stiff floorcloth in a bucket. Dad spruces the place up now and again: patches up, paints a room, swaps the fridge.

I walk through to my workroom with my empty plastic bag. The room's at the back, facing across the yard. Two Ikea shelves stacked with videos and DVDs. My PC. In the blind spot to the right of the window is the armchair that belongs with the corner sofa and the other chair out in the living room. Above the blind spot, shelving units with the TV, video and surround system.

I empty the wastepaper basket and start picking up the congealed tissues that lie scattered across the floor. One of the paper balls splits as I pick it up, sticking itself to my fingers, and naturally goes all over my trousers and onto the rug. I rip the cardboard packaging open, stick the DVD cover up on the shelf and feed the player.

Then Dad rings. Still clutching the packaging, remote control and plastic bag, I slump into the chair. I barely listen to what he says; bending forwards, stomach squashed against my knees so I can hardly breathe and the cordless phone wedged between my cheek and shoulder, I gather fistfuls of tissues to put into the bag. But then suddenly the hairs on the back of my head go on end: without any room for discussion Dad tells me he's coming round next week to check the flat. 'I see,' is all I manage to say before he goes on to inform me that he's planning to get a lodger in. *Fuck-fuck-fuck.* Dad says it would be lunacy not to rent out now. What he really means is that it's lunacy not to sell, but since I've evidently dug myself in, he'll make do with renting.

'OK. I see… Which room did you have in mind?' The words falter from my lips. I let the bag drop, short of breath from stooping to pick the wank wipes up, and deeply shaken, I find myself rubbing my hand across my forehead. In the reflection of the darkened TV screen I see my face illumined, my mouth already forming a grimace. I attempt to unravel more toilet paper with my other hand, sending the roll in a trail out of the door. I sit there with three squares of paper and the remains of musty spunk on my face, trousers and hands, and my father answers, unsurprisingly perhaps, that it was this room he had in mind, since it's the largest.

Artificial Desire

For those first hours it's as if everything's stopped still. As if I can't breathe: in a single snap of his fingers, Dad has taken away the only safe haven I had in all the world. My own special room. I go on tidying, on autopilot. In the background the video hammers on, but I'm not up to focusing on it, with its muffled sounds of screaming black girls. And the oven rattles as the thermostat stops, rests, then starts up again without my putting the chicken on. My first reaction is that I've got to move out: I can't stay here any longer. I start to plan my move: how I'll put all my videos in neutral covers and hide them between books. I'll have to buy some books for that. I've got enough money to buy a place of my own, and in the end I'm in high spirits: I can have a new start, a new life, perhaps I'd even grow to be somebody I like.

Then it comes clear to me that it's unlikely to ever turn out that way, that running away would be futile, and quitting my job is a financial impossibility. I'd be dealing with the same faces; the same faces would continue to surround me. I begin instead to imagine my new flatmate. Perhaps they might turn out to be a friend, somebody who might make me feel better, somebody with a life I could become a part of. Something new. I put the chicken in the oven and eat it without cutlery or trimmings, standing at the kitchen worktop.

Standing at the kitchen worktop with hands and chin covered in chicken grease. Fat-ass Rino.

The whole weekend I sit in front of the screen with my new films, as osmosis makes my hands reek of genitals. Spit. Dick. The skin on my fingers starts wrinkling. I wank each film to its conclusion, from one scene to the next, wipe myself, eat, continue. The palm of my hand grows smooth and dry. Smooth-shaven black babes, with oiled butts, hips, thighs, white-soled feet, thick lips and white teeth.

And I eat continually: I empty the freezer, I take a shower and go down to McDonald's, ring Peppe's Pizza and Dolly Dimple's, choose the longest queue at the supermarket so as to avoid the cashier who has great boobs but makes nasty comments, pad down to 7-Eleven for more Coke, crisps and ice cream. Come Saturday afternoon I sit on the floor in front of the TV, a half-empty bottle of Finlandia between my legs. And the remote. *Shag you. This is dick. You like dick? You want dick? Huh?*

I roll over. Imagining a woman. A woman. Lying there next to me on the floor. *Shh…* she says as she wraps her arms about me. *Everything'll be fine. Just relax, it'll be just fine.*

I'm here…

Dream

I have this dream. Of a room. The room doesn't have to be very big. The size of the showers at the swimming baths, perhaps. The walls are clad in smooth, almost soft, tiles. A gentle orange or almost pink light. A room. They are waiting for me here. The room is filled with women. Just women. Packed close. There is only one entrance and exit. The women are smiling. Waiting with large eyes. Fine-scented oils drip from the showerhead in the ceiling. There is enough space for just one more.

I slide in. I am enveloped by bodies: slithering between smooth bellies and breasts, oiled limbs and hands, sinking against hip after hip, eased round the room, sliding, my mouth filled with soft, smooth cunt, smooth tongues and breasts. Covered from head to toe, fucking bodies and in between bodies.

The air is filled with breath, sighs and groans.

I close my eyes.

They all become one.

And they're waiting.

For more and more, without end.

Cock Teaser

On Sunday, I finally put on some clothes and go out to see Edel. She's after money, again. Or a free meal ticket. Something at least. That's what it was last time. I don't have very high expectations. My tweed jacket is already itching from sweat. I regret putting anything so heavy on. My shirt's going to be transparent by the time I reach the restaurant. And since it'll be soaking wet and transparent, I won't take my jacket off in the restaurant. I'll stink. And when I eat, I'll sweat even more.

I sweat because I'm fat.

And why the fuck do I dress like an old maths teacher anyway? And why do I bother going out with Edel? She doesn't like me. She won't sleep with me. She just wants to give me a hard time.

This has got to stop. I've got to come straight out with it: *'This has got to stop. You've got to stop playing games.'* Short and to the point. And then leave. Or: *'Fuck you, Edel, you're not gonna fucking piss around with me, you lousy little cock teaser!'*

Something like that.

I've got dried, yellowish-white gack at the corners of my mouth. I push my finger under my shirt collar, loosening my tie.

Edel

She arrives at the table half an hour late. Dressed in a matching peach-coloured suit. It looks ghastly. She thinks she looks sophisticated with its being simple and in the one colour. A suit, of sorts. As if she had any career. But she's been on sick leave for something like the past five years. She's going nowhere.

Unless she marries money.

'Oh, can't we sit in the window instead?' is the first thing she says. So we move over to a table next to the window. Edel browses through the menu, making the waiter stand there as she pretends to search for a specific wine. She finishes up ordering a glass of the house red.

'I think you should pay this time,' she smiles, smoothing her hand over the pages of the menu.

I've *always* paid, every time we've eaten out together.

'How are you, anyway?' She scans the pages indecisively. 'And your dad?'

'Oh, not so bad...and well...Dad, he's...'

'What is your problem?'

I look up at her.

'I really don't understand why you have to swallow your words all the time. You just drag your words and talk so unbelievably slowly, it's practically impossible to understand a word.'

I lift a hand from the table as if to say something. I really can't grasp what she's talking about.

'What is your problem? Are you trying to give me a bad conscience about something, or what?'

'Of course not.'

'Right, then. Let's find something to eat. But can you please try to talk more clearly?'

The waiter arrives with her glass of wine. She dives into it, staining the inside of her lips purple in the process, pushed forwards as they are by her equally rapidly stained teeth.

I have got to do something to change my life. Something. That's for certain.

'I've made my mind up,' she says. An instant later she pulls a terrible face and lays the menu carefully down before putting her hand on her stomach. I know what's coming next.

Last time she did this there was the most infernal moaning throughout the rest of lunch. She'd just invited me back to her place. I was meant to hang around here for a while, take it easy, and then drop by her place later. She wanted a bit of time to herself first, to relax, let her food settle and make herself look nice. *You just enjoy yourself, eat my dessert too, and we'll see each other later.*

I ate my dessert. Alone. Then spent the rest of the evening trying to call her. When I finally did get the courage to go up, her flat lay in darkness.

'Oh dear, just as we were going to have a nice time together and everything, I have to get this pain again.' Edel gets up and goes to the toilet.

I hate knives and forks. They never sit properly in my hands. I'm no good at using both at once. It's best just to use the fork and break bits off.

I try to remember when I last had a good time.

Wotsits

She places a morsel of food into her mouth gingerly, lays her fork on the table, leans back in her chair and begins to cry.

'What's up?' I ask.

'There was a pregnant woman just walked by,' she says in a whispered tone.

'Oh, I see…' I say.

'I don't know if you've given it any thought, but I could have been a mother now.'

'I see…' I repeat, staring into my plate, sauce drizzled decoratively on the edge in thin stripes. The corners of my mouth are stuck together, glued with gacky spit.

'It's possible that I'll never be able to be a mother again, even if I were to meet a man I wanted to have kids with some day. And I get such dreadful pains down below.'

Edel's always talking about some obscure sexually transmitted disease she believes she caught from me: but I've even had the tests done, and I'm completely free of any infections. And she gave herself away once, so I know she had problems from earlier: 'You blokes. You want to shove it in the whole time, but we have to carry the can and sort the mess out after.'

'I could have been a mum again now,' she says with a sad smile and distant look in her eyes, scrunching up the napkin which she holds to her face.

'That's sad…' I say after a moment.

Then she stares at me sternly, drops her napkin and arches her back with arms folded. 'Oh well,' she says with a sigh, raising her eyebrows before leaning forward to lift her fork to her mouth.

'I *have* thought about it,' I say.

And then for some reason, I've no idea why, but it falls silent and I'd rather have changed the subject, but find myself telling her about some documentary on the Discovery Channel. One of those 'beginnings of life' programmes, with all those pictures that anti-abortion protestors on American Christian channels love showing. 'The Body'. The first episode was about conception, which I somehow ended up recording: mainly because there were lots of naked people in the trailer and also because later in the series they were going to show a girl going through puberty. On impulse later that night I visited a tasteless American pro-life site. But whatever, it was then it hit me: what it was we were taking away. I suddenly notice I'm feeling emotional too. And I tell her about those closing images that made me sad: the embryo in the rubbish bin and the embryo in the womb with its tiny fingers, its hair, its hand close to its little nose and its round, pink tummy.

'Those pictures must have been of a really *late* abortion,' she interrupts.

I nod. How would I know.

'Irresponsible hussies. And you had to bring that up now.'

But then, I'd wanted that baby. I'd managed to convince myself that we might have had something going between us. That there was no turning back and that Edel wasn't so bad after all, if I only got to know her better. *We all have our good and bad sides*, I thought. In fact, I was pleased and excited about it in those early days. But when we met next, Edel told me the doctor had told her she shouldn't carry to term. And that she didn't want it anyway.

'But it was good we managed to catch it early,' she says earnestly, taking a mouthful of wine and gazing out onto the street.

'Yes. According to this *documentary* it could have been anything at that stage anyway,' I laugh, 'a little marsupial, an elephant, a kangaroo. A fish even.'

'Yes, it's true, isn't it!' she says animatedly. 'It can't have been more than a wee clump of nothing,' she adds, flashing a hurried glance in my direction as she places her glass back on the table, smiling. 'There'll never be anything between us, Rino,' she sighs with a melancholy look. Her eyes slightly glazed from the wine.

And so we sit in silence for a while, finishing our lunch. My food has gone cold from waiting for her to stop crying. Edel passes the occasional comment on what some of the women are wearing as they pass by, and she stares at a strange man with a doddery walk and a little carrier bag round his wrist that she laughs at, but acts as if it's nothing when I ask.

Payment

Edel sits, twiddling the hair behind her ear. She finished her second glass of wine extremely fast, and now she seems rather satisfied from lunch and a little tipsy.

'But it *almost* feels as if we should have had a child together,' she says suddenly, her tongue searching her mouth for bits of food. 'Sometimes I dream about it at night, that we have a little boy together. I think it must have been a boy we had, I feel it inside me, female intuition, I suppose.'

I latch my lips to the straw and hunch over the table.

'Perhaps you should pay maintenance anyway?' she winks.

'(...)'

'D'you know what?' she smiles. 'I've got an idea. I can have all the money he'd have had!' She laughs.

'Who?' I ask.

'Our son. For clothes and stuff, education.'

We both laugh. At least I pretend to laugh, not so much so she'd think I'm insensitive, but enough so she can see I know it's a joke and that I'm not accusing her of fishing for money. My straw gurgles noisily amongst the ice cubes. I order another glass and use the empty one to cool my neck and cheeks.

'Did you get that test done for sexually transmitted diseases I told you about?'

'Yes, of course, ages ago,' I answer.

'That's good. You've got to be careful not to go spreading it around, you know.'

She's asked me this several times now. But the moment she's the least bit tiddly, the fact I tested negative always seems to slip her mind. And then she jumps straight to the conclusion that I had something, but that it has finally come to light, and all with her assistance.

She lights a cigarette.

'You know something? I really think you could have paid a bit towards things. Paid for the gynaecologist perhaps, or something. Done your bit. Don't you reckon that would have been the right thing? To do your bit?'

For a moment Edel says absolutely nothing. She peers across at me, then allows her eyes to wander, stares through the window, fiddles with her hair and brushes her suit, orders another glass of wine before fixing her eyes back on me.

'Yeah…right…sure,' I mumble.

Then Edel reels off a whole list, from unpaid gynaecologist bills and restaurant expenses, to her daughter's nursery fees, clothes and things from the chemists I can't catch the names of. All with the shared but tenuous link of my having spent thirty seconds inside her.

'How much are we talking about?' I ask.

'I'm sorry, have I made you feel guilty now? You shouldn't, you know.' Edel rests her hand on mine and leans across the table, trying to catch my gaze: I'm aware of looking rather sorry for myself. It's ages since anyone touched me.

'No…course not.'

'Ah, you are just so sweet sometimes,' she smiles, bringing her hand up to my cheek. And I realise that if this means she's going to invite me back to her place again, that's fine by me.

'I can transfer it this evening if you give me your account number again.'

'I really have to go soon,' says Edel, drawing her hand from my face.

Dogs

It's gone midday. I'm standing at the window of the living room, in my tracksuit bottoms, drinking a cup of coffee. Dad's already been here and painted the room, unscrewed the blinds, filled the gaps with putty and painted round all the frames. He got me doing the vacuuming, and I was still standing there in my underpants with the vacuum cleaner when he left at about eleven. It was freezing in here; the windows had been open for almost four hours. I was halfway through. Dad wants me to scrub the cupboards out as well. He's left me two new pairs of trousers and a pullover; I can barely remember when I last bought clothes for myself.

From the balcony I can see flocks of schoolkids with their rucksacks and cigarettes. I'd give anything to be fourteen or fifteen, slim and attractive. I wouldn't even mind being a girl. If I was going to be fourteen or fifteen and attractive, I think I might even *insist* on being a girl.

I'd kill to be a fifteen-year-old girl.

Men can never get raped. It seems. Men never say no. Men are just dogs, open to persuasion at all times. Deep down men don't have genuine preferences. Men have no personality. If all you want is just to sleep with anything or anyone, if you have no preferences, then you have no personality. You're nothing but a mutt.

Neither have men got the right to say no. Some turn-around that would be, and hell would she be insulted. And should you suddenly get it into your head to express your preferences, should you say what kind of a woman you want, and so much as seem to want to step out of your league, you're a chauvinist. That's why I don't want to sleep with just anyone. I want to decide who to sleep with. I want to sleep with someone I judge to be pretty. I'm picky. I have personality.

I don't want unconditional love. I want to be chosen because I measure up.

Why should I make do with someone just because they're willing to make do with me? Perhaps I like slim women, perhaps I like fat women.

But right now I want a teenage schoolgirl.

Talent

You're beautiful. You're pretty. You *want* everyone to admire you. But you are so fucking, fucking greedy. You get pissed off when you realise that men are ogling the snapshots of you on the net. When it dawns on you that these peeping Toms, these voyeurs you hate so much, wank in front of your glam shots. You'd have preferred people to be blind, and just hear about how beautiful you are.

You want control over who scoops up the crumbs you leave behind.

Then you're peeved because you don't get left in peace.

But shall I tell you what real *voyeurism* is? Voyeurism is all those weekly magazines you read at the hairdressers. Paparazzi pictures that go to the highest bidder in the news agencies. The TV cop shows you doze in front of before turning over in bed. The family reunions on TV that make your granny sigh. The poor gazing in at the rich. People forced into being adults so others can remain as children.

Another thing I hate is adverts. Adverts just tell you how you inadequate you are. Porn does the opposite. You're always adequate in porn. I am not inadequate. And let me tell you this: I am everywhere, people like me are everywhere, we've got our lenses trailed on you, we live underground. Every time your boyfriend takes pictures in to be developed, an extra copy gets taken by the part-time photography student. We know what you want, we know all your habits, we know what you really like, we've got you on computer, we've got you on film. I've got you on video.

My wishes, my desires, are simple: it's you that's complicated. It's you that makes things complicated. Not me.

This is dick...you like dick?

The Real Thing

I'm drunk again. If I hadn't wanted to be a teenager, I'd have wanted to be a porn star. I'd want to be Ron Jeremy: all the best male porn stars are ugly. But perhaps I'd have liked to have a mask. And I reckon my porn alias would have been Captain Naff, or then again, Captain Vile, Captain Goo, or maybe Captain Cock.

I'd have made a movie called *Fuckenstein*.

I search the net, with no results, for this kind of doll I saw on *Sex Sense* on Discovery Channel. Not an ordinary blow-up doll, but a realistic, handmade one, moulded in the same kind of latex they use for special effects in Hollywood.

I mean, these dolls just look so totally real. Like real women. In every shape and size: black, white, Asian, small, big, small tits, big tits. And apparently this latex feels just like skin.

After a lot of trouble I manage to log into a chat room under the alias Captain Cock. I write to say how I'm new to the forum, and that I'm just curious to know if anyone else knows about these dolls and how much they're likely to cost.

While I await a reply I click onto the escort girls' ads. I'm gob-smacked every time: all these call girls are in Norway. They show pictures of them. Though it annoys me their faces are blanked out.

To get some practice I log onto Peppe's, glance through their menu and choose a pizza. Then as I phone them, I browse the escort ads and fantasise that I'm calling the girls up, and not Peppe's.

'What d'you want?'

'(…)'

'What size?'

'(…)'

'OK. Big. Any extras?'

If only it were that simple.

'Anything special?'

I want her to suck me, and then I want her to give me a massage. Can she make food too?

Meanwhile, I've received an answer to my query.

I saw a programme with the dolls you're talking about, but haven't found more out myself. I think they're about $30–40,000. But don't forget nothing's better than 'the real thing'. :) Dig the alias, by the way!!! :P

Signed by a guy calling himself 'JonasMelonas'. And when I take a look at other discussions he's participated in, I see he's very concerned to have it clear what's in the price. *Are you paying by the hour? Or are you paying for how many times you can cum? I like her to spend a little time and not just go off as soon as you're 'done'.*

Fuck that for a lark. I am gonna have a wife. For fuck's sake. I've got enough money; I'll fucking buy myself a wife. Not like a whore, but one who'll live here, suck me, make food and clean. Why not go the whole way?

Perhaps that would get Dad to ditch these new plans.

Call Girl

The doorbell rings. I press my dick in under my trouser waistband and lift the receiver on the entry phone.

'What floor?' she asks.

'Top,' I say.

I lean into the spy hole on my front door and listen to the hurried steps coming up the stairs.

I turn the light off in the hallway.

She's Vietnamese. Korean. What do I know? She glances down at the order, then up at the door, then she shifts to rest her ass against the banisters, legs apart.

Slowly, soundlessly, I open my flies.

She leans forward and rings the bell. Her fringe hangs in two long locks as she leans forward, staring impatiently down into the floor.

I hold my breath. My fist slaps rhythmically against my crotch. As she leans back again, she lets the bag swing between her legs, and the way she holds the handles together in her clasped hands shoves her breasts up, and up, and I blow my load.

I put newspaper over my cum, close my flies and wipe my hand on my stomach under my pullover. Seconds before she gets to the bottom landing I shout down the stairwell.

I'm pissed.

I need food.

Treadmill

'Could you go up on the treadmill, sir, and run for me, please,' asks the sales assistant, loosening the laces on the shoes.

My feet stink. I ought to have gone home to change, but instead I got the tram straight down to Grensen. And here I sit in my socks staring down at my trouser legs. They ride up as I sit down, finishing halfway up my shins. I've never noticed that before.

'Pardon?' I push my glasses back into place and peer up at him.

'Could you run on the treadmill over there, please, sir?' He points towards a stand with a wide band under it and passes the other shoe to me. I lean forward and do up the laces. My clothes cling to my body, as if I'm being crushed by a huge hand squeezing the breath from me. When I've finally done them up, I'm already hot and sweaty under the armpits.

I push my foot into the floor. He leans towards the treadmill, looking at me expectantly.

'These are perfect. I'll just take these, please.'

I just want to get out of the shop as fast as I can. I don't want to go up on any treadmill.

'Sorry, sir, those are only for trying,' smiles the assistant, pointing at the heel where the shoe size is written in heavy marker-pen. 'If I can just see how you run first, before we find your shoes. How often do you go running?' he asks. 'On a treadmill or outside? Cross-country or asphalt?'

'I don't generally go running,' I answer.

He leads me onto the treadmill and presses a button on the dashboard in front of me. I only just manage to grasp the handles as I trip and am left dangling there with the band scraping the toes of my shoes. I right myself again and start to run. My feet thunder into the apparatus. There's a video camera behind me, and on a screen in front I watch my feet tramp against the fragile mat. He's asking me another question, but I'm no longer listening. My breathing is heavy, I'm sweating and I should have taken my jacket off. He covers his face with his hand, and a silence in the shop tells me that I have everyone's attention.

I am a joke.

A huge, fat joke.

Mucho Mas

I'd have liked to have some friends. I drink a Diet Coke sitting in the window seat at the bar with the bag containing my new trainers between my feet. I'm sitting in Mucho Mas, watching Gry and Stine: the way Gry puts money in the till and does the adding up in her head and ignores the waiting customers until she's ready. The way she dries her hands on her apron after wiping the cloth over the counter, and smiles.

I shouldn't really eat Tex-Mex. Sometimes I like to sit here, but right now there are too many people here so I've ordered a take-away. It's good in here because it isn't like the other cafés. I can just have my food and then go. In the other cafés everybody sits around chatting. To see and be seen.

Gry asks if I want to read the paper while I wait. I shake my head.

She's a girl I'd certainly have liked to get together with, that's for sure. I think we could be good together. If only I could show her that I care, that I'm not like the others, but that I could really, really care for her. I wish I could tell her that I think she's cute. Some day I want to say it. Just casually, when I go to pay. I only ever eat here on the days she's working. If there aren't too many people, at least.

Not that I could actually ever do it.

For others, perhaps it's just a question of courage.

My dick's huge. That's got to be a plus. I have a huge dick. Just that alone could be reason enough for a woman to like me. In fact, I had the biggest dick at school, and college too. I'd swear that if I measured my dick against anyone else's in here, even on a day when it was really packed out, mine would be the biggest. It runs in the family. If I'd still had any friends, it might have brought its rewards. Then my friends could have told people about it, spread the rumour. But I don't have any friends, so nobody can say anything to anybody about it. I'm just fat and dull. And a coward.

Gry is sweet.

I'm not in love with her, but I like her.

It could turn out to be pretty difficult to sleep with a girl I respect. Leastways for the first few times.

Only Once

But what do I know? I've only done it once. If that even counts as once. With Edel. According to my definition, you are no longer a virgin when you've cum inside (or on) a woman.

By those standards. I am a virgin.

After a company party, nearly two years ago, Edel wanted us to share a cab home. We were drinking from a bottle under my jacket, and as we swung round a corner I fell on top of her. But we neither of us laughed. After we'd kissed she invited me back to her place. *A wee nightcap.* After paying the cab I followed her in.

I needed the toilet. Because I had such a huge hard on, I leaned over the toilet bowl so my tie fell in: I stood there, heels against one wall, hands on the other wall over the toilet and pissed in an arc beneath me.

She gave me a tall glass of Schweppes grapefruit with vodka. *A wee nightcap.* I lied and told her she was pretty. To make her feel better. I tried saying all the things you're meant to say, nice things, but nothing seemed right. And it was hard to keep coming up with more compliments. Nothing seemed to touch her. More than anything she seemed bored by it.

She went to change. When she got back, she took my glass, drank half of it down in one large swig, then opened her dressing gown and pulled my head between her breasts, took my hand and guided it to her crotch. I had to take all my clothes off myself. She didn't touch me once.

In the double bed she'd just lowered herself onto me, when the kid started crying in the other room.

After that she told me she was totally turned off. And even trying to touch her was out of bounds.

'You're my first,' I told her and tried to stroke her on her back.

'Oh, really,' she said after a brief pause, 'of how many then?'

'No, I…' was all I managed.

'So you'd planned on sleeping with lots of others after me then? What a nice thing to say!'

'That wasn't what I…' I ventured.

'No, you're not used to handling the ladies,' she added.

Her kid banged on the door and came in the bed. At first, it was told to get off back to its own room, but then she relented and the kid crept in. But then, as my foot rubbed up against Edel's leg, she said it was probably best I order a cab.

Two weeks later she rang, told me she was pregnant and that she'd known it since the day we'd slept together.

But I hadn't *cum*.

I hadn't climaxed.

OK

Gry is standing in front of me with my take-away in a bag. She offers me my receipt and some change. I shake my head, lift my hand for her to keep it. She gives a little bob and smiles.

'What have you got in there?' she asks.

I open my bag.

'Ah, trainers. That has to be good, doing a little bit of running.' She blushes.

I don't think she meant to say I was fat. That's just how it came out. Gry's not like the others: she treats everyone equally. I open my mouth and try to say something, but nothing comes out. So I nod and smile.

'Oh well. Enjoy your food,' she says and goes back behind the counter, drying her hands on her apron.

I plod up the street, towards home. I am going to enjoy myself. With my food. Alone. In front of the TV.

I glance down at the food and the trainers. Suddenly I feel a warmth. A feeling that something is about to happen.

Closeness

I open something that I initially take to be a bill. But it turns out to be a form from the National Health. THE NATIONAL HEALTH SERVICE it says. The Institute for Medical and Health Research.

Sexuality and Health, it has written on the cover.

Inside the form is an accompanying letter:

A study of sexuality and health

You are one of 10,000 people living in Norway, between the ages of 18 and 49, selected to participate in a study of sexuality and health.

Gaps in our knowledge. *A great deal is written on the subject of 'sex' and it is easy to have the impression that we know everything about people's views of their own sexuality. This is mistaken. Fundamental gaps in our knowledge remain. The institute has therefore decided to carry out a study into health and sexuality. Similar studies are being carried out in other European countries.*

You have been selected. *You have been randomly selected from the register of the Central Bureau of National Statistics. Everyone who has been selected for participation is of equal importance to our study. This is applicable whether you have had sex or not, whether you are young or old. Your participation is completely voluntary...*

So I've been chosen. I am the chosen one. The single, totally randomly selected fat virgin.

I almost don't believe it. I don't believe it: they must surely have found the only person in the country who's over sixteen and still a virgin. And how my virginity could be of any possible consequence to anyone is beyond comprehension. It's certainly no help to me.

You are anonymous. *Neither your name nor any other personal information are shown on this form. Information given by participants will only be published in the form of assembled statistics and tables. Your answers cannot be traced back to you.*

No lonely person is ever anonymous. Ever.

Damned if I'm going to answer: hidden away, right at the bottom of those statistics and tables, there'll be one lonely number, one single unit.

That unit is me.

The virgin.

How to complete this form. *It's important that you complete this questionnaire alone, so that you can answer as honestly as possible. When your form is complete, place it in the return envelope for postage. Postage is* *pre-paid. We would be grateful if completed forms could be returned as promptly as possible.*

I put the form down on the table, take my glasses off to rub the corners of my eyes. For a moment I sit there wondering whether I know anyone in the statistics office. Somebody I might have gone to school with, for example. Somebody who'd want to take the piss. The thermostat in the coffee machine clicks. Fill this questionnaire out alone? And in what way do I have any choice in the matter? Am I about to drive back home perhaps and ask my dad for assistance, or what?

I have to laugh.

We would like to thank you in advance for your assistance in making this a worthwhile survey.

Signed Per Magnus, Department Director, and Hein Stigum, Project Leader.

I glance quickly through the questions and then close the form again, go into my bedroom and put it in my bedside locker. Take my glasses off again. Roll my shoulders, try to stretch the ache away.

I refuse. I'm not fucking well going to send in that form before I've had a screw. No fucking way. I've got to have a screw. Before I go insane.

Right now I'd be content if someone just touched me a bit; I've got a headache. I'd be happy just to have a little physical contact. That's what I miss most.

No one has touched me for years.

I've heard it helps.

You

For you I was born. For you I grew up. For you I have spent my life waiting, and for you I will die. I am dying now. I love you in a world where people do nothing but fuck each other up.

But you are much too distant from me. So distant. A million miles off. Light years.

If you only promise you'll care for me, if you'll only be here for me. If you only give your word to stay at my side, through thick and thin.

And not go off at the first sign of trouble.

Then I will be all yours.

Gry and Stine

I eat up all my food. Put the cutlery in the dishwasher. Turn off all the lights in the flat. Belch guacamole. Wander down to the toilet. Then Gry and Stine and I have sex together. They turn up on the landing and ring at my door. *We thought we'd drop by to see you, didn't we*, Stine giggles. Gry opens her eyes very wide and then shuts them again, smiling, just as I've watched her do with customers she likes or knows, like a cheeky Bugs Bunny. I hold the door wide with an outstretched arm. Check them over.

'Is that OK then?' says Stine.

'Yeah, sure, of course,' I say. 'Come on in.'

I walk over to the drinks cabinet and mix us some drinks, but it soon becomes apparent that that's not what they've come for. They drag me over to the sofa. I take Gry around the hips from behind, stroking her beneath her blouse as she bends forwards and undresses Stine.

'It's so huge!' They kneel in front of me. Stine watches with interest and guides it into Gry's mouth. Wanks me against her lips. Strokes her cheeks. With my hands round her waist I turn her slender body round and press myself into her.

'Fuck! I'm cumming!' I roar and pump her and pump her before my body tenses and arches back. And this is one lad who's eaten his spinach: I spurt my first sticky spunkload over Stine's back. A long strip that gushes over her shoulder. With Gry's breasts squeezed round my dick, the next load lands in the grooves where Gry's tongue and lips meet Stine's mouth.

How it would be for real is way beyond my imagining. I know nothing about how it would feel, apart from its being slippery, warm and sticky, totally different from a wank, and that my dick would smell afterwards.

Still

It's so amazingly quiet in here. I lie on the bed. My heartbeat ceases pounding through my ears and there is nobody here but me.

I pat my head and run chubby fingers through my hair, and fantasise that someone else is doing it. And that someone is stroking me on my chest: turning my hand over, I stroke myself down from my chest and across my stomach.

It is Gry. She turns over and sighs into my ear, the faintest gasp.

My tailbone aches. I reach down with my fingers to the thick stickiness at the base of my dick, and I pull a scrap of toilet paper off.

Who the hell would want to sleep with me here? Who'd want to share this with me? Nothing but emptiness, unclean skin, a computer, strip light, rolls of toilet paper and dust.

The sodden paper hits the wall.

Nobody *I* can think of, that's for sure.

Why

I am lonely and a misfit. Why don't I go to therapy? Why don't I just pay a prostitute or ring a sex line number, travel to Thailand or go to a strip bar?

That would be cheating. It wouldn't be real.

Pride. But then again, I'm just a coward, a fucking coward.

Oslo City

I wake up, get out of bed and put on my clothes, but swap the tweed jacket for a grey hooded pullover and pull on my trainers before taking the tram to the centre of town.

Something has got to happen now. I'll go with the flow, just put everything aside and let myself be pulled along, down, towards town. I'll hire a prostitute, or whatever. But then, instead of going down to Tollbugata, an impulse grabs me and I find myself in Oslo City Shopping Mall. They were talking about it in the canteen, and I've read about it in the paper: there are gangs of young girls down here who bet on who can do the most in a day, in the toilets. It's a status thing, apparently.

For a moment I stand next to the escalators on Level 1. I buy an ice lolly for myself, so as not to look too suspicious, but start to grow tense, not even tearing the whole wrapper off, before I've completely forgotten to eat it and it starts to drip. Then when I fetch napkins from the ice cream bar, the assistant's so obliging I don't dare stand there any longer and finally move off to Oslo Central Station.

In the walkway between the old Eastern Railway halls and the concourse I see a short, little man in his fifties being stopped by three girls. I don't see them at first, but turn as I hear one of them talk to him.

'Excuse me, sir, you got ten kroner spare?'

The man stands there saying nothing. She walks ahead of him, the other two following behind, forcing him to stop and make a detour round them. I freeze almost completely. Begin to walk slowly. The girls are all wearing Miss Sixty trousers and pullovers cut short at the waist.

The one who's asking is the prettiest of them, with long legs, ruddy-brown skin, a light blue top and blonde, sun-bleached hair tied back in a ponytail. She's pretty. She looks as if she's got money enough. And she modulates her voice so as to make herself charming. Pretty. Bright. Polite.

The man doesn't give them anything.

I hover around them. But they don't ask me. I'm expecting them to, but they don't, and neither do they ask anyone else. Instead they trail off in the direction of one of the platforms.

Back in Oslo City I take the escalator up to the top level and gaze out over the whole mall. I follow a girl who goes into the pet shop, where she stands next to the ferrets.

I stand at the railings. Take the escalator down to the level below.

'S'cuse me. You got a fag?' she asks and I automatically pat my pockets.

'Sorry, no,' I answer.

'OK, no worries,' she smiles. She turns away, allowing her gaze to rove among the passers-by.

'But I can *buy* some cigarettes,' I say suddenly and feel something stream through my body.

'Jesus. Fucking ace, man. You're sweet, man. I'll wait here.' She moves towards the exit, all the while texting on her mobile.

For a moment I stand there utterly paralysed before eventually moving over to the Narvesen kiosk. Shit! She didn't tell me what cigarettes she wanted. Shit-shit-shit. And I probably ought to buy some condoms here too: this isn't going to be her first time, that's for sure. Although I won't catch anything if she just sucks me off. I stand there, my hands shaking, wondering whether I can go out and ask her which cigarettes she prefers. I ought to get some cash out too, in case cigarettes aren't enough. But I don't want her to only suck me: I want to cum inside her. It's not like I'm paying a prostitute. She chose me. She asked me if I had a cigarette. Where are we going to do it? The toilets are probably under surveillance after all the newspaper reports. Will the cashier phone security if I buy condoms as well?

'Fags!'

The assistant looks quizzically at me.

'I mean cigarettes, please.'

'What brand?'

Coke

As I walk towards to her, on my return, she begins to move to the exit. Passing through the swing doors I shove my hands deep into the pockets of my grey hooded pullover, tugging it over my dick that stands rock hard under the waistband of my trousers.

I tear the cellophane off the pack and toss it onto the ground, tear off the silver paper and toss that onto the ground too. As I stretch the packet out to her (*'Here…here, take it!'* it feels as if I'm yelling, she reacts so slowly), I note that the flap on the top of the packet is torn and dangling.

'Blimey, stressed or what?' she laughs as her fingers dig after a fag.

'No, I just…'

'On Coca Cola?'

'What? Did you want a Coke too? Just take the whole pack. I don't smoke, anyway.'

'Oh, right, cheers, mate.'

She sticks the cigarette in her mouth and turns the top of her body so as to put the torn packet into her rucksack. She crouches over her school bag and I get small glimpses of her hips, a little bit of ass and crotch. Her hooded pullover rides up over her back and I can see the string of her knickers and the tops of her buttocks. A tan line. From the sun bed. White knickers, black top. Brown skin.

Pussy. Your soaking wet pussy!

'So, how are things with you then?' I ask and observe myself clapping my hands together. A peculiar, sploshy sound. 'All right, eh?' I add.

'Yeah, OK, innit? And yourself?'

'(…)'

'Haven't you got a light then?'

The first match snaps. The second refuses to light, and before I get the third lit a guttural sound emits from my throat that really puts me out of gear. I can't hold my hands steady and a hollow, shivery feeling fills my body. I go weak at the knees as I lean forwards. I'm sure I'm going to get arrested any minute. If the police take their time, if they need to catch her in the act so as to be able to arrest me, then I hope I'll cum straight off. So it's done with.

Then they can do what they want with me.

She bends forward with half-closed eyes, fingers locked around the base of the cigarette.

'Shit!' I say, handing her the matches.

'No worries,' she says. 'Hangover?'

'D'you want…er…would you consider…'

It's like porridge in my mouth, and before I get the chance to finish she yells over my shoulder, 'Catinka! Over here! Here!'

'And who's this then?' asks her friend.

'Just someone I bummed a fag off of. What was your name?'

They both look at me. She stubs her cigarette out on the concrete, and I know it's over.

Whatever *it* was.

Ski Shopping Centre

Fuck you. I'm gonna fuck you. Shaft you so bloody hard. Fuck you. I dart into Oslo Central Station, consider for a moment whether to go in the toilets and wank, but suddenly find myself sitting in a half-empty train compartment with a ticket to Ski.

First I eat two McFeast Burgers at McDonald's. The fries break, pulverising into a mush as I press them down into the ketchup. They glue themselves to my fingers like lumps of mashed potato. I'm far too heavy handed, but my body is raging. I have to eat the clumps off my fingers, scraping my fingers hard against my teeth. My body is itching. As if I'm suffering from withdrawal. I suck on my Coke straw and when the girl behind the counter shouts that my apple pie is done, I neither thank her nor say anything: I just go over to the counter, pick up my pie and turn again.

Back at my table I force the pie down. The hot, sweet filling scalds my gums and when I reach out for napkins, my hands are covered with so much ketchup and sticky caramelised apple that the napkins break up into tiny little pieces that get stuck to my fingers. I flick my hands in vain, the napkins refuse to come off. In the end I'm so furious, and itching so badly under my clothes, that I slam my hands down into the table.

The Touch

You can – can't you? Just go out of the house, walk a couple of hundred metres down the road, and find yourself someone. Anyone. Whoever it may be. A man or a woman. Go straight home within the hour, maybe not even right home, just right into a café, right into the toilets, no knickers on, in it goes, bang-bang-bang, and it's done.

It's that easy, that fucking easy for you. Isn't it?

You've got the touch.

Security Guard

I drink my Coke. The buzz of the Coke beginning at the back of the tongue and spreading up into my head. My tongue rubs at my scalded gums as I watch the security guard go up and down the escalator.

Peeping Tom, I think. From the corner where I stand and sip on my Coke, my cover for standing and hanging around, I can see how the security guards move in circles, how they stand waiting before they position themselves on the escalators and glide down with their eyes glued to the asses and naked midriffs of a flock of schoolgirls before them.

Fucking peeping Tom, I think to myself. He gets paid to go round here and spy. Perhaps that's the dream job. I could swear that he's got a girl-friend six years younger than him, minimum. And what kind of bribes must a bloke like that get offered? Do they suck him off to get off from being reported?

He is here every day, after all.

Oh go on, do us a favour, mate. Couldn't you let me take that dress home with me, and I'll give you a blow job!

(The security guard seen by security camera locking himself into the staff loos with two fourteen-year-old girls and a boy standing guard.)

I walk round again, just watching. I take the escalator up, browse through the jeans not far from the changing rooms: slender, bare calves and thin socks with a soft, gentle touch of pink or blue. Asses as good as naked apart from thin summer fabrics. Soft skin. Bikini stripes. Smooth, bronzed skin. Small Vietnamese girls, dark Latino babes with dark, black eyes that sweep the entire room. Blondes with stick-thin legs. Buxom brunettes. Cleavages so soft they look like you could stick a spoon in their creamy flesh and sup it up. Tiny girls with thick lips. G-strings that show, forming an arc just under their love handles. Hands hidden in long sleeves. Plastic bags. Rucksacks. Wrists softened with lotion. It's like I'm being force-fed, like I'm having it shoved down my throat from every direction: from the screens in the TV shops, the posters in the perfume departments and clothes shops, flock after flock, bodies either going up or down the escalators, as if writhing in one great hive, oiled. An ecstasy thrilling from my head to my toes, into my fingers. Like sticking your head in a soft peach pie: all I have to do is open my mouth and move my jaw. If I was attractive, I'd never be able to choose. There are women everywhere. Gorgeous women, girls, bodies, skin. Tastes. Smells. Flesh.

Three boys play a computer game at a stand in Spaceworld. Nobody takes notice of me before I put the straw in my mouth, and rather than a sip it makes a loud gurgling sound. The boy with the manic thumbs flashes a sideways glance up before continuing the game with half-opened mouth.

'You lot will have to go now,' says a voice from behind.

At first I think I'm about to be thrown out too, but then the assistant hands the machine over to me with a welcoming motion. The paper cup makes a gurgling noise again. I gaze up at the machine, take the straw out of my mouth. What must he think? I am, after all, an adult.

I can't stand computer games.

I hate the fucking things.

The boys hang over the balustrades by their elbows, torsos in gentle, loose arches, their shoes barely touching the floor as they peer down at the people below them. It seems they've got things sussed.

That ought to have been me. Should have been me. Could have been me.

Little Girl

Standing in Narvesen's, I flick through nearly every magazine with naked pictures in it with my sticky fingers. *FMH, Loaded*: I think they're shit, they only titillate and then censor everything. It's only soft porn. But I still can't do it, I can't bring myself to walk over to the till with the magazine. Somehow or other I can stand here with it and take a sneak read, but I can't walk those few paltry metres to pay the lady at the till. I will never see her again, and yet it's totally and utterly impossible.

I stand at the till. The cashier is hanging back a bit, a telephone to her ear. She smiles, I smile back, she apologises and hangs up.

'Hi. Could I buy a phone card, please?' I ask, getting my wallet out.

Shaft you. Shaft you so *fucking* hard.

'What amount?'

Big. Mega-gi-normous. *D'you want to come with me in the back room and fuck me? Wow, it's sooo huge... Cum all over my tits, let me unbutton my blouse so you can cum on my tits.* Her breasts are spilling out.

'Er, I don't know, what have you got?'

Suck me? For how much, then?

'We have fifty kroner, one hundred and one hundred and fifty.'

How much is your pussy?

'I'll have one for one hundred and fifty then.'

'We've got two hundred as well.'

'Super! I'll take that then.' I wrench the notes from my wallet and place them on the counter in front of her.

'Your phone card, sir.'

'Super cunt.'

She looks quizzically at me.

'Super, thanks,' I say. 'Just super.' I shove the phone card in my back pocket.

'Goodbye!' she says as she closes the till.

I'm already on my way out.

I stand next to the bin some way from the exit, tearing the plastic wrapper off the card, when I feel a tug at my trouser pocket. I turn quickly round.

She looks up at me. 'I'm lost,' she says.

'Right.'

'You have to help me.'

'OK,' I answer.

'I can't find my mummy. We need to go to reception,' she says, hands clasped in front of her and head tilted.

The plastic wrapper sticks to my fingers, set fast to the sticky film of sugar. For a moment I'm standing there flicking my fingers hard around me to no avail.

'Is it stuck?' she asks and leans forward, eyes filled with curiosity and rising on tiptoe for a moment.

'Why don't you go to reception on your own, since you know that's where you have to go?' I ask, finally free from the plastic.

'Just…because,' she says and shrugs her shoulders.

'Because what?'

'I don't know where it is.'

'OK. We'll go to that man over there,' I say, pointing at the security guard by the exit, standing with his hands on his belt and feet planted wide apart.

I've gone two steps towards the guard when I feel her grab my hand. She peers up at me. I freeze.

'Why are you holding my hand?' I look around. A lady going up the escalator turns to stare at us. Three sullen teenagers with rucksacks sit on the edge of a flowerbed.

'I don't want to go on my own.'

I shake my head and start walking in the direction of the guard.

Two metres on and she starts sobbing. She stops, rooted to the spot, standing there stiffly as she howls. I have to tug her up to keep her on her feet.

'Get up,' I bark.

Now everyone's looking.

'What's the matter?' I whisper sharply.

'You're ho-ho-holding my hand so ha-ha-hard,' she says on an in breath. 'I want to-to-to go to my-my mummy,' she sobs.

'That's where we're going!' I say. 'We'll find your mummy now.'

'I'm frightened.'

What the devil's happening? Two minutes ago she was Little Miss Cool. But now, of course, just as she's about to be rescued, she has to go and fall apart. Shit! And the security guard over by the exit starts to shift, changing position. People turn around and I can see how this might look: it could look as if I'm trying to pull her after me, to the exit, instead of the guard.

And what would I say? What could I say? She could suddenly start making stuff up. And *I* know why I've come here: I'm desperate, I've got to get it all out, something's got to happen for me, I was here to find release. And what would they find in my house if there was an investigation, if they ransacked my home? Pictures on my PC? But if I had been kidnapping her I'd have had a car, I'd have had a car and dragged her into the car park. I would have worn a mask. I'm not daft. I'm neither stupid nor backwards.

But what motives would I have had to try and kidnap her?

None.

She's just crying. She's crying and I have to stay calm.

'Hi,' I smile and nod at the guard.

The guard comes over and crouches down in front of the little girl.

'I think someone's lost,' I say, smiling.

She's still crying.

'So you're lost, are you?' asks the guard gently. Finally, she lets go of my hand.

'Can you take care of her?' I ask. I smile. Smile and point at my watch.

He peers up at me, one eye narrowing.

I smile again and give a nod.

Without turning back I walk straight out of the shopping centre, towards the railway station, and jump onto a train just as the doors close.

Phone Box

Getting off at Nordstrand, I wander around for ages in no particular direction. I'm hot. My shoes have turned an orange-brown colour from the grit that still lies along the sides of the road. There's nothing out here, no shopping centre, just big houses.

From inside the phone box I've got a view of the football pitch through a gap in the shrubs. I stick my phone card in the slot, open my flies and whip my dick out. The air in the phone box is cold, like someone's trailing a chill, delicate fabric over my warm dick and groin.

My breath hangs frozen on the air.

As the team coach sets out red and white striped cones on the field, the football team warms up. A girl with short, straight legs and track-suit bottoms made of thin, artificial fabric bends forward, touching the ground with her hands, stretching. Her top slips forward. She stands with her ass in the air, *ass in the air ready to be taken*, her midriff bare, the underside of her boobs visible. Sports bra. Another girl lies on the grass, legs sprawled, leaning forwards with her hands around one of her ankles, her inside thighs, her groin almost showing under her shorts.

The payphone emits a stream of shrill noises. I just manage to bring my spit-covered hand down towards my dick when the payphone starts bleeping. I press my dick back in my trousers and look round. But the payphone's almost screeching.

I thwack it, thump it hard, even as I lift the receiver, trying to say *hello*. But it still won't stop bleeping.

Then I notice the display that says REMOVE CARD.

I remove my card, and stick it back in again. I get a dial tone but I've lost all interest now. I can't cum: not even with the girls right in front of me on the sports field, with their long hair, breasts that bounce, bodies that slide, clothes getting dirty, almost transparent with mud, sweat and water. It's impossible to rid myself of the unpleasant feeling of being stared at, of being discovered. Of someone watching *me*. Not one, not one lonely person is ever invisible. A film of sweat spreads across my stomach. It's as though my tongue's swelling, a prickly, faintly nauseous sensation.

I try to call again, dialling a random number.

'Hi, this is Trude.'

I hang up.

Ring again.

'Hello. This is Bjørn Espen.'

I hang up.

On the next number nobody picks up.

I can't cope with this any more. I zip up my flies, wedge my half-limp erection under my belt and burst out of the phone box, door slamming behind me.

Some way down the road I realise I've left my phone card behind and nearly turn back. But I walk on instead. Without direction.

Nordstrand

It has clouded over, there's a bitter wind blowing along the road. At a bus stop I shove the empty Coke bottle and cigarette pack down into the rubbish bin by the shelter and zip up my hooded jacket. A moment later I check the bus times, but it's almost impossible to decipher the notices covered in spray paint. I want to get home. To my room. My video. To wank.

I'm standing with my shoulder leaning against the shelter, protected from the wind, when I hear shuffling steps approach. At first I think they're boys, then perhaps a boy and a girl. One of them has a cap and the other has a bag slung from her shoulder reaching far down to her thigh. Then I realise they're both girls, but as to whether they're first year sixth formers or still at school, I can't decide: they can't be more than five feet two inches, but they've got curvy hips and thighs, short, sturdy legs and buttocks that bulge under the soft fabric of their trousers. I try to work out if they've come from the football practice, but I don't recognise either of them.

They circle around me. The one with the bag lets it drop and sits on the bench less than half a metre behind me. The shelter fills with noise, motion, clothes, bubble gum. *I'm not shifting*, I think to myself, *I got here first.*

But I finally give up, I can't bear it. The thought that they're going to be exchanging glances about my fat ass and the clacking sound that intermittently explodes into a sharp smack from the gum that one of them is chewing drives me from the shelter.

I wander off a couple of metres, then move in closer again. They're whispering, or perhaps I'm just imagining it.

When I get back I position myself on the corner, just to the side of the shelter, and secretly spy on the one that had the bag: she's practically lying down on the short bench, wedged up into the corner, legs out in front of her, black tracksuit bottoms with stripes down the sides riding over her hips and her back is naked against the pistachio-green bench and her red hooded jumper. She's left the laces on her huge, sloppy shoes untied. They're shoved up against her friend, who texts away, jaws working at the little clump of gum. She looks pure and innocent compared to her gum-chewing slob of a friend. She's sweet, I think, she makes me smile, I get a *tender* feeling from looking at her. There's something relaxed and healthy about her.

'Is it…is it long till the next bus?' I force myself to ask.

She shrugs her shoulders.

'Don't think there's any buses for a while,' she answers.

I pass by the shelter, managing to catch a glimpse of a little more belly and back, and end up several metres beyond the shelter, some way up the road, before carefully edging my way back.

'Jesus, there's a pack of fags in the bin,' I hear one of them say.

A split second later and the gum comes shooting out from the shelter and lands on the asphalt in the bus bay.

'Excuse me, sir. You got a light?' asks the other.

'No. I don't smoke,' I say, moving away from the shelter again. Now she's lying with one foot rested on the ground and her crotch splayed out in front of her friend: I can follow the contours of her knickers from where they disappear from her naked hips and into her cotton trousers. Her bulge: swollen, soft flesh.

She slips down from the bench to open her bag. I turn away.

She can do as she pleases, I think. *I can't be arsed to help her. Slapper.*

But when I get back, I see that she must have found a light in her bag after all, and that they're *both* smoking, the one I'd thought was the sporty kind included. She's lying in the same position, one knee up and the other foot resting, and she's already smoked her cigarette down to a butt that glows all the way to the filter.

Then I see the splats of gob next to her sloppy, unlaced shoe. In a wide, but tight radius. She spits, glances up at me, then spits again. The asphalt is covered in splats of gob, large and small.

'I'm thirsty,' she whispers.

And continues to expel small, gungy, almost dry clusters of gob.

Bloke

Their hair is wet from swimming. And they're warm, despite there being a chill wind. It's almost pleasant that there's a bit of a cold wind blowing.

'Is that nice?' she says, pressing her fingers against her friend's swelling crotch on the bench. Her friend closes her eyes and nods. She turns to look at the man standing at the bus stop. Imagine how it would be to be discovered. She turns back and lets her fingers circle her crotch. Her friend's leg falls heavy to the side. Her lips part.

'Wait. Stop. He's coming back.'

The girls sit up again.

'Sorry, but d'you know if there are any buses coming soon?' asks the man.

'No. I don't think there are any buses from here for a while,' she answers and the man disappears again.

The friend lifts her ass, tugging her trousers down towards her, so as they go just below her buttocks. If anyone were driving past now, it would look as if she has her trousers on, when in fact her ass lies warm against the cold bench. She pushes her index finger inside her friend as she lets her middle finger slide upwards to circle her asshole.

Her friend wets her hand and shoves it down to her crotch. She lets out a little squeal, a whimper of delight.

'Wait. Wait. Stop. He's coming back,' she says suddenly.

She fumbles for a cigarette with her wet hand.

'Excuse me, sir,' she says, 'but can you light my fire?'

'No, but you can bite my wire,' he laughs.

The girls laugh too. They haven't heard that line before.

'What are you two up to?' asks the man.

'I'm fingering my friend. D'you wanna watch?' she says.

He certainly does.

It's not cigarettes they need.

Inside the shelter he takes his dick out. Then the friend beckons him over and takes it in her mouth. She groans.

He cums all over her naked stomach, over her face and her friend's hooded jacket.

Fillip

I'm still wearing my outdoor clothes. My shoes have left footprints all over the flat, from the front door to the bathroom and into my room. I stand at my desk with my hooded pullover open, breathing with my mouth open as my fingers pound at the keyboard. My right hand guides the mouse over the links on sexhound.com. I spit on my left hand and wet my dick. An uncontrolled spasm in my right leg prevents me cumming: my knuckles go like jelly, my foot gives way, ruining my co-ordination. I have to shift my whole weight to my left foot.

At first it's impossible to get a link that works, then a sudden stream of pop-ups starts, even though sexhound is supposed to be dead-link and pop-up free. As an FFM Blowjob mpg goes onto repeat in the background, I stand there, trying to close the screens, only to experience them popping up again, and to top it all off my computer generally crashes at this point. Then the phone rings.

New pop-ups continue to heave and swell, and at first I decide I'll let the phone ring on. I click the screens closed and massage my crotch so as not to lose my erection, but then, as the phone starts up again almost the instant it stopped, I think it's got to be Dad and perhaps he's standing outside, and it might be important, but the pop-ups won't stop and in the background the film clip goes on moaning. I pull the computer plug out, wipe my hand on the tissues and clothes that lie strewn across the room and hunt for the cordless phone.

In an effort to catch my breath, I clamp my hand over the telephone for two seconds before answering.

'Yes, hello?' I say.

'Hi, it's Fillip, why the fuck don't you pick up then, eh?'

Shit-shit-shit.

'Oh, hi. Where are you?'

'Where d'you fucking well think I am? I'm in Spain. But I can't hack it 'ere any longer. It's bloody baking.'

'It's cold here.'

'Hey, listen up. There's this opportunity just came up to rent my flat out over the summer, can I stay over at yours?' Fillip breaths with a kind of whistling sound.

I knew this was going to happen. That he'd ask me this.

'You'd get paid, and everything.'

'Er...' I begin.

'Cash in hand, if you'd prefer.'

'Dad's renting it out,' I say.

'And me ma says you can have a holiday out here if you fancy. I fixed a new flat up for her, you know; with a lift, the works.'

'Dad's done it up. We're renting it out.'

'How much d'you want for it, then?' Fillip's sipping at something. 'I've got the cash, you know.' He burps, a squidgy bubble that bursts in his mouth before whistling out between his lips.

'Sorry, it's already gone. He's moving in next week,' I lie. I pick up my trousers, clutching them in my hand and flop back into the chair.

'I'd only need the loan of your sofa, really. Gonna be driving a truck all summer. Can't you have a chat with the bloke who's moving in, then? I won't get in your way, honest to God. I'm driving liquor across from Germany, *Deuts-che-land*. Could get you sorted with loads of booze, mate.'

'I don't think Dad'll like it.'

'Ha ha, scared of the ol' boy then, are you? That's a good one.'

'You know how it is,' I say.

'Nah, nah, it's OK. I'm not totally thick, you know.'

'When are you coming back home?' I ask.

'I'll be over your way in three weeks. My ma's booked tickets for next week, but we'll probably take a trip down to the summer cottage before coming to town.'

Fillip could have been a friend, but he hasn't ever been quite. He only rings me if he's bored or needs something. At the same time as he's gentle as a lamb, he's nothing but trouble. He's nearly forty, but behaves like he's fifteen. I got to know him when I was doing a summer job at my dad's company nearly ten years ago. We used to go around together. He took me with some of his mates to his cottage on the south coast. He lived in Bastø as a kid. He was in the papers once when he dived from Vrengen Bridge at Tjøme, but that was years ago. Then, resisting arrest at some time, he got a punch on the nose, and now it whistles, forcing his voice into a thin, nasally tone, despite his being such a big bloke. In those early days, when I first met him, it was a bit exciting. He was like the Fonz: his friends were all at least five or ten years younger than him and he promised us booze and loads of available females. And barbecues. The weekends always ended up with booze, mixed grills and a knees-up with the locals when we went out, on pretexts of checking out the ladies. South coast ladies. Ladies on vacation. The restless wives of the rich. *Horny as hell.*

Then one day we all grew out of it. Or simply couldn't hack it any longer, and I broke contact with him, after he'd driven in a single stretch from the summer cottage back to Oslo, more or less pissed out of his head, following one tragic weekend when we'd both been left behind on our own. I didn't hear from him for years after that, until he suddenly rang me from Spain.

Summing up those lost years, he told me that he'd done time for drink driving and smuggling booze. But he'd been put on disability benefit now, and he'd more or less moved to Spain with his mother.

'You there, mate?'

'What? Yeah, sure, I'm here.'

'Anyway, better be off now, and sort myself a bit of totty.'

'You what?' I ask.

'*A nice bit of totty*, know what I mean?'

Fillip can have a jovial, but at the same time rather arrogant, laugh.

Running

When I wake at around eleven o'clock, I shake all over at the thought of the day before. I can't conceive what was going through my head. It's absurd and alien. I'm just not like that, for God's sake. I do a bit of work, then nip out to buy a kebab.

Later that afternoon I put the new trainers on, but end up sitting on the stool in the hallway. Inside my head I try to imagine how it's going feel: to walk down the hall and out onto the street. I don't even know which direction I'm going to run in. I've just pictured myself running. Suddenly I see how pathetic this is going to look. What people are going to think.

I'd prefer to wait until it's darker out, really. And then I start stressing about having to take my key with me. I'm frightened I'll lose it and get locked out. I'd have to ring at the neighbour's. Then it occurs to me I might get thirsty and I get some money for a soft drink. The money for a drink poses a problem as well. I swap the coins for a note and put it in my shoe.

Then I go running.

Maria

In Alexander Kielland's Square I buy a bottle of water at the petrol station and shuffle on homewards, my tracksuit clinging cold against my body. When I get back, there's a girl outside the gates, leaning against the wall and texting on her mobile. The hairs on my legs are sticking in streaks of sweat, it's bugging me, and I put my key into the lock quickly, stretching my arm in front of her. As I walk past, I see her press my doorbell.

I lock the iron gate.

She leans against the wall again, continues to text.

I stop next to the wheelie bins by the gateway and wait to see if she'll ring any of the other doorbells. It's impossible to say how old she is, but she looks too young to be doing market research, she looks more likely to still be at sixth form college. She's slender, her body almost boyish with narrow hips and long legs. Approximately a head shorter than me, perhaps even shorter. She smelled sweet. Dressed in a grey skirt and something that could be either a short coat or a long jacket. She turns one of her knees inwards towards her other leg, head bowed forward. It looks as though she uses hairgrips.

She doesn't ring any of the other bells. Then, suddenly putting her mobile in her handbag, she goes.

It was only my bell she'd rung.

I just can't think what she wants with me. What *she* wants with *me*.

When I run back and out of the gate, she's already disappeared around the corner.

A car speeds off.

A Memory

'It...it isn't...before tomorrow,' I say.

She's standing there in front of me in the stairwell, smiling, wide eyed. She has smooth skin, perfect eyebrows and red-brown lipstick. In her hand she holds a cup of coffee from 7-Eleven with a napkin round it. She smiles. 'Oh, so it *was* you!' is all she says, stretching her free hand out, giving her name and telling me she's here to look at the flat.

She does use hairgrips.

'The viewing? I know, but I spoke to your father, and he knows my father and he said it would be fine.' She smiles, lifting up on her toes for a moment.

Dad's been over and tidied up the flat while I was out. I'd hardly had a moment to catch my breath before she'd rung the doorbell again. He's chucked all the rubbish into my room. There are smelly socks, under-pants, newspapers, toilet rolls and clothes all chucked in there and scat-tered across the bed and the room.

The moment she traipses in the flat, Dad phones. I tell her she can take a look around, but I make sure to close the door to my room. She nods and peeps round, stepping cautiously out onto the balcony. It all looks put on, as if she's just feigning interest for the sake of politeness. I would never have wanted to move in with me, that's for certain.

In the kitchen as I still chat to Dad on the cordless, I discover she's put her paper coffee cup down.

I pick it up carefully.

Looking inside, I see it's empty.

She's left several thick lipstick marks around the edge. The remains of sugary cappuccino froth are left in a circle at the bottom. The imprint of her lips is clear, with tiny details, cracks and wrinkles.

Dad asks me if it's OK. What's supposed to be *OK*, I haven't a clue. But I answer that it's *OK* anyway. We hang up.

I place the paper cup on the shelf over the fridge.

A moment later she's standing right there.

'The flat's absolutely brilliant!' she says.

'How old are you?' I ask, filling my water bottle.

My glance wanders up behind her, towards the paper cup standing on the shelf just over her head, and then down at my sweaty feet.

'Oh…I thought you were older,' I mumble, not absorbing her answer.

'Oh, whoops,' she says, laughing. 'How old are *you*?'

Rather than answer I pretend not to have heard, and as if I've been distracted by a noise or something, I walk into the living room for a moment.

'Have you got a boyfriend?' I ask and try not to look too conspicuously relieved when she says she doesn't.

Party

He's been here for over two weeks now. Without break. Most of all I want to stab him to death with the kitchen knife. Stuff the pieces into black bin liners. He stays behind in the flat when she goes out, and lies about dozing the whole day, or sits in the kitchen eating and reading old papers, or sometimes lets himself in with her key and starts making dinner for her. Every damn morning of that first week I was woken by the harsh, scraping noise as he set the heavy frying pan on the hob and turned the knob. Everything has to be fried. And he's totally blind to the extractor fan, which unsurprisingly meant the first thing he did was incapacitate the fire alarm with the broom. Once he came dragging in with a fish that he gutted and cleaned in the kitchen; there were fish scales all over the place, added to which he stubs his cigarettes out in whatever he finds. Whether it's on the kitchen worktop, in the sink or in the cups and glasses. There are stubbed out cigarettes on practically every piece of china, it's like eating out of ashtrays. And the entire flat reeks of fat. Bacon. Bacon and fry-ups, every morning, until these last few days when funds finally seem to have run dry: he doesn't get up till late into the day, at which point he commandeers the bathroom for an eternity with his mobile, and chain smokes before consuming a big bowl of cornflakes, overflowing with sugar or strawberry jam.

My milk. My jam. My sugar.

His cornflakes.

They've piled up almost an entire week's worth of washing-up in the broken-down dishwasher. He's nabbed all my returns bottles, but never manages to take the rubbish out.

'The dishwasher's broken,' I say.

It stinks. The dishwasher reeks of rotten food. Dad said he'll take a look at it when he's got time.

'Oh, OK,' the two of them answer from in front of the TV. Håkon didn't meet my gaze at all. Instead his mouth formed an irritated O as he blew his cigarette smoke out. He scratched his forearm, scattering (and chewing) bits of skin and scab from a newly tattooed dragon down into the sofa cushions.

Already, during the course of that first or second day, he was in my room asking if he could borrow the TV and video player, and put them in the living room. It felt daft to refuse, besides which it did seem rather odd for those two things in particular to be in my bedroom. As if all I ever did was lie in there watching porn, sleeping, eating and wanking.

'We've rented a video,' he said.

In other words he'd counted on being allowed to borrow the TV. The video player had never been out, so either he'd guessed there was one in the flat, or he'd been snooping in my room when I was out.

'OK,' I said.

Two days later I heard him taking the TV into Maria's room (where the cordless phone also seemed to find itself most of the time) after I'd gone to bed. And late the next day, when he'd finally got up, he brought it back out without offering a single word of apology or explanation. Håkon shuffled round in his underpants, fetched himself some cereal, cornflakes, before sitting himself down at the PlayStation wearing the earphones. On his way out, as if to justify his presence in some way, he asked if I wanted anything from the shop.

'Anything from the shop?'

'No.'

Creaking

I haven't watched a porn film for two weeks. Other than dodgy films downloaded from the net. Apart from once when they were out, and I was nearly caught in the sofa with my trousers round my knees: hearing the key turn in the lock I had to go running into my room holding my trousers up. Luckily they went to their room quickly, but the video player made an enormous clunk as it spat out the tape.

I like porn best on video.

Her bed creaks.

Sometimes I sneak into the bathroom so I can hear them better.

Hand Towel

It feels really peculiar going out into the flat. Generally they sit glued to the television, which stands next to the door of my room: it's like they're sitting there watching me.

But I like my new room: the change, the break from my old routine.

I brush my teeth. I ate breakfast while Maria was in the shower. After I've washed my hands and face I try to find my towel in the tangle of used ones. Of course, someone, and it's not me, has used *my* towel to wipe the floor.

Håkon has chucked a pair of trousers and two T-shirts onto the floor. I get the urge to kick them over towards the toilet and purposely miss when I piss.

Then suddenly there's a tingling travelling from my inner thigh and up: Maria uses these towels too. Feeling my way to the warmest and dampest of them, I search out her most recently used towel. I dry my hands on it but picture all the places she's used it to dry herself with.

Then I sniff it all over. In one place, down in one corner, I'd swear it smells of cunt.

Cunt.

Fluff

Maria stands in the kitchen wrapped in her robe with a towel in a turban round her head as she hacks a crispbread to pieces between her front teeth for breakfast. Her legs poke out from under her robe. A cleavage forms between her breasts, and there are pink flecks on her skin from the shower. She rubs one foot against the back of her leg, and looks up at me before opening her mouth to crunch into the crispbread. Open mouth. Tongue. Teeth. Transparent spit.

Floating in the toilet bowl is a cluster of blonde fluff.

After having stood there with my hand resting on the door handle, listening out for Maria's every movement round the flat with my eyes closed, I'm so sensitive to the least trigger that I jump when the toast pops out of the toaster in the kitchen.

Carefully I close the door. Then I crouch down, push my glasses back up and study the little island of hair that bobs about on the surface of the water. Like miniature water-repellent scythes. It's as if they rest on the surface in tiny grooves.

I fish them up with my middle finger and lay them in my hand. Eventually I have almost a handful. In the cupboard behind the mirror I find an old tin box into which I scrape the hairs from the palm of my hand.

Cunt.

Shower

I'm standing in the shower when Maria comes in. She flushes the toilet because I forgot to before putting the toilet seat back and sitting down.

I don't move.

Through the shower curtain of clear vinyl I can just make her out as she stretches out to unroll some toilet paper. Several times over, I consider whether I might reach over for my glasses that are lying on the side of the sink. But there's no way I can get away with it. All I can see is a blur of colours: the robe slipped open to one side, knickers stretched between ankles, head tilted to one side as she waits for the urine to stop running between her legs. One of her breasts.

The water thunders from the break created by my dick in the running water. For two minutes now I haven't moved a muscle, apart from to turn my face and squint at her. With my fingers folded round my dick, bent to one side. She gets up, pulls her knickers up, flushes and stuffs a toothbrush in her mouth before scalding me by turning the cold water on.

Then she starts chatting in a rush of excitement, all the while staring at herself in the mirror, toothbrush still stuck in her mouth as she runs her fingers through her hair, tousling it to make it stick forward.

After a while it dawns on me that she's waiting for an answer. She's not *telling* me something, she's *asking* me.

'Ah…' I say, as steadily as I can, '*okay*.' My voice comes out like a great, heavy lump in this tight space.

'And then I was wondering if it would be all right to do my room up a bit, like paint it and wallpaper it and stuff? Would that be all right with you?' She flings her toothbrush down and spits in the sink. So much for Dad's efforts.

'I'm sure that'll be fine,' I mumble.

Håkon comes in immediately afterwards. He pisses while still smoking a cigarette that he chucks into the toilet bowl when he's finished.

He doesn't flush.

Fluff II

The front door closes, Maria locks up. Quickly I open my magazine and find the picture of Kobé Tai where she's lying on a coffee table with her head upside down and a dick in her mouth and take a little of the fluff from Maria and strew it over Kobé's sprawling pussy.

There's a noise. I leap to my feet, listening in case she's come back for something.

I've waited hours for her to leave the flat.

With hair on the pussy, it's almost like real.

Moving-in Party

Later in the day I'm sitting at the computer when I hear the front door open, and the sound of footsteps. Maria's suddenly standing in my doorway, wondering if I've got any music. Without knocking. She just opens my door: 'Oh, are you in here?' she says. 'I didn't think you were home. I just wanted to see if you had any music, that's all.'

There's a woman sitting on the sofa in the living room dressed in a tight black dress, and smoking a long, thin cigarette. She doesn't greet me, just looks at me with a cautious smile, not slipping my gaze even when her phone rings.

Håkon sits beside her, browsing through some comic magazine as he scratches between his toes.

'Were you thinking of anything in particular?' I ask, feeling how my throat has swelled completely.

'Not really. Who were you thinking of inviting, by the way?' asks Maria.

'Inviting? To what?' I ask.

'To the moving-in party, of course,' says Maria, 'I asked you about it earlier. When you were in the shower.'

'Oh, right, of course,' I answer and raise a hand in greeting to the woman on the sofa. At that very moment she looks down, says something decisive into her mobile and gets up.

Before I can protest, Maria goes straight over to the shelf with the CDs.

'Just a friend, perhaps,' I say.

'Tons of Bruce Springsteen here, I must say. Def Leopard?'

I haven't got a single *friend* I can invite. Perhaps the odd acquaintance, but no friends. And I'm not going to invite Fillip.

Her friend laughs.

'Type O negative. Danzig. I didn't know you were some kind of hard rock guy,' says Maria, holding two CDs out in front of her. 'That's not exactly lightweight either,' she says, throwing a glance in the direction of my PC. 'Hey, d'you mind if I pull the blinds up? It's really dark in here, I can't see a bloody thing.'

In my attempt at grabbing the mouse to close the screen, I knock a glass of juice all over my desk. As the two of them start giggling (hopefully the woman about something said on the phone), I automatically make a grab for the toilet roll and in that instant realise how it must look in here.

I haven't tidied in here for over a week.

I've just been so amazingly horny.

'Ah! You looked so cute just then!' says Maria.

I have been just *so* amazingly horny and my entire room is littered with wank wipes. There's a plastic bag hanging from the door stuffed full of crisp bags, chocolate wrappers, paper plates and plastic cutlery, but most of all it brims with tissue papers. Like flypaper, yellow stains, yellow against the cream-coloured tissue. There's even some on the scattered clothes.

Maria's pulled up the blind, and it looks as if there's been a snowball fight, little balls of screwed-up paper tossed all over the place. Like some pen at the zoo.

Maria notices absolutely nothing. Or it doesn't bother her. She's wearing a skirt with black and white checks, a white blouse she's tied in a knot over her midriff and black nylon tights. Her foot rests on a pile of screwed-up, sauce-drenched kitchen roll.

I sit there and stare at the paper towel. Her toes touching the yellowed paper. At worst, inside it there's a blister of old, uncoagulated slime: I imagine the paper bursting and everything oozing out.

'Wow, do *you* have Stina Nordenstam?'

The way Maria says '*you*' brings me round somehow, breaking my reverie, besides which, I have a sense of being watched by the woman on the sofa.

There's a girl standing in my room. She's trampling in my semen.

I think she's...sexy.

I think *it's* sexy.

Somehow.

And all I want is for her to go away.

Fluff III

The door closes. Maria puts a CD on. The smell of cigarette smoke creeps into my room. They leave the flat. I squeeze Maria's pubic hairs around my dick just before I cum: I stroke my hand across Kobé Tai's picture, scoop the hairs together and arrange them round the base of my dick, where her cunt would have closed itself around my dick.

The Weekend

I stand next to the kitchen worktop, waiting for the coffee to finish percolating. It's hopelessly early, but I thought if I stood here, perhaps

I'd get to see more of her. Up to now I've only seen her either in her robe or fully clothed. But I heard her walk through the flat to fetch something out of the fridge before going back to her room again. So it occurred to me that if I were to get up earlier, I might catch her rather more lightly clad.

Maria dumps a bag in the hall.

'Coffee?' I ask.

'Oh, no thanks. We're going away for the weekend; popping over to Håkon's parents. His mother's ill.' She sits down on the stool and starts slipping her shoes on. Glances up, bends forward and ties her laces. 'Sorry Håkon's been here so much, by the way.'

'Not to worry,' I say.

'It wasn't the plan, but he got thrown out of his place.'

'Oh?' I say.

'Yeah. He had problems with the rent.'

Håkon pulls the chain in the bathroom and pads out into the hall. He grins, his eyes heavy with sleep, and without saying a word, he nods. Shoves his feet into his shoes where he left them: kicked across the floor, unlaced. Then, when he's finished putting his jacket on, he stands there stroking the back of her neck.

I hate him, I hate him and I'd like to kill him.

'We've got to catch that train,' she says.

Håkon nods. Maria gets up and pulls the bag straps over her shoulders.

'It would have been lovely to have that moving-in party,' she smiles.

I'm alone at last.

Bed

I open the door to her room. It smells sweet. Lightly soapy. The bed's made. The window stands ajar.

I stand there for a long time at the end of her bed before finally daring to stretch a hand out to touch the duvet cover. A feeling of being watched comes over me. I wait for ten seconds as if everything were normal, then walk out of the room, but without closing the door. Cautiously I steal back from the doorway, looking across the room and through the window into the backyard.

There's nobody up on the roofs, and nobody at the windows.

I come back into the room and close the curtains decisively. And from then on try to memorise the room to the smallest detail. How the duvet is folded, how things are placed and how they stand in relation to each other.

She has several boxes under the bed. Shoe boxes, cardboard boxes and a beer plastic box with wheels so it can be rolled out.

In the exact same moment I open one of the shoeboxes, I become aware of a slip of paper that floats out and lands in the middle of the floor. I pick it up and read it, it comes from a Filofax.

The topmost line reads OSLO.

Calida knickers
1 x white
6 x champagne

Lejaby bra
2 x black
2 x white
2 x champagne

Swimsuit
TL Ice Oil (cuticle oil)
Sticky clothes brush x 2
IKEA duvet cover sets x 2
Make-up bag for handbag
Mirror for make-up bag (DKNY)

At first I think the note must be about knickers with the brand Calida, and bras, but then I don't see what the terms black and white mean because I get it into my head that for some reason she's put eight bottles of champagne on the list. And so white must mean white wine. But for what? I wonder at first. The party? Black…

After a while I realise it's got to be about colours.

Then I desperately start trying to guess where the slip of paper might have come from. It can't possibly have been in the shoebox because I hadn't opened that yet when it came fluttering down. Or had I? Could it have been on the window ledge? Or the top of the cupboard?

I decide to just shove it under the bed together with everything else. The shoebox contains nothing but odd bits. Things.

I have no idea what I'm looking for, but I can't stop myself: I go down on my hands and knees along the edge of skirting board, roll onto the floor and peer up into the bed slats, pull out the bedside cabinet drawer that's almost empty. I'm standing there with both hands shoved between the folded garments in her wardrobe when I'm startled by a noise from the hallway.

Quickly I get out of her room, closing the door. Then open the door again to check that the room's the same as I found it, dash in, pull open the curtain and dash out again.

Was the door open, or was it closed, or had it been left ajar?

I stand and listen for noises on the landing. But there aren't any. What I thought might be Maria coming back for something turns out not to be. There's nobody there. After years of sitting here alone in my flat, I'm suddenly frightened that people are going to barge in.

Eventually I open the front door. There's nobody there. But a free magazine lies on the doormat.

Soft

On the bathroom shelf in a toilet bag there's a little tin box containing a handful of mild cigarettes. Carefully I open the lid and peep into it, before switching the bathroom fan on and placing one in my mouth. It doesn't have much taste to begin with. I watch myself in the mirror. I wonder if it'd suit me, perhaps I'd lose weight if I started smoking. I blow smoke up towards the fan. The smoke creeps through the flat, settling in a layer on the air and floating into the rooms.

I remember the car trips when my gran used to smoke. I twist the cap off a lipstick and screw out the red-brown stick. My mouth's drying out from the cigarette and I throw the butt into the toilet. It hisses briefly and then an oily, brown stripe settles to the bottom of the bowl. While I was smoking, I've read all the ingredients on the various lotions, oils and shampoos she has. Creams for cellulite. The room is stacked with packs of cotton wool, Q-tips, bath oils, eyeliners, lip gloss, mascara brushes, tampons and tubes. Small pieces of coral, sponges, hemp gloves. Kolokrem to darken her eyebrows and eyelashes permanently. I take a sanitary towel out of a green pack of Always: it's soft, she's going to put this in her knickers, on her crotch, and wear it there all day. I imagine it lifting her ass, like in the advert.

The flat is completely still. I grow aware of my creeping about, as if it were the middle of the night, as I systematically remove all the caps, tops and corks. I take off my clothes, rub Veeta hair removal cream on a little area of hair on one side of my stomach and wait a few minutes before scraping it off.

As I light another cigarette, my hands smell of a hundred things at once. They smell sweet, a little dry, almost of earth, and wood from the pencils amongst her make-up things, and my lips taste almost bitter from her perfumes. Soap.

It stings from the cream. So I rub some lotion in. Eventually I've moisturised myself from head to toe. Everything's soft, sticky, sweet and strange.

That afternoon I venture into her room again. At first I just sit on her bed peering round, then I let myself fall back into the soft, soft bed. Her pillow against my face. The smell of hair and sleep and body and genitals. This is where she lies, warm and dry, packed in cotton and feathers and wool.

Everything is soft, squishy and peculiar, and smells like nothing I've ever smelled before.

Present

Fillip stands on the landing, legs planted apart. He is breathing heavily. He leans against the wall with a plastic bag dangling from his wrist and a pack of Heineken under his other arm. Taking a deep breath he hands me the bag, untangling it from his wrist.

'Present from my ma,' he puffs. 'And from me too,' he adds with a short-winded chuckle.

I take the bag. I can feel there's a bottle in it. It says Supermercado in green print on the plastic.

'Ought to have had a lift here.' He wipes a sleeve across his forehead and tugs a can of beer loose from the pack and opens it. The can looks almost fragile and small in his hand, like the drinks cans they hand out on planes. He carefully squashes the aluminium ring down with his powerful index finger, flicks off the froth and drinks half the can in a series of little, gurgling sips.

'Aren't you gonna let me in then?' he asks, belching, automatically taking a stumbling step forwards and then back. He leans against the wall again. I open the door and move back into the hallway.

'Jesus, what do you smell like? Have you been in a lady's beauty salon or something?'

Totty

'Well, well, hasn't he made it lovely in here; a woofter, is he?' laughs Fillip, standing in the middle of Maria's room, indicating its contents.

'It's a girl,' I say.

'I can see that. I'm not totally blind, you know.' Fillip drains his can of beer and crushes it. The room amplifies the sound of his tight breathing. He still hasn't put his pack of beer down.

'Shall we go out, then?' I ask.

'Sure, but aren't we going take a peek at my ma's pressie first, eh?' Fillip nods toward the bag with Supermercado printed on it, on the living room table, as he tears off another can and slurps up the foam that trickles from its opening.

Fillip takes the bottle out of its bag and sends me off for glasses. Into them he pours what I take to be a coffee liqueur, and we traipse out onto the balcony.

'How's about that sofa then?' asks Fillip.

'Nothing doing. I think it's going to be difficult.'

'She a bit of all right, then?'

'Sort of,' I say.

He smiles.

'She's very young,' I add.

'Posh too, eh?'

'Hmm, don't know,' I laugh and straighten my back.

'Any nookie for you then, been down her knickers yet?'

'Nah, it's a bit difficult. She's young,' I add.

'Down in Spain, you know, there's no problem getting a bit of totty there. You should see this Brazilian girl down at the massage parlour. But then again, all you've really got to do is go down to the beach and take your pick.'

Out

Fillip breaks the rest of the pack of beer apart on the kitchen table. Shoving strong, thick fingers between the cans as he rips the plastic off.

'Know anyone who wants to buy some fags, then?' Fillip stuffs the cans into his jacket pockets. You might almost suspect him of having bought the jacket for the purpose.

'You grab a couple too. Can't be bothered carrying the whole load myself.'

Fillip hands me four cans, expecting me to stuff them under my jacket.

I take two, one in each pocket.

Fillip peers at the two remaining cans in astonishment, then lifting his gaze, glares at me.

I pretend to be looking at my watch, but eventually force myself to meet his eyes.

His nostrils make a whistling sound. He shakes his head as he puts the last two beers in a bag. Then he starts laughing. Despairingly.

Angus

We're sitting at a bar in town. Fillip went marching past all the café terraces on Thorvald Meyer's Street and Markveien, wearing a sceptical look, as he knocked back a good few beers on the trot out of the bag. I've consciously increased our pace so as to reduce the opportunity for embarrassment along the way. Reaching the fountain in Olaf Rye's Square, he was forced to stop, his fringe wet with sweat. He wiped his forehead with his sleeve and stuck his finger into the opening of a can, laughing squeakily at all the middle-class teenagers he was seeing. 'Nothing but posh kids round here these days! Never like this before!' At every place we've passed he's asked, 'Is this where you hang out, then?' followed by the same spiteful, high-pitched laugh.

Then he wanted to know where I usually go.

I don't go anywhere.

He seemed a bit disappointed, as if he thought we'd go out and meet some people, that I'd have a few friends up my sleeve for him to hang out with. We went into Schous, but the bouncer was sure he'd seen Fillip before. Besides, he had a bag of beer.

Unable to put the stoppers on him, I've had Fillip relate his entire life story again; Bastø, the dive from Vrengen Bridge and all the rest. I try being tactful; I don't know how he'd react if I interrupted him. But then, it's not as if we have very much to talk about. I've nothing to contribute. I've already told him about Maria, and whatever else I have in the way of other stories is so little, they're probably best kept in reserve. Wait until he asks. Put that way, it's best he talks like the clappers.

'Did you know I've got kids?' asks Fillip.

I nod. He's told me before.

'Two of them. You don't believe me, do you?' Fillip laughs, easing his backside into the barstool.

'Course I do! Course I do, mate.' I nod affirmatively before hunching back over my drink.

It was one of the first things he told me when he started taking up contact. '*I've got kids, never have thought that, would you,*' he'd said as suddenly as now. And I hadn't. Truth was, we never talked very much, so I assume it's something he likes to brag about.

And without him being held the least bit responsible for them. Quite the contrary: according to Fillip, that was all the women had wanted from him. Kids. He refuses to say who they are, apart from telling me that he thinks I'd recognise one of them. A media personality.

'I don't have to pay maintenance or anything.'

'No. Right,' I say.

'One of them, well, she's a good mate of mine, the other one I don't know her so well, but she was fucking gorgeous, wealthy, you know what I mean. Though it's not as if both of them weren't gorgeous.' Fillip fumbles with his glass and smiles. 'I haven't looked this way all my life, you know,' Fillip adds, patting his belly.

I try to laugh with him.

'But one of them, she's a really, really good mate, we've kind of got things sorted between us. It was just something that happened and sometimes I go over and visit the littl'n. Take him to the fair and stuff.

But the other one – well, she was a sweetie, she invited me back to her summer cottage and just opened the drinks cabinet.' Fillip comes to a halt and starts laughing.

'And?' I say.

'Nah. I've said too much already.' Fillip looks at me, weighing me up with a hesitant grin. I lean forward, sipping my beer. Then waving care aside, Fillip leans forward. 'Oh, what the hell,' he says. 'Then she took me in with her, and told me I could drink until it was all gone. So I stayed for a few days, you see, and she lay there on the bed, took all her clothes off and lay down on the bed and told me I could stay till the cabinet was empty. D'you follow? You know what I'm talking about?'

I nod.

'Are you sure?'

'I think so.'

'She wanted me to give her a kid. Her old man probably couldn't get it up, you see. She took her clothes off and spread herself across the bed, and I lay there and shagged all week, and she never put her clothes back on, not once. In the end there was just a bottle of wine left, but I don't drink wine. Next time I saw her, she was expecting.' Fillip laughs and points to himself.

'Are you the registered father, or what?'

'No way.'

'Crumbs – what do you think about that, then?'

'Nah, it's totally cool.'

'But isn't that a bit sad?' I ask. 'Don't you want to see the kid?'

'Why should I? He's doing just fine.' Fillip tilts his head back and empties his glass.

'I think you told me that before,' I say cautiously after a moment.

'You think so or you know so? You can just tell me, I'm not totally dumb, you know.' Fillip burps a flabby burp and slides down from his barstool.

When he comes back he's adjusting his belt. Clearly without having washed his hands.

'D'you see anything of that single mum these days?' Fillip slides back onto his stool again.

'No, not exactly,' I answer.

'So you've not been getting any nookie, then. You still haven't had a good shag, mate!' Fillip laughs.

I shrug my shoulders.

'You needn't get embarrassed, I won't plague you with it.' After talking in hushed and secretive tones for the past half hour, he's suddenly talking embarrassingly loud.

'But you do get the urge to shag, don't you? You do like the ladies?'

'Sure, yeah...'

Limbo

Finally arriving at String's, Fillip insists on going in first, to suss the place out. Whether it's worth it. Worth the money. Or worth the *beer*. Fillip's loathe to put his beer down outside only to be cheated. We've walked up and down Skippergata trying to find somewhere to hide the cans. But Fillip was sure we were being spied on by teenagers and an alcoholic who wanted to steal them.

He reckons it'll be a waste of money if we both pay just to get cheated. I don't see the problem really; I'd pay a hundred kroner just to not have to stand out here. But Fillip's determined we shouldn't be idiots; that we shouldn't be taken for a ride. And since it's my first time this has got to be something special. He's got little drops of relish in his moustache from the burger we ate in Stortorvet. So going in together with him doesn't seem like the best idea either. Just as I'm giving in, Fillip smuggles the beer out of his jacket and into a bag and passes them to me. And as there's clearly no question about who possesses the relevant expertise to suss the place out, we hurry over, Fillip walks up the red carpet and sidles in through the door.

'Aren't you coming in, then?' asks the doorman.

'No...I'm...' I say, holding the bag up and trying to roll my eyes. Right now I don't feel in a fit state to go in. All that beer's repeating on me; I felt reasonably all right after we'd eaten, but now I'm burping the whole time. I don't feel attractive enough: I want to show myself at my best at least. I mean, I'd like to be as unrepellent as possible. I'd like there to be some chance of the strippers *liking* me. After what must be about a quarter of an hour, I'm considering leaving the bag and going home.

'Great bloke, that brother of yours,' laughs the doorman. Fillip's obviously talking with the wardrobe attendant.

'He's not my brother, he's just...' I begin as someone knocks into me from behind: four lads come blustering up the stairs. I want to say the bag isn't mine.

The bouncer stops the last two for ID. Beyond the entrance I can hear Fillip's argumentative voice and jovial laughter.

But instead of giving me the thumbs up for us to go in, Fillip stretches out for his bag and walks back out towards Karl Johan Street.

'Fucking hell, there's nothing but a load of thump-thump-thump music in there; not even any pretty girls. Still, I know another club,' sighs Fillip, 'a proper club. How much cash have we got on us?'

'I don't know,' I mumble. 'Cash isn't the problem.'

'D'you fancy a bit of the real action, then?' Fillip looks at me seriously, sniffing hard through compressed sinuses.

'Now?' I ask.

'There's plenty of clubs…clubs where you get to touch the goods too, I know loads.'

I shrug my shoulders, fling my arms out and laugh. Why the hell not? Isn't that why I'm here? Isn't that why I've come along? Isn't that what I want more than anything?

'We've gotta drink the rest of these first,' he says, handing me an opened can.

Fillip waves a taxi over. The heat of the car nearly makes me pass out. I take off my glasses and massage my cheeks. We drive west, my head's swimming, I'm starting to feel really, really drunk.

The Club

Fillip's already out of the cab. I pay. He seems to be rummaging through the bag of beer again, but I can't imagine there are any cans left. The cab rolls off behind us and we trudge into the back courtyard of some office buildings, where the muffled sound of music creeps from behind a heavy fire door.

They're not keen on letting us in to begin with. The two men at the door look first at Fillip, then at me and then out over the courtyard, without moving their hands from the door handle. But as they're about to shut the door, Fillip gives them a name.

'Quick-quick-quick!' says one of them in a broken accent.

We pay and get a fluorescent stamp that lights up from the UV light behind the counter. I hand my jacket to the cloakroom attendant. '*Keep your wallet,*' says Fillip, and then we're in.

We are in.

The dancers are up on two small podiums, each taking a corner of the room. Pressing their hands on their knees, they glide their bodies from side to side in a slow skating motion, the music is low, their high heels are clacking. They've still got their underwear on. In another room further in, others are standing around playing cards at a casino table. The central room with the strippers is quite dark, but with a pair of UVs beside each stripper.

'I need the toilet,' I say.

'Already?' laughs Fillip, making wanking motions with his hand.

'No, I need a shit.'

Now!

I wash my hands and stick my head under the cold running water. Cooling my face at the same time as trying to get as much cold water down me as possible.

I almost seem to be sober again. I feel calmer, comb my hair. To make my hands less clammy I hold them under the cold water till my fingers go numb.

I smile at myself in the mirror. *This is it. It's gonna happen any minute*, I think, *it's gonna happen now, for real.* They take off their clothes and I have money; anything's possible. I point at myself in the mirror. The sweat has stopped pouring. It's cold in here, chilly. I'm sober. I'm ready.

'It's gonna happen now,' I whisper and smile. 'Go get 'em.'

Fillip has found a table directly under one of the podiums. He sits there with four shots of tequila and two pints in front of him.

'Drinks on me!' he says, pushing a tequila and a beer across the table.

More than anything right now, I want a glass of water.

Fillip stretches out a hand, and at first I don't understand what's going on. Something seems to be glittering in the UV, then I realise he's shaking salt into my lap, distracted by the stripper as she removes her negligee. I hold my hands up in front of me before finally managing to turn the salt pot the right way.

Fillip laughs apologetically. I get up to brush it off when suddenly Fillip leans forward and starts to help me. I freeze. It can't look too good with Fillip fanning my crotch. I pull back, pushing his hand away.

'Chill out, mate, sit yourself down!' Fillip pulls me down by the elbow.

He pours salt onto the back of my hand before raising his glass. I try to drink only half the glass, but since Fillip drains his to the bottom, and I can't predict if he'll be offended or not, I drain mine too. There's no lemon. Or perhaps Fillip didn't want any.

I check my clothes for salt again, and that's when I first notice the snags on my shirt. In the UV light my shirt looks like it might have belonged to an old wino. I'm covered with small clusters of snags, round the arms, on the sides of my stomach, and the insides of my trouser legs. My clothes look old and worn. As if they were soaked in grease.

'Do you want to see the show or what?' He gives me a clip round the head with the flat of his hand, then leans forward, teeth lit below his moustache, every pore visible, each tiny blackhead, each flake of dandruff, and my nails looking like plastic in the blue light.

I turn my gaze to the podium. The stripper is clearly finished. She stoops down to fish her knickers and bra up before mincing down from the podium.

'Yeah, sure,' I say, but my speech is slurred again by the tequila.

For a while nothing happens. Most of the guests have left for the casino table. In the mirror behind the podium I can see that Fillip's clip round my head has ruffled my hair. I try to smooth it with my hands. My face looks totally crumpled.

'Nervous, are we, eh?' asks Fillip.

'No, I'm just a bit…'

I was about to say *pissed*, but Fillip interrupts me.

'Need a bit more to drink if you're nervous, it helps, you know.' He grabs the salt and pours some on the back of his hand before passing it over to me.

I try to refuse with one hand, but he's not looking and licks his salt.

'Cheers, mate,' he says.

We drink, then Fillip points behind me.

'Look, here she comes again. Look, take this.' He shoves a couple of hundred kroner notes over. 'Roll those together and stick 'em in her knickers.'

After a pause the stripper who was dancing on the other podium gets up onto ours. Then the music starts, louder this time. She twists around the pole. I reckon she must come from Eastern Europe. She has a bruise on one thigh, but her skin is stunningly smooth and lovely, although she could have worked up a better tan. She smells of lemon. She meets Fillip's gaze several times, but I don't quite dare look her in the eyes. She leans into the pole, writhing with her hips. She's still not taken any clothes off.

Every time I shift my gaze, it feels like my head goes with it. My hamburger's repeating on me in unpleasant, sour belches. Fillip drums his fingers on his glass and wipes his moustache. When I look back, she's on her knees with her fanny thrusting towards me, hips gyrating. She smiles at me and winks.

'She wants you to stuff a note in her knickers,' says Fillip.

But it's all happening too fast for me. I'm pissed. This isn't how I want it to be.

'Go on then, you do it,' I say.

'I've done it before, mate, it's you who needs it. Go on, get in there!' Fillip gives me a slap on the shoulder. 'Stick a note in those knickers of hers, what's the matter with you?'

I sit there with the notes lying stiffly in front of me. She's already moved on to another group as she lets her bra drop to the floor.

'I've gotta go home,' I say. 'I'm so fucking pissed, mate. I've gotta go home.'

'Could at least finish your beer,' says Fillip.

'I've gotta go,' I repeat, getting up.

Fillip shakes his head despairingly. Incapable of taking my gaze off the floor, I reel toward the exit, cloakroom ticket clutched before me. Then it hits me: I didn't get to see any cunt. I didn't get to see any cunt. But it's too late to go back now. I stagger onwards, stumbling over some chairs.

Shit, I think, *shit–shit–shit*.

Arnold Lane

I wake early. Fillip has already vanished after a night spent on the sofa. The flat reeks of stale booze, sleep and burned pizza. After working a few hours I start to wonder when Maria actually said she was going to be back. Whether I'll manage it in time. I stand there, taking a piss as I contemplate the room behind me in the mirror. The washing machine. The shelf with washing powder. Maria's shelf of toiletries. The feeling starts tingling through my body again. The laundry basket.

I wash my hands in scalding hot water. I don't know why I've never thought of it before. I soap myself twice. Dry myself.

First I take off the lid. It's totally silent in here, aside from the traffic noise that sneaks up from the street, neighbours chatting in their kitchen, somebody walking in the flat below. My hands are trembling. On the top lies a pink T-shirt with oval sweat marks. A half inside-out pair of jeans. I pull out all the clothes. Dirty, little socks. Bras. And once I've disentangled the jeans I have a total of three pairs of knickers. A lacy pair in hard, synthetic material, a cotton pair with blue and white stripes and a thong. I stand there listening for footsteps in the hall.

In my room I lay the cluster of hairs in Maria's knickers, having smelled them first. Their smell was almost too strong, more than I'd expected at first, and there was some white stuff, but it's given me a really big hard on. I wrap the material in a loop around my dick, tighten it, pull on it, it dangles over my scrotum. I stop, listening for steps on the stairwell. Someone lets themselves in downstairs. I go on.

Fuck you, fuck you so hard.

Eli

The telephone rings. I'm standing in the middle of the room with the knickers tight round my dick and I let it ring. But then when it rings again, it occurs to me it might be Dad calling to say he's on his way over to repair the dishwasher. I fumble after the handset, then holding my thumb on the receiver I take two deep breaths to steady the worst of my heavy breathing.

'Hi,' I say.

And fuck you, I think. Fuck you to hell and back. Why d'you have to go and ring me right *now*? What kind of fucking, shitty coincidence is it that you've got it into your thick skull to ring me right *now*? After all these years?

'Oh, hi Rino… Didn't expect this, did you?' she laughs tentatively.

'No,' I say. I try to be short, without seeming bitter. It would just be childish to be bitter after all these years.

But she dumped me. We were even engaged. She was in another class in my year at school, but I never noticed her until college. In the second year we were engaged. But she was an insane born-again Christian.

'No, I'd never have thought,' I repeat.

'You sound different. It's so strange to talk to you again, after all these years,' she laughs.

'Yeah, isn't it,' I say, allowing my office chair to roll in semi-circles.

We'd lie in the basement room for hours necking. With the cassette tape I made for her droning in the background. And my dad walking backwards and forwards across the living room floor above. She'd love it when I let my thigh sink between her legs as I groped her enormous breasts. And she'd lie there, for hours, rubbing herself against me. Rubbing her crotch against my thigh. My thigh used to be quite sore after. She always wore dresses, and she'd pull them up so I could get closer. But under her dress she'd always have tights and under the tights she'd always have knickers.

Everybody thought we'd be an item. *Everybody* would come to us and tell us it seemed so right. We stood together in the schoolyard every break, I even went to her bible meetings. And it was obvious what everybody meant about our being the perfect match: I was big and strong, she was little and chunky, had broad hands and dressed conservatively.

We already looked old.

Or, as boring as one another.

'Right, so how are you?'

'Well…er…everything's fine,' I say.

'Yes, but what are you doing, what are you up to? What's become of Rino, eh?'

She's so pathetic I could puke. As if she's been lying there sleepless every night wondering *what happened to Rino.* She's probably given a toss about it. She dumped me. She found someone else and went off to study, since when I've not seen her. *I*, on the contrary, have spent many a sleepless night thinking of her. If it had been up to me we'd still have been together. It wasn't a phase from college days just to look back on, for me. There haven't been others since her and I hate her for it. She broke my heart.

And why? Because I couldn't bear it any more: I was nineteen years old, we'd been together over year, and not only that, but we were engaged, yet she still refused to sleep with me. It was the same over and over, every night we were together: rub, rub, rub. Until my thigh nearly came out in a rash. Sometimes I could finger her. But that was the limit. She was allowed, but not me.

In the end I said we had to, or I wasn't going out any more. She said she had to think about it. One evening we even tried, but I couldn't get it up. A few weeks later we were finished.

And now Eli, who swiftly found herself another boyfriend, by the way, only a month after dumping me, and who, to top it all off, felt obliged to share the details with me in break times the Monday after (*How was it, then?* I asked. *Fantastic*, she sobbed), now she wants to know how I am after all these years.

My tongue rolls about in my mouth searching an answer.

'OK, I suppose. But what are *you* up to? How have things turned out for *you?*' I return the question.

It goes quiet at the other end.

'Right,' I laugh. 'But isn't it Sunday today? Shouldn't you be, well, at church right now?'

She laughs back. 'Oh, no, I can't pretend I'm terribly religious any more,' she laughs. Almost cheekily. A touch flirtatiously. 'Leastways, not practising in any way. But how are you? You got any kids? Are you married, how are things on the love front?'

'I live with someone,' I answer. Telling her nothing more, I ask, 'So what do you look like?'

'What d'you mean?' she asks.

'Like, how you're dressed, for example?' I swivel my chair so it's fixed.

'Well. I've lost quite a lot of weight since you saw me last.'

'Oh?'

'Yes, it just happened when I hit twenty, the kilos just dropped off.'

'Really!' I tighten the knickers round my dick.

'I train a lot too, I like to keep fit.'

'How are you wearing your hair?'

'Well, I've coloured it. You might not even recognise me now, I think.'

'Are you wearing a skirt or trousers?'

'What, usually, you mean?'

I rub the knickers up and down my shaft. With my left hand I open the video file on my computer, while I hold the telephone against my shoulder with my chin.

'Usually I wear skirts, but right now I'm wearing tracksuit bottoms, I like wearing them when I'm relaxing, but I wear trousers too sometimes. Anyway, I don't dress like before. If you see what I mean.' She laughs.

'Are they tight?'

'Pardon?'

'Your trousers, are they tight?'

Are they tight around your pussy, I think, do they squeeze your crotch as you move.

'Hello?'

'Well, you know...do you tend to go around in loose trouser suits or jeans?'

'What, usually?'

Your cunt.

'Well...'

'What do you mean?'

Does it make you horny, do you get wet, do you cycle home from work, rubbing yourself against the seat?

'I was thinking like at work, what work do you do?'

'Oh, right, like that, I see. I work as a nursery school teacher, there's not exactly any dress code there.'

'But *tracksuit bottoms*, yeah?'

'In my time off, yeah.'

'What are you wearing on top?'

'A hooded jumper, I'm going out for a jog. But what do you work as?'

Tracksuit bottoms. Soft cotton, airy, flowing, slightly tickly.

I press the phone against my chest, coughing to disguise the fact I'm orgasming. Maria's pubic hairs lie strewn across the floor. I dry the cum up with the knickers and throw them onto the bed.

'Rino?' asks Eli.

And again.

'Rino?'

The Window

'I had to close the window in your room,' I shout out into the flat.

'OK,' answers Maria from her room.

'I thought it was getting very cold in there.'

'That's fine, really,' she answers.

'No point having a draft!' I shout.

'I understand,' she shouts back. I listen out for anything in her tone to suggest she's suspicious, that she's realised I've been in there.

'D'you want some liqueur?' I shout.

I don't hear her answer and add, 'There's some in the bag in the living room.'

I go cautiously from the kitchen into the living room, and stand at the door to her room.

'Is there something wrong?' she asks.

'Nope,' I answer.

'OK!' she smiles, takes her toilet bag and towel from her baggage, slips past me and out into the bathroom.

She opens the washing machine. Her clothes are still in there, I haven't got round to hanging them up. I disappear into my room.

I stand, listening.

Håkon

I've decided to give her notice. She's got to go.

I know what I'm going to say as well. That it's a bit rich that her boyfriend's been staying with her for the last two, almost three weeks. Non-stop. They never do the washing-up. Besides which, she irritates the life out of me: with all her talk on the phone, she says *sex* and *sexy* the whole time. She's so vulgar. Somehow. And what's the telephone bill going to come to? She brings people home that I don't know, who barely bother to say hello. It lacks respect. And I'm used to being on my own anyway. She might even understand that. *'I'm used to being on my own, and I like it best that way. This wasn't my idea anyway.'* Added to which, she flutters around in her undies or her robe as if this were a sauna. She gives scant regard for the fact that I live here too. It makes me furious. Does she think that I'm so ruddy bowled over at getting up to the sight of her boobies every morning? What if I had friends around? Would she still sit there with her tackle on display then as well? I know what I'm going to say. I've got a good enough lot of arguments. All the same, I know what really lies at the heart of this. I'm worn out. Just aside from having messed about with her underwear. If Fillip continues turning up all summer, she's bound to leave of her own accord anyway. But that's not how I want it to be: I want her to move out before I lose face. Completely.

She seems to think the word sex is sexy. It irritates me. She says *sex*, with this horrible s-sound at the end. As if what she's saying is somehow shocking or daring. It seems have to passed her by that it's the most clinical term around.

'We had sex,' she says to her friend on the phone.

And the first day she was here, I'm *convinced* she had sex with one of her girlfriends in her room. She hadn't even unpacked, they must have lain there straight on the floor. They laughed all the way up the stairs and held hands as they went into her room. *You're so lovely*, I heard her say.

It's funny to think that somebody's had sex in my old room.

But it was impossible to hear anything, so I can't be certain.

Sex this. Sex that. Sex on the phone. Sex in the papers. *Just wait, dear, mummy's having sex right now.*

But then again: I'm not getting any of it.

But most of all, the issue is I've been messing about with her underwear.

Maria sits at the kitchen table with a glass of drinking yoghurt and three crispbreads she munches as she stares into thin air. I pour some liqueur into a glass, and pluck up the courage to sit opposite her.

And there isn't any chemistry: there could never be anything between us.

'Is there something wrong?' she asks suddenly.

To make things easier I decide that she can carry on living here until she finds another place. She doesn't have to worry about next month's rent either. *Of course.* It's not her fault. I can pay. She's just so young. It's best to deal with it now before things get even more difficult.

'Er, no,' I answer and look down into my glass.

'There's one thing I forgot to tell you. You haven't got the whole deposit yet.' She leans forward and bites into her crispbread, looking up.

'Oh?'

'But Daddy put the rest in just before the weekend, so you'll have it in a couple of days.'

'Oh right, fine,' I say, drinking my liqueur.

'I hope that's OK.' She scratches her leg, lifts her glass of drinking yoghurt.

'Yeah, sure,' I say, realising the moment's lost, that it's too late and it'll be impossible to say everything I wanted now. Maria leafs through a magazine, but I try to restrain myself: my foot shakes and I clench my fist in frustration under the table.

'Are you doing anything this weekend?' She peers up from her magazine, wiping yoghurt from her upper lip.

'Huh?' I say.

'I just thought, I've been talking with quite a few people and it looks like this weekend suits most of them.'

'Oh, for what?'

'The moving-in party, the one we talked about.' Maria gets up and goes over to the sink with her plate, brushes away the crumbs, rinses her glass and adds it to the pile of washing-up.

Something awakens inside me. I'd forgotten about it completely. The moving-in party. In a flash I see it all before me, all my expectations fulfilled: people in the flat, me drinking, going with the flow, talking to people, and in time I'm conjuring the contours of a woman who listens with interest to my every word. I imagine meeting Miss Right. And at last it's going to happen. And perhaps *she's* there. Anything could happen. *It* could happen. It really could happen! I've been an idiot not seeing it. If nothing else it might turn out to be a breakthrough, and the rest can follow. I'll go jogging. I'll train. Go on a sun bed. And jog even more. It'll be brilliant!

I knock back the rest of the liqueur and I'm at the point of whacking my forehead in excitement, and roaring *Wow! That fits perfectly. Brilliant! Wow!* but nod emphatically instead, and give myself an enthusiastic slap on the thigh.

To cover up just how thrilled I actually am, I get up abruptly, go into the living room, pour myself another glass of liqueur, count two seconds to pull myself together and then take the bottle in the bag into the kitchen. Maria refuses politely, she's got to go to bed soon, she has a lecture tomorrow. She yawns.

She starts tidying the kitchen worktop, puts the sandwich fillings away, the peppers, radishes and cheese back into the fridge. We talk a little bit about what we need to buy. I offer to go to the Vinmonopolet for some wine and to buy some food perhaps.

'Listen,' I begin, 'you know that woman who was here the other week? Was she…was she your aunt or something?' And I feel the heat spread embarrassingly over my face. My cheeks are certain to have flushed red just from the obvious association.

'Who? Lara?' Maria laughs, half turning away.

'Yes…well, no…I only wondered,' I add and shrug my shoulders.

'You better not go telling her you thought that.' Maria shuts the fridge door, leans back on the kitchen worktop, her hands tucked behind her.

I laugh, turn my glass, drops of liqueur sticking to the inside in long threads.

'Did you think she was nice?' Maria smiles.

'No, I just…'

'You ought to be careful of her. *Be warned.*' Maria gets up from the bench with a knowing smile and wags her finger. 'Anyway, I'm off to bed.'

I nod.

Maria goes out to the bathroom. I sit on the sofa, put the telly on and channel flick. She brushes her teeth, there's a trickling, then I hear her flush. Then she comes out and stands at the end of the sofa staring towards the screen, picking at her nails now and again.

'Is he coming later?' I ask after a moment.

'Who?' she asks.

'Håkon.'

'Oh, him. No. I shouldn't think so.' She shifts her weight to the other foot. Standing there till the end of the news.

'Listen, I see you washed my clothes, thanks ever so much, it was really kind, but I'll manage it myself next time, all right?'

'OK,' I say without taking my eyes from the screen.

Run

I can scarcely wait. I go running on Monday and Wednesday. On Tuesday I go on a sun bed and get heat rash, my skin turning a reddish pink and itching when I try to work. Maria comes home late in the evenings, chats briefly but sweetly and excitedly about all the people who have accepted the invitation. Then she goes off to bed, disappearing early next morning. I take myself through a series of various sit-ups and push-ups from a fitness magazine every evening.

And I've begun to have second thoughts. It's almost as if I want it over with. To be done with it. Nothing spectacular's going to happen. We're going to have a party. Then everyone will go home. At the end of it all I'll tidy up, go to bed and get up to another day. That will be exactly the same as any other.

But if no change comes of it, then at the very least I'll throw her out.

On Wednesday, back from a run, the telephone rings. It's Maria wondering if I want to come out for a bit. I say I ought to work, but Maria insists, *oh come on*, it seems like she's had a bit to drink, then she adds that she's sitting together with someone who wants to meet me.

'Really?' I say.

'Yes, come on!' says Maria.

Fru Hagen's

I have a shower, decide the sit-ups can wait until evening. Spend forever choosing what to wear: the usual (shirt, tie and jacket) or hooded jacket. Having decided on the hooded jacket I stand there combing my hair, first this way then that. Then I ring to see if they're still sitting there waiting. She says of course, and to just come. So I brush my teeth and comb my hair again. Clear my throat and pretend to put my hand out to myself in the mirror before letting myself out and walking quickly down Thorvald Meyer's Street. I see them from a distance. There are people standing outside Bar Boca and Mucho Mas, the whole street is filled with people and I'm rather nervous of sitting down amongst them.

Maria is laughing about something as I arrive at Fru Hagen's.

I have the distinct sense of the noise dissolving around me. I want to leave again. Then she sees me.

'Rino!' shouts Maria. People stare up at me, then over at her, before picking up where they left off. Maria pulls up a chair.

'This is Lara,' she smiles before I manage to sit down.

I lift a hand in greeting without shaking hands. A wave and a little nod and sit down.

'We're celebrating Håkon and me splitting up.'

'And she wants to treat you to a well-earned beer for being so patient in putting up with it all,' says her friend.

'I'm so glad it's over,' says Maria, smiling.

'I didn't think you had a boyfriend in the beginning,' I say.

Lara gives a little laugh. Then her mobile rings. She signals to Maria and points at the receiver. Maria smiles back and shakes her head, in mock despair, before turning back to me.

'I didn't really, but then it just suddenly happened that way. He simply turned up and refused to go away. Couldn't take a hint. You don't have to be fixed up just because you fool around.'

'No,' I say.

'What about you then, have you got a girlfriend?'

'No, I'm single,' I say.

'Oh, are you *single*?' laughs Lara, putting her mobile down on the table.

'Yes,' I mumble.

Håkon II

It soon rings again. Maria speaks to him for less than a minute, but when she hangs up there are two streaks of tears running down her cheeks.

'Are you all right?' I ask.

'No,' she answers.

'Perhaps we should be alone for a bit,' says Lara.

'No, it's okay,' says Maria with the back of her hand covering her stained cheek. She tries to smile.

But since none of us says very much in the next quarter of an hour, when she comes back from a visit to the toilet, I get up, excuse myself and leave.

Personally

On Thursday Maria gets up and tidies the flat. She apologises for yesterday, empties the dishwasher, scrubs the kitchen worktops and washes the floors. Today she just wants to stay in and relax, she tells me. I give the garden chairs a hosing. Soon after she sits sunning herself between two chairs as I tidy my room and vacuum the sofa. Trying, all the while, not to stare at her too much. Lara clearly slept over, they were rummaging about in the bathroom and living room early this morning before I heard the front door go again. At three o'clock Dad drops in with a mate of his to mend the dishwasher. They have a beer in the kitchen, Dad and his mate both teasing me about Maria, pointing with their elbows out towards the balcony and winking. It goes a bit far in the end, as his mate gets tiddly, and Dad lowers the temperature by reminding us that he knows her father.

When Dad and his mate are finished, I make myself a couple of sandwiches and amble out onto the balcony. She shades her eyes with her hand and peers up, I nod hello and sit down in the plastic chair.

A moment later it creaks. Maria glances up. I look across at her. At first I understand nothing, before the chair suddenly skids to the left. The white chair splits at the joint, my sandwich flying out of my hand, and it takes a moment for me to grasp what's happening, I'm sinking and tipping backwards, and I barely manage to throw myself back up.

We laugh.

Everything's fine. I put the broken chair aside and sit carefully down in one of the others.

We don't say much. The sun warms the back of my neck, it's gorgeous.

'Do you reckon your father would be cross if I decided to move out in the autumn?' she asks a little later.

I cough, mouth full of sandwich. *Wow!* I say to myself. *Fantastic!* Suddenly things are looking up. It couldn't be more perfect. Given I couldn't achieve it myself: she now wants to both continue living here, and yet simultaneously move out.

'No…I don't think so,' I say, chomping on my sandwich and letting my gaze glide past her, over into Birkelunden Park, trying not to reveal my own huge enthusiasm at this.

'Great!' she says.

'That should work out fine,' I add and chomp on.

Maria repeats how great it is as she studies her toes.

'But what's the reason, anyway?' I ask after a pause.

'It's still not certain, you know, but I want to travel.'

'Oh? Where?'

'Don't know yet. Almost anywhere. I've thought about India, Thailand, Australia or South America. Mexico perhaps. I want to go to India or Australia most.'

'With Håkon, or what?'

'No. I'm pretty certain it *won't* be with him.' She laughs, letting several pages flick through her fingers. 'Probably one of my best mates.'

'Lara?'

'No, she can't probably, we've talked about it. But I've got a friend who's at college in the US, she's really my best friend, so long as I don't have to put up with her boyfriend it'll be fine... Have you travelled much?

I shake my head.

'That's a shame. Why not?'

Because I've never had anyone to travel with, I think to myself. I've never had friends so I've hardly dared contemplate it. And I feel sick with anxiety at just the thought of it now.

'I haven't really had anyone to travel with.' I brush the crumbs off my hands and take another sandwich.

'You could have gone on your own, then.' Maria tilts her head.

'Oh?' I say.

'Yeah, it can be good to travel on your own too, you don't always need someone with you. If you travel alone you don't need to worry so much about other people and that sort of thing. You're a lot freer to change plans and be more impulsive.'

Sure. If you're sick to death of company, it might be fucking brilliant, but when you've always been on your own, there might just be a point to having someone with you so as not to feel so totally alone in the world.

'Yes, well, it's your own fault if you're too much of a coward.'

I'm stuck for words for a while after that: it probably wasn't meant unkindly, and I don't feel that angry or hurt, but nonetheless it sits there.

'But then, I don't reckon it's likely to be the US, really.'

'Hmm?'

'I don't reckon we'll go to the US, considering my friend's already been there so long. Perhaps I'll go to the US and meet her and then perhaps go on further to Mexico.'

'Oh, I see.'

Face It, You're Fat

After a while, it clouds over and grows chilly, so we trek back into the flat. Maria lies down browsing through a catalogue with a blanket over her as she drinks cup after cup of tea or hot toddy, while I channel flick. On a couple of occasions I even forget I'm not alone: once I manage to take my sock off to see what's making my foot itch underneath and another time I dig my finger so far up my nose, I have to turn away from her without taking my finger out and walk bent over double to the bathroom, for fear of what might come out at the end of it.

When I come back, she doesn't pass comment, so perhaps she didn't notice. But I am convinced she's farted.

I don't pass comment either.

I suggest impulsively that we go down to the video store on the corner and rent a film. But before we get on our way, Ricki Lake Show's topic of the day confronts me, hitting below the belt: *face it, you're fat!*

And the guests' common denominator is that, as fat people, they dress too provocatively.

Ricki Lake: What do you mean she's fat? What does *fat* mean?

Samantha, the sister of an overweight stripper in a tight-fitting pink dress: 'Well, Ricki, if you weigh 200 pounds, you're fat! And when you're fat you shouldn't dress like that.'

So now I know. This is exactly what I needed to hear right now.

A black guy in a Hayes 79 football shirt who's convincing nobody and who's fatter than me anyway grins with white teeth. 'I don't want a fat girlfriend.'

I rattle my keys.

'What did you say?' asks Maria.

'A video.'

'Yeah, OK,' she says, getting up without taking her eyes from the screen. It's so damned engrossing she goes on standing in the middle of the room, as if turned to stone, remote control stretched out in front of her, totally unable to press the off button.

But the crassest bit of all has to be the mother who reckons her daughter's just jealous because her boyfriends find her more lovely than she is.

'I don't care what you say. I *know* I look great,' she says, shaking her head manically.

When the audience boos, she gets up and starts pretending to strip. More than anything she looks like the baby in Ally McBeal, grinding her hips before putting her hands on her knees and shaking her ass.

'Do you see what I mean? She does that in front of my friends and even boyfriends.' The daughter sinks back into her chair, head in her hands.

'You're embarrassing your daughter!'

'Oh, she's just jealous.'

'Je-sus,' sighs Maria.

'Stay with us. After the break we'll see today's guests after they've had a make-over with our stylists, and see how fabulous they look in their new outfits.' Ricki Lake smiles and there's something about her that I can't quite bring myself to dislike.

Maria pulls a pair of tracksuit bottoms on and we go down. And the moment we walk through that door, this feels like something new: I'm going to walk through that gate together with someone. Just for once I'm not walking alone. I'm walking together with a girl.

And somebody could take her for my girlfriend.

It could even be quite embarrassing, since she's obviously younger than me. Maria walks with hurried steps, skipping over curbs, shivering slightly with her hands tucked in under her armpits as she asks what films I like. I swing my key ring on my index finger, trying to saunter along a bit casually. 'Don't mind, really,' I say. And as we stand in front of the shelves, I notice myself drawing closer to her, little by little, until we're standing side by side and looking *together*. I like the way she pulls the covers out, the way she holds them in front of her, closing her fingers gently round their spines. She turns her nose up at most things, but after some to-ing and fro-ing we agree to rent *Copland*.

Maria stands choosing some sweets from the pic 'n' mix, bum slightly swayed to one side, while I line up at the cash desk. I smile. The Pakistani bloke behind the till juts his jaw forward by way of greeting, as he works to get something out from between his teeth. I push the cover out in front of me, opening my wallet.

'And she's having some sweets as well,' I say, pointing towards Maria.

He doesn't answer, but runs his fingers over the keyboard.

'Hang on, there's something showing up here. Ah, you have a late return. You'll have to pay a fine,' he says.

'What? From when?' I ask.

'You rented one movie with that Raquel Darrien and one Austin Powers.'

'What?' I ask, pushing my glasses up.

That's ridiculous. Why would I have rented a soft porn movie? I've got access to just about everything in the whole world. Besides, I hate Austin Powers. And I hate Benny Hill.

He turns the screen towards me.

Maria puts a bag of sweets on the counter.

'What's going on?' she asks.

'Nothing,' I say.

'Trivialities,' he smiles.

The Vow

It is evening. Maria has hardly moved from the sofa. After the film she's dropped off a couple of times with a travel brochure on her chest, snoring a little before an abrupt awakening, followed by yet another round of tea and trips to the loo.

'Is Håkon coming tonight, or what?' I ask.

Maria laughs, lays the catalogue over her face and scratches between her eyebrows before bringing her arms back down and smacking the catalogue down in her lap.

'You know what, at first I thought Håkon was just sweet and scatter brained. He's *unbelievably* irritating. He has all those bad traits that are a bit charming and a bit cool, it's just that he's also such a fucking jerk.'

'Oh?' I say. 'In what way?'

'No, there's so much. It's a bit personal.'

'Oh, right, sorry.'

I flick briskly through the TV channels. If she gets off to bed soon, I might get to watch Canal+ or Playboy Channel, if I turn the sound off.

'No need. It's fine.'

Maria puts her travel brochure aside, sips her tea, rolls onto her side and continues, her eyes still turned towards the television.

'No, honestly. For example, he goes on at me the whole time about having this threesome. And then he goes and suggests it to Lara, without even asking me first.'

She looks up.

'So I feel more than a bit daft when Lara comes and talks to me about it. She even thought it was my suggestion. A threesome, with my friend, kind of. And that I was the one to suggest it, but didn't dare ask her myself.'

The remote control's getting clammy in my hands.

'But I'm going to be celibate now; from next week I'm not going to sleep with anybody for six months. At least! Apart from girls, maybe. Boys are foul.' She laughs. 'Boys are all pathetic and childish.'

My head's about to burst.

'Have you done loads of crazy things with women, then, Rino?'

She stretches and yawns.

'Well, I don't know. Just the usual,' I answer.

We have been out renting a video. That's totally wild. Maria and me.

A video.

Friend

At around midnight the phone rings. She gets up and takes the call in her bedroom before disappearing into the bathroom.

Maria returns from the bathroom and stands next to the sofa, her knees pressing against the armrest, catching the end of a documentary about an injured rhinoceros on *Animal Planet*.

'I'm going to go and stay at a friend's,' she says.

I nod.

'It's been a great day, really nice,' she adds. 'I presume you'll be staying up a bit longer.'

And with that she strokes my forehead, letting her fingers run through my fringe.

'You're so sweet. It's like you're so calm about everything.'

She smiles.

The front door slams. I try to remember the last time anybody touched me.

It feels like years.

It feels like I've got armour plating, inches and inches of thick, thick skin.

I lie like that for ages.

Shit

On Friday I pick up some booze from Vinmonopolet, go jogging and do some sit-ups in the living room in front of the TV. Maria doesn't come back home. She's nowhere to be seen. I suspect her of not giving a damn about the whole thing. I sit and do some work, and then start drinking some of the rum and vodka, drop off in front of the telly and wake up with the noise of people on their way home in the street below, before tumbling into bed.

I am woken by Maria knocking on my bedroom door.

'You've been so brilliant!' she waves excitedly at the flat.

I feel happy.

Clammy

'Fuck! What a penthouse!' yells one of Maria's mates.

A glass slips from my hand onto the kitchen floor and I'm halfway out of the living room before finally realising that it's the flat he's talking about, and not anything I've left lying about or that he's found in my room (although even there I've tidied everything away, thinking it might just be possible that someone would stay the night, or something).

'Fucking ace flat, man. Wow!' He flings his arms out as he stands in the doorway onto the balcony, before adding, 'Fucking hell, Maria, who d'you give head to to get this, eh?'

I'm still standing there with a bag of ice cubes when I'm pointed out as the owner of the flat. He stalks across the floor and grasps hold of my hand so I almost lose my glasses.

'I just gotta say it, man,' he says, 'I just gotta say it.'

I clutch the ice cubes against my hands to stop them getting clammy.

The Slip of Paper

This is so weird: every time someone rings the doorbell, they ask if they've come to Rino's and Maria's. Rino and Maria. That's what it says on the doorbell downstairs. And it feels totally unreal: every time I walk past and see it. *Rino and Maria.*

'Hey, it's Marathon Man, isn't it?' says a guy out on the balcony. 'You're that bloke who goes jogging round here, aren't you?'

For a split second I wonder what he means, what he's getting at. Over time I've begun to take my route round the football pitch, and some-times when there's girl's football, I walk past slowly, or run round several times, and around midday I've developed a liking for running up along the Aker River and round Foss High School.

'You what?'

'Yeah, I've seen you running round here.'

'Oh yeah, fucking right, man. I've seen you too!' says his mate.

'Have you?' I manage to stutter.

I experience an unnerving sense of bewilderment: I don't know whether to feel flattered or worried that he's seen me out.

'Yeah, don't you usually go in Boca and Hagen?'

'Well, not really,' I say.

'Jogging's bloody brilliant. I go jogging myself quite a bit,' the other one adds.

That makes me feel I can relax again at last. We talk a bit about training, I tell him about my sit-ups programme, he listens with interest and asks me to draw the exercise for him on a napkin. As I stand drawing, his friend shoves a slip of paper in front of me.

'What's that?' I ask.

'Oh, it's just an invite to a party I'm arranging.' He scoops his invites up and knocks them into a neat pile against the railings on the balcony.

'What, is that for me?' I ask, thrilled.

'Bring a lady friend along, it's gonna be a fucking brilliant party, you've gotta come, courtesy of me.'

I take his hand.

'Thank you, thank you very much indeed!' I say.

'Yeah, right, it's cool, man. No big deal.'

I let go of his hand, stare at the note and put it safely in my wallet.

'Wow, smart wallet,' he says.

'Would you like something to drink? Can I get you one of my beers?'

'Don't worry, I'm sorted for a bit, but thanks anyway, might take one after.'

'Oh, sorry,' I say.

'No stress, man. Cool pad you've got here, by the way.'

'Yeah...yeah. Right,' I say, draining my bottle of beer to the bottom.

'This is just such a fantastic flat, it *so* is,' says a girl standing next to me without introducing herself. 'If Maria goes off travelling this autumn, you have *so* got to tell me if it's available.'

She rests a hand on my forearm and smiles.

I look at her.

Then down at my arm.

Then up at her again. She's amazingly slim. With huge, white teeth. She's wearing a short blue dress with bare arms.

If Maria goes off and travels.

If Maria moves out.

Maria travels. Moves out.

Telephone

I should eat. But I'm slimming. It seems achievable now, losing weight, but the alcohol's going straight to my head. I spend all my time refilling bowls with snacks, clearing tables. I don't say much, just try to smile at the guests instead.

Eventually I can't help myself and eat some nibbles: by the time they reach the living room the bowls are half empty. Slightly tipsy, I juggle them through the dancing guests. Remarks flying at me, all the time, about how fantastic the flat is. Lots of them assume it's a new purchase. And when they hear it isn't, they wonder why I don't sell now, when there's so much money to be made.

'Anyone here by the name of Rino?' a guy suddenly yells out in the living room, turning the stereo off.

'Rino?' a girl's voice says. 'What kind of a name is that?'

'That's the guy that lives here,' I hear someone whisper back sharply.

Rino and Maria is what's written on the bell.

'Oh, yes,' she blushes. I recognise her as the girl I was talking to earlier. She guides a potato twist stiffly to her mouth after having somehow studied it, then stomps out onto the balcony.

She is definitely struck from my list of possibles to live here.

'Yes?' I shout back. I already sound a bit pissed.

'There's a call for you!' He tramps toward me, handing me the cordless phone.

Just as I bring the receiver to my ear, somebody turns the music back up.

'Hello? Who is it?' I shout, hoping it isn't Fillip, who I've been trying to avoid all week.

It's Edel.

'I see,' she says. 'Having a nice time, are we?' She hangs up.

Arse

When I come out of the bedroom, Maria's in the hallway talking to a man in black wearing a broad-brimmed hat.

'How's everything going?' she asks. Maria has a fantastically distant gaze. She smiles with narrowed eyes and a drunken giggle.

'Great! It's going brilliantly!' I smile as best I can.

'This is Henning. He's a poet,' says Maria, giving him a pat on the belly.

'Hi there. Henning here.' He takes my hand, says what a fabulous party it is before apologising and saying he's going out for a bit. My guess is he comes from Bergen.

'Are you famous?' I ask.

'Well, no, not exactly,' he answers and laughs. He drinks straight from a bottle of what I take to be homemade wine before turning to Maria and adding, '*You can work your ass off to change language and still never get famous.*'

I squint questioningly at him.

Rather than explain himself, he rests a hand on my shoulder and laughs.

'Anyway, we're off out to do a weather check. In fact, we're going to run around Sofienberg Park naked.'

I look at him.

'Want to come along?' he asks me just as Maria's returned from the kitchen and given him a hug.

'Me too, I want to come and bathe naked too.' Maria's voice simpers like a child's.

'We're going to *run* naked,' Henning corrects.

'Oh, whatever,' says Maria, shrugging.

'You can't come anyway, you're too drunk,' he laughs.

'Well, I don't think I'll...' I shake my head and try to smile. Henning raises his arm and a short brunette rushes out into the hall.

'Oh for heaven's sake, spring has sprung! And if we go on like this, chances are it'll get to be a tradition,' chuckles Henning, grinning with the bottle to his lips.

'Well, yeah, I suppose so, I could time you all or something,' I mumble.

'That'll be absolutely splendid,' laughs Henning.

Witness

I'm about to be run over by a car as I cross the road, hovering at the back of the group with my mobile where I've found the stopwatch function.

They stop by a tree.

'Kit off, everybody!' says Henning.

'Isn't he going to run too?' asks the brunette crossly.

'No, I'm timing you,' I say, trying to laugh.

'Yeah, yeah, don't bother!' says Henning, unbuttoning his trousers. His shoes already lie kicked to one side and he's walking barefoot on the grass.

'I think that's cowardly,' she says, taking her pullover off.

'Somebody's got to look after the clothes,' I mumble.

'But you go jogging and stuff, don't you?' asks the guy next to me.

'Yeah, that's right,' I answer.

I'm regretting this. I really ought take my clothes off and join in so as not to lose face, only I can't bring myself to do it. Nobody says a thing. They take their clothes off in silence. So, to have something to do, I walk over and draw a start line in the gravel on the path.

Henning puts his shoes back on.

Then they start sprinting. Giving a toss about my start line. I shout *Go!* behind them, but it's totally out of place.

What's more, she hides her buttocks behind her hands for the first twenty metres to make sure I can't see.

Where

'Where are you, mate?' asks Fillip. The harsh sound of my mobile suddenly ringing in the dark startled me, and before I'd managed to see who was calling, I'd already picked up.

'What d'you mean?'

'Where are you? I'm standing outside your flats, but you're not answering when I ring the bell. I've been across to Sweden and got some beer and stuff.'

'Right...no...I...'

'Some bacon, too. Your neighbour's having a party.'

'Oh?'

'Yeah, there's a load of daddy's boys with their lady friends out on the balcony.'

'I'm at the old man's,' I say quietly, watching the naked sprinters.

'There must be masses of booze up there, I reckon.'

'Yeah, right.'

'Loud music, that's for certain.'

'OK.'

'And loads of ladies.'

'Look, I've gotta help Dad with a few things, so I've really gotta go.' I press my thumb over the microphone and talk into thin air as if I'm answering someone.

'Aren't you coming back to town tonight then, mate? I can wait down in a pub or something, then we could go over to your neighbour's or out somewhere – thought we could fry up some of the bacon.'

'I don't think...'

'I can just walk down to the park and drink my beer while I wait.'

'No…er, I can't. I'll call you tomorrow.'

'OK. Won't pester you, mate.'

'Nah, you're all right,' I laugh.

'Bye.'

'Bye!'

Taxi

They have vanished from sight over by the church. I'm looking for the stopwatch function, but just as they come back into view, my mobile rings again. Fillip's laughing.

'You should be here, mate.'

For a split second I think Fillip has managed to get in. That he's got into the party and that I'll spend the remainder of the evening trying to gloss over all my lies, and at the same time defend myself from the embarrassment of what's certain to follow. (*Why don't we fry a bit of bacon for the ladies? I can go home and fetch some more beer.*)

'Really?' I clear my throat.

'I'm standing down in the park, and you'll never guess what they're fucking doing here!'

'(…)'

'There's a whole bunch of people running round here starkers!'

Fillip laughs. Resulting in the phone sounding like a faint echo. My gaze following along the edge of the park, I spot him on the far side, his mobile clasped to his ear, the hand with the plastic bag and beer lifted to his mouth.

I think the game's up at first, and take a couple of steps to go and meet him.

Then I dash backwards into the bushes.

Fillip raises his beer can to the joggers. Henning and his friend wave back, laughing. The girl stares stiffly ahead, but it's obvious she's laughing too.

'Are you there?' shouts Fillip.

'Reception's bad,' I whisper. They have less than fifty metres to go, and if Fillip follows them round with his gaze, he's going to see me squatting here in the bushes with my hand clasped around the receiver to smother the echo.

'D'you hear me? Masses of ladies… Fucking hell, flat as pancakes or what!' Fillip sneers.

'Yeah, yeah,' I answer, 'but the reception's awful.'

I hang up and watch as Fillip stares down at his mobile with incomprehension before sticking it in his pocket and crossing the road to the park. That's done it, I think to myself; now they're going to start asking themselves where Rino is, and they'll end up shoving him in my direction, because he's such a pain: because we're both such a pain. Because I shouldn't have come. Because we're just a couple of annoying peeping Toms.

I start to fight my way through the bushes. But fucking hell, why do they do it, then? What's the point in running around naked if you don't have any witnesses anyway? What the hell's she making such a fuss about? She's the one who's taken her clothes off in the park. And besides, it was Henning who invited me.

The branches catch my jacket. I stand, head hanging, resigned, and more than anything I feel like screaming. But just as they reach their clothes and I'm about to come out to meet my humiliation, I hear Fillip shout, 'Taxi!' And I turn around to the picture of Fillip stepping out into the road with a taxi in front of him like some caught beast as he knocks back his last drop before crushing the can in his fist and putting it back in the plastic bag.

Fillip dives into the taxi. I breathe a sigh of relief and try to stop myself from staring at her but my gaze is constantly drawn to her crotch and breasts. Henning's dick flops up and down. She has a large, black untrimmed triangle as well as the flat chest, but I reckon she's an artist too. She runs straight over to the clothes, and they begin to dress quickly. Henning laughs as he catches his breath.

'It was a good job I was here to look after your clothes,' I laugh hesitantly, gathering myself with a sigh and trudging out from the bushes.

'Absolutely,' Henning says, pulling his trousers on.

They've barely got their clothes on before they're traipsing out of the park, in the opposite direction to home.

'Aren't you coming back to the party then?' I ask.

The brunette doesn't answer. She stuffs a jumper down in her bag and moves swiftly off.

'I think we'll probably go out somewhere,' says Henning.

'Will you come to the after-party then?' I ask.

'Yes, why don't we do that, that's a splendid idea,' says Henning. 'We'll talk then.'

He bounds off, skipping to catch up with the others. I ramble back in the direction of the flat.

On a Silver Platter

The flat is full of people. As it's never been before. The doorbell's ringing all the time, people are coming and going, whizzing in and out of the flat, down to 7-Eleven; someone's found badminton rackets and they're down in the park playing; a couple sit, sobbing in the stairwell; others are dancing and snogging in the living room; one guy's tried to sleep in my room. I've got an acid taste in my mouth from all the excitement and lack of proper food. And I'm gradually getting rather drunk with all my nervous drinking. I tried mingling to begin with, but it was hard to think of things to say. And I can't remember any names. So I've ended up sitting in the kitchen, picking the twigs and leaves off my jacket. Apart from which, I've already been on one errand to buy more mixers.

'Hey, what are you doing sitting here?' Maria more or less tumbles into the kitchen, tagging a boy along I've not seen before. She's been in top gear for the last hour, falling around on the dance floor. Her stockings are laddered on her inside thigh, like little pouches of spider web. She drinks from a huge glass of water, which she refills.

'You're not feeling sad, are you?' she asks, taking a drink.

'No, I'm just...' I begin, feeling the irresistible need to massage my temples.

'Oh, but you are!' She puts her glass aside on the kitchen worktop.

'No, honestly.'

'Something's the matter, I can feel it.' She blinks her eyes in a futile attempt at concentration and giggles, 'I f-e-e-el it inside me.'

That said, she crosses the floor to me. 'Give me some space! I need to sit down!'

'Oh?' I say, straightening up.

Before I realise what's going on, Maria has settled herself on my lap. She dangles her legs and wraps her arms around my neck.

'You're not allowed to be sad. Today we've got to be happy, you see.'

I stare down at the floor and nod. My neck feels restricted.

'You're not allowed.' She bows her head and peers into my eyes. Then she rests her cheek against mine and whispers, 'You're not allowed.'

Only when she risks tumbling off my lap because I need to shift my legs do I dare hold her around her waist.

'Amazingly nice flat,' says the boy suddenly, standing next to the kitchen worktop.

'Thanks,' I say.

'How much d'you pay in rent?' he asks, filling a glass with water.

'Why don't you just go and put some music on or something?' says Maria, head tilted and one arm stretched out, twisted childishly and demandingly, a finger pointed in the air.

'Yeah, sure.'

'Now you mustn't go being cross. This is Rino, he's lovely, but he's a bit sad, he's… This is the man I've given my vow of cilla…ciliba…celibacy to, you see.' She laughs at her own awkwardness, sitting with an exaggeratedly swayed back and legs dangling. She drinks some of her water and smacks her lips.

'Yeah, okay,' says the young man, leaving.

At first we sit without saying a word.

'I've been so stupid,' she says sweetly and brightly.

'Oh?' I clear my throat.

'Yeah, look, I've ruined my tights.' Maria sinks back on my lap to lift her knees. I have to use both hands to stop her toppling back and hitting her head on the window. 'And I haven't bought any new ones.'

I gaze at the smooth skin on the inside of her thighs, revealed by the bubbly holes in her tights.

'Feel here. They're ruined!'

She takes my hand and guides it towards the rip. My fingers yield limply and without will against the inside of her thigh.

'Go on, feel then!' She shakes my hand. I stretch out my index finger and she guides it towards the rip again.

'Feel! Here it's completely cold. And here it's warm.' She moves my finger against the fabric of her tights and then against her bare skin.

'You're not allowed…' She turns to sit astride my lap. Her lips close to my earlobe.

'You not allowed…' I still have my finger inside her tights. As she shifts, the holes unravel one after the other.

'You're really not allowed to.' My ear tickles, I can hardly breathe and she's leaning against my dick.

Maria's mouth is cold from the water. She clutches at my neck and runs her fingers through my hair. I try as hard as I can to kiss her, but it's been so long. I don't understand why she's doing this, but I feel as though I'm about to cry: I'd completely forgotten how it felt.

'You are so calm and safe,' she whispers.

Her skirt's ridden up, she's sitting astride me, I can see her knickers, they cut into her sleek thighs.

'What's happening?' I suddenly hear the boy ask from somewhere behind me.

'We're just having a nice time,' says Maria, clearing her voice.

Then she puts her feet on the ground. She leans forward and kisses me again, tracing the tips of her fingers over my cheeks. I close my eyes.

'Still, I'm going to go and dance now. I love that song. Come on!' She takes me by the hand. I open my eyes. The last thing I want to do now is dance. There's a bulge in my trousers.

'Wait a bit,' I beg her.

'You'll have to come later, then!'

She runs from the kitchen, snatches the boy's hand and immediately she reaches the living room, turns the volume to full.

She is completely wild. She must be crazy.

Nauseous

I sit waiting for Maria. But she never turns up. I go in search for her. She's not out on the balcony. She's not on the dance floor either. And I don't dare ask anyone where she might be. It's too embarrassing. She's too young and too drunk. I'm too old. She's not in her room either; in fact, the boy she brought with her into the kitchen is there, on her bed reading comic books. He meets me with a blank expression. It's when I need to go to the toilet that I find her. Lara is standing behind her, holding her hair back.

'Oh...' I say.

'It'll be fine. She always pukes, then she's fine again afterwards. It would be brilliant if you could find a towel.'

'Sure,' I say.

'Rino,' moans Maria with her head down the toilet. 'You're so lovely, Rino!'

She stretches her arm up behind her and waves with her fingers.

'Lara?'

'Yes.'

'Rino's lovely.'

'Course he's lovely. Are you feeling better?' Lara bends down, just as another wave of vomiting starts.

'Just put it on the side of the bath.' Lara indicates the towel I'm holding out, and I'm on the point of leaving when Maria calls to me.

'Rino! Can't you hold my hand?'

Not knowing what to say, I give a short laugh.

Maria stretches her arm behind her and waves her fingers at me again.

I look at the hand. Then just as she is about to pull it back, I step forwards and grab it. It feels like holding a dog on a lead while it's having a shit. I kick the door shut behind me.

Maria vomits several times on the trot as she grips my fingers so tightly they turn white.

'You're both so sweet and lovely, you ought to be together,' she says.

And then, just as we thought she'd finished, one long, explosive fit of vomiting makes her pull her hand away and grip hard around the porcelain.

'I need a shit,' she says. She lifts her hand from the toilet bowl and lifts it up to her face to wipe her mouth.

At which point I leave.

On a Silver Platter II

Lara comes in the kitchen. She asks for a glass of water. I get a newly washed glass out of the dishwasher.

'She usually snogs half the party, but she seems to have restrained herself a bit tonight,' Lara smiles. 'How long have you owned the flat?' she asks, and for a while we chat about nothing in particular, with me losing track now and then because I've got so drunk and more than anything I'm concentrating on keeping my balance and answering her questions as best I can, until she asks me what I like reading.

I shake my head, my mouth refuses to open.

She practically chases me round the kitchen: she seems short sighted, I thought I must have something on my face to begin with, and so I've felt it several times and wiped the corners of my mouth, without finding anything, but every time I take a step back, she takes one forward.

She lifts her chin and lets the wine glide in.

Soon after she kisses me.

It comes suddenly: my first response is to back off, but I simply end up banging the back of my head and my heels into the fridge door, and knocking a bottle off the worktop. Then I just attempt to hang in there.

Her hands lock behind my neck.

Her little, wet mouth against mine.

Her tongue in my mouth.

She kisses me on the neck. I struggle to bring my arms down. My arms stick out like two stiff, thick branches until she guides my hand to stroke her back.

Soft fabric under my fingers. Am I allowed? Am I really allowed? She really wants this? I can't take it in: I have to force myself to touch her.

Lara moans in my ear. Kisses my neck. Then she leans her head back, her nipples erect in her black suit. I have to force myself to hold her round her hips and doing it makes me dizzy. With her fingers clasped around me, she pulls me down to kiss her neck.

Lara's hips between my hands. The top of her ass against my fingers, the cleft under my hand. I take a sneak look down the front of her frock.

She doesn't stand still for an instant, her body twists this way and that, her hips moving in a circle, her hands stroking me up and down my back. She traces her nails from my earlobes, over my cheek and down over my neck. She takes my head between her hands and looks me in the eyes. She whispers closely and quietly in my ear.

'I want you to fuck me, Rino. You can fuck me, exactly as you want. You're so big and gorgeous.'

She strokes my mouth with her index finger, letting her fingertip glide over the lower lip of my open mouth.

I'm going to screw her stiff.

Like a huge, heavy animal I press myself towards Lara, pushing her, almost running across the kitchen floor before we reach the other side: I kiss her up against the wall, stroking her breasts and ass, I squeeze the backs of her knees, let my hands slide under her skirt. She bites my neck as my fingers slide over her knickers, she pushes her hips up and pulls me towards her, pressing me in the small of my back, her fingers cold under my trouser waistband, but she doesn't push them all the way down. For a moment I wonder whether it's right for me to be doing this; whether Maria might be offended considering we were snogging each other first. But then she had another boy in her room; she's too drunk, too out of it and too young.

Besides, I'm not thinking. My body shudders. The head of my dick's going to burst.

'Yeah! Go for it!' I hear a boy's voice say behind me. 'Lara the go-getter.'

Lara laughs. Her hair clings wet to her neck. The two of them say something to each other, and then, as if his life depended on it, the boy insists on shaking my hand and saying 'great party', and a load of other stuff, and then suddenly there's a whole pile of people standing about in the kitchen: some wanting water, some just getting something, while others, with their lips smacking, are about to raid the fridge. 'Lara's snogging a bloke in the kitchen!' someone shouts on their way back to the party.

Lara wants to dance.

'Here?' I ask.

'No, in the living room. Come on!' she says, taking her glass and cigarettes with her.

Lara dances.

Gradually, I start to loosen up too. While I'm dancing I knock back a bottle of wine. Lara leans forward, making a wild hollering, almost clucking sound, then laughs. I spill wine all over my shirt and laugh too. I dance. I have an invitation in my pocket: I have been invited! Lara leans forward again, her breasts forming the perfect cleavage in the front of her frock. She takes my bottle and drinks from it, I stretch my arms in the air, the living room is crammed with dancing people. And at the edge of my vision I see people out on the balcony, talking, holding glasses and cigarettes. Maria has clearly come round again and leans out from a group of people over by the table, one by one they all lean over the table, but it's no concern to me, a bloke sitting on the floor in front of the stereo is changing the CD, it's gone quiet, somebody starts shouting, then I shout too, then the music starts again. Lara sways towards me, pressing her hips against mine, her mouth is cold and tastes of wine, she holds round my hips and lifts the bottle to my mouth, I stamp around, and even if it no longer really bothers me that I'm probably making a complete arsehole of myself, I don't really get the point: I want to screw, not dance, not drink.

I want to go in my room.

The Key to the Kingdom

The sweat's pouring. I rinse my head in cold water, the chill of the water nearly making me piss myself. I catch sight of my dick in the mirror. I grab hard around it, it's huge. With a towel round my head I position myself over the toilet. *Fuck you, fuck you hard, feel my dick slide in.* My underpants are full of sticky fluid, like thinned resin, it's seeped through the material and onto the inside of my trousers. I can't remember the last time I had a reaction like that to anything, perhaps once or twice to a really good porn film, but it's a long time since I've been so turned on.

Fill you up. Slide into your wet cunt. As I tug on my tie, I do the same to my dick, and piss all over the floor and my shoes. And when I finally realise it, to my horror, a great stain appears on my trousers too.

Fuck. *Rino. You're gonna fuck. I'm gonna fuck. I'm gonna fuck!* Under the shower vomit suddenly gushes from my mouth, it's all been too much at once. I keel over with my dick stuck out of my trousers and sick hanging out of my nose and mouth.

That's the last I remember.

The Creep

Whores

I should really have struck while the iron was hot. But I haven't dared to ring her. And for nearly a week I speculated as to whether I was still a virgin or not. When I first came to after the party and tried to reconstruct what had happened, I couldn't remember any of what had led to me waking in the oven-hot, stinking room where I found myself, deserted in bed.

Naked.

And as soon as I considered the fact that I was lying there naked and in bed, I realised something wasn't right.

I hadn't gone to bed.

At first I just opened my eyes and lay there with an empty, light feeling in my body.

I was naked. I rubbed my crotch and sniffed my fingers.

Cunt?

Perhaps that was the smell of cunt. It was possible. But it was a long time since I'd smelled that last. It looked as if I might have cum over my stomach and the inside of my thigh, but that could be cunt juices too. I tried hard to remember if it had happened, and for a moment I could picture Lara on top of me, but it was just fantasy. I sniffed at the bedclothes and checked the clothes that lay on the floor, but there wasn't a trace of anything, apart from a faint smell of perfume on the sheet.

So if I had slept with anyone, I couldn't remember it. To no longer be a virgin, you've got to remember it. You've got to drop your load, and then you've got to remember it too. I could remember Lara shouting in my face.

Then it all came back, how I'd puked in the shower. I doubt anyone could have faced sleeping with me after that.

Slightly relieved, and after drinking enough water, I got my runners. My head was aching from all the drink, but otherwise I was okay. Light. There was an empty, liberatingly light feeling in my body. It was hot out, my lungs moved freely, but my legs soon felt like logs. Crammed full of lactic acid. No sense of fatigue, it was easy to breathe, but my thighs had stiffened completely.

In the end I bought myself a bottle of water and a newspaper and strolled about before lying on the grass in Torshov Park. I couldn't stop smiling after a while: I felt new-fucked. I remembered how turned on Lara had been. She had wanted to go to bed with me! That much was clear. And it wasn't certain that my being sick would have been an obstacle, if she'd *really* wanted it. (I'd have fucked Maria even though she'd puked. But technically, that might have looked more like rape.) So perhaps, given the situation, Lara might have too.

I folded my newspaper and got up, determined to go straight home and call her.

Surprisingly, when I got back home the whole flat was clean and tidy. I found Maria in her underwear on the sofa in the living room, moisturising her legs. She smiled when she saw me.

'Crikey, you were a bit wild last night,' she laughed.

Maria was too, and is probably quite unaware of her own behaviour: she hasn't said a word about our snogging session, and there's no sign she remembers anything of it. It must have been repressed.

I *think* I asked, or I think I at least mumbled, '*Did I get any action last night or not?*' I'm almost sure I said it so as to be audible. I know I *thought* it, and that my lips definitely moved. But I was too beside myself with curiosity and nerves about the answer to be certain of what came out of my mouth or entered my ears. And there was no response.

Maria leaned forward to reach her ankles. She twisted to the side, her G-string making it look as if her ass was naked: if I held my index finger in front of my eyes and squinted, that's what it would look like.

'Hmm,' said Maria.

Having interpreted Maria's 'hmm' as an affirmative 'mmm!' to my question of whether I'd had any action, I had to fight to get my next breath down into my lungs.

'So, Lara's…' I began. Maria sat up straight and patted her hands dry of body lotion.

'We had to undress you,' she burst out laughing, 'you were soaking wet from head to toe.'

Then, in fragments, it came back to me how things had unfolded the night before: the shower. The vomiting. The party smashing the door down to find me. Maria and Lara taking off my clothes. Seeing me naked. Washing the sick off me.

'So nothing happened then...?' I mumbled.

'Like what?' asked Maria.

'Oh, nothing,' I answered.

Still, for a week I was convinced that Maria was in two minds about whether Lara had gone to bed with me or not. She made quite a thing of it even, joking for ages about Rino and Lara's 'affair', and that Lara probably had a bun in the oven. But then another time she told me Lara had spent the night in her room. Which of course didn't exclude her being with me first; perhaps she just used me and left me lying there. Something like that. Women like to just screw too, without commitment.

So, despite Maria's constant hints and jokes, I am now pretty well convinced I'm a virgin.

And ringing Lara has become too big a deal. Over and over I stand with the phone in my hand and try to call. But I can't. Once I rang, but hung up moments later. It's too much of an embarrassment, too: they undressed me, the mere sight of me must have been pretty scary if you ask me (apart from my dick, of course).

Yet I've come to some sort of decision that despite everything, the next time I see her, I'm going to be honest and straight upfront. And say something like, 'Hi, d'you know what, I find you really attractive. I like you, and I'm not just saying that.'

Something like that. If she only knew. That deep down I actually care. That it's something more for me. That it means something.

And that it isn't just sex.

Maria

And even though I keep finding fresh reasons to throw her out, lately it's becoming more and more of a habit having Maria around. And chances are she'll disappear in the autumn anyway. If the party's anything to go by, there are plenty of other girls for me to pick and choose from who'd like to move in. If any of them are desperate enough, I might even get to exploit the situation a little, who knows what might happen.

She's not especially domestic; just now and again, like after the party, she makes a massive effort. For the most part she's bloody messy. Apart from the kitchen table. Everything around the kitchen table is extraordinarily and meticulously tidy. Little by little she's dug a corner for herself with cups, Kleenexes, a pencil case and her various lifestyle magazines.

And we do things together. It's quite strange, really. She's taken me out for a beer twice. We don't say much. I sit with my beer or a coffee and watch Maria, who sits texting or talking into her mobile or reading the papers. It's no problem. I don't have much to say, most of all I'm pleased at having an excuse to sit outside, and that I don't have to sit on my own. And we chat about films.

We're not exactly friends, perhaps. But then, all her friends seem to have such hectic lives, and once I overheard her call me her substitute boyfriend. Maria says she wants to take things easy and chill out. She should perhaps have been doing exams now, but I've noticed her filling forms in for unemployment benefit and we're fast approaching summer.

'You should grow a beard,' she said once. 'Then you'd have a girlfriend within two weeks. Tops!'

Very encouraging.

Once when we were out she got pretty crazy and drunk, losing things all over the place, and then wanted to walk home barefoot, and as she mucked about taking her shoes off, I ended up carrying her shoulder bag. Then she wanted to us hold hands: we walked side by side, and she took my hand in hers; it felt totally natural and rather strange.

As we walked along Thorvald Meyer's Street, she whispered, 'Pretend you're my boyfriend.' And as she went round chatting with lots of people, some of whom I recognised from the party and from our visits to town, she held onto my hand tightly.

I stood back, saying hi, feeling daft and cool in equal measure as she chatted on.

On our return she went to bed as soon as she'd brushed her teeth.

Another time she wanted to fly. She wanted me to lie on my back, then I had to put my feet on her stomach and lift her while I held her hands. She squealed like a little kid. We ended up play-fighting. Somehow. We laughed tons. I bent her arm behind her back. When she tried to get loose, she ended up pressing her ass up against my dick.

Which was, of course, rock hard.

Perhaps it was just that I'd stopped laughing. But then it might have been that she'd noticed my dick against her ass.

'Let me go,' she said.

Slowly I let her go. She stood completely still. I didn't want to let her go instantly either, it would have looked too conspicuous. Then she got up abruptly and went to the bathroom.

Brushed her teeth.

And went out.

Paw

At first, I went into my room to wank it off.

But that wasn't enough. After lying next to that buxom ass, it suddenly felt so pathetic to give myself a hand job. To take myself in my *paw*, as I once read on the internet. I wanted to screw. To shove my dick into something at least.

Something squishy. Moist and soft.

What a hellish venture that turned into. I went into the kitchen on the hunt for something I thought could bear some resemblance: fruit, food, cake, whatever. I sliced into an orange and tried to shove it on in the bathroom. For a while it worked. But the orange flattened somehow and went hard after a while. And the juice made it sting and start to itch.

Besides, the orange could look like a little head. A tiny little head with a gaping mouth. That was a real turn off.

I washed.

For a moment I considered going down to Sultan to buy a melon. But it felt like I stank of fruit and dick and I couldn't cope with the paranoia of standing there and choosing a fruit.

Instead I ended up with two bread bags filled with warm water. I smeared the bread bags with Maria's moisturiser. They looked almost like an ass. Or two breasts. Like being breast-fucked. But the bags were bulging with water and totally uncontrollable, so I transferred to using just one, slightly looser bag that I put over my dick to form a groove, a kind of grotto.

Sod's law, the bag burst just as I climaxed: I sat there on the bathroom floor, water all over me and my trousers round my knees.

Afterwards I sat there slicing and snipping up the orange, Maria's orange, by the way, and the plastic bags into tiny pieces to cover up what had been going on. And that's the thing I hate about it ALL.

Women have their own shops where they can go and select themselves a dick. There are international chains selling rubber and plastic dildos. A whole industry. And there are innumerable vegetables they can masturbate with, and viewed statistically the chances are I've eaten tons of these vegetables.

But a man who shags an object is a joke.

A dildo is altogether different. That's something for debate on chat shows and at confirmation dinners.

A man who shags fruit.

That's a problem. A case. A tragedy. That's someone who's sick in the head and needs treatment.

That's me.

That's more than you need to know.

Whores II

As the tram passes the A&E on the way home, I overhear an exchange between two friends.

'Crikey! I almost forgot to tell you,' exclaims the first, pointing towards the Old Bridge. 'Right over there, when I was crossing the bridge, there was this bloke last weekend that flashed at me. And then, just when I caught his eye, he went and climaxed. And the only thing I could come up with to say was, "Flipping heck!"'

They laugh.

'But wasn't it disgusting?'

'Nah, I don't know…I just wished I'd made some totally cool remark.'

'Yeah, I know what you mean.'

They laugh again.

'At least something. Just to show it hadn't bothered me, sort of.'

'Yeah, right.'

'But I just couldn't think of what it could have been. Straight after, I thought of loads of things I could've said. But then we went for drinks and stayed out really late, so I forgot them all.'

'You should've written them down, you know what I mean?'

They laugh.

'And then I sat there with this really stupid feeling of guilt afterwards. Like it was my fault, because I looked him in the eyes. And that was what made him cum.'

My head's about to explode. I'm certain women want to be raped. Just so long as the circumstances are right. They want to be raped on their own terms. They want something out of it for themselves. They want some sort of added value, which is why they're whores too.

I mean, when a girl prepares to be flashed at. When she wants to find herself in that situation with some cool remark and even spends time planning it. That means she likes being flashed at. She wants to walk away from being flashed at with added value, a sort of pleasure. You could even call it sexual pleasure. In addition to her being urban, modern and hip. It's perverted! It's certainly more than the flasher gets out of it.

'Have you thought about that?' I want to scream. 'That you're actually sitting there, saying you're looking forward to the next time you get flashed at? So you can be cool?'

Even the feelings of guilt afterwards are a bonus prize: it's so bloody feminine to have a bad conscience about absolutely everything. And just as feminine to give absolutely everything and everybody a bad conscience. Which everybody should sort of know doesn't work on men, of course, because men are psychopaths, aren't they? We're incapable of bad consciences. Are you less of a woman if you don't get a bad conscience if you try to give someone a bad conscience even when the person you try to give a bad conscience to doesn't get a bad conscience?

On Discovery last night they said it was a scientific fact that women actually like ugly men! In a test they got groups of women to smell T-shirts of men and to look at pictures of the same men, then they had to choose who they found attractive.

The women who were ovulating liked the ugly men and the others liked the good-looking ones. From smelling the T-shirts. It's a hormonal thing, a scientific fact. So if you look at what's *natural*, then women like ugly men. But none of them want to admit it.

With the ones that were on the Pill everything got turned on its head and nothing applied.

By ugly people we mean asymmetrical. And if you think who's ugly, of course it has to be the losers.

But doesn't that actually mean the losers ought to have been the winners?

And who are the losers? They're all the ones you never give a second glance, the ones you pass in the street and don't bother with: they're the ones you actually want. Repulsive, lonely men. The men you really like, deep down, except you're too vain or too fucked up to admit it.

And who therefore lose out as a result of idiocy.

Which in turn means everybody loses.

American Pie

But symmetry doesn't apply to women. At least fewer women than men, and I can't remember whether symmetrical men smell good while the asymmetrical ones smell bad, but I'm on the verge of insanity. I'm tired of being desperate. This desperation drives me to shower every day. To smear myself with nice aromas, pluck my nose hairs and powder myself with talc to sweat less.

I've got to get a fuck. I've got to screw soon. I can't bear it any longer. I've got to have cunt. And I've resigned myself to the thought: it can be a whore, she can be whatever, she can be fat and ugly as hell. I don't give a shit.

I don't want to die a virgin.

Sometimes I think I'm going to die soon, like it's going to happen tomorrow, and the only thing that torments me is that I'll die a virgin. There are loads of fourteen-year-olds more experienced than me. There are people born long after me who have more of an idea, who have done it hundreds of times and take it for granted. But nobody wants to sleep with fat people. They'd rather employ anyone than fat people. The ugly and the fat suffer most discrimination.

I'll give Fillip a call. He can take me to that club again. I don't give a shit: I've gotta fuck! Gotta fuck!

Shit... Did I say that out loud? Or did I just think it?

No one turns around, but the girls in front of me sit in frozen silence. No one says anything either, apart from a dark-skinned man who glances up for a moment and looks round, his mobile pressed to his ear.

After Sandaker Centre I sit completely still until the very last minute, when I quickly get up and dive through the doors as they snap closed behind me.

Anonymous

'Have you taken your post in today?' asks Maria without looking up. As usual, securely ensconced in the corner in her permanent place.

I shake my head.

Maria puts her pen down and looks up.

'I got this weird form in the post today.'

'Oh?'

'Yeah, some kind of sex questionnaire.' She laughs. Then pushes the form across the table and lifts her teacup to her mouth in both hands. I nod and push my glasses back up on my nose.

'Aren't you going to read it?' she asks. 'There are some unbelievably weird questions.'

'Oh, really? OK.'

Slowly I pull the form towards me. I soon recognise that it's a form like the one I received earlier in the spring. NATIONAL HEALTH SERVICE. Sexuality and Health. Not so long ago I'd received yet another one, with a different letter accompanying it which said they hadn't registered any reply to the previous one, and were therefore trying again.

Which did not make me feel less paranoid. In the least.

I am now totally convinced there's somebody sitting in the Central Statistics Office eagerly awaiting my reply. Who, for reasons unknown, thinks it vital that Rino be represented too.

Questions 1–5 to be completed by all. Question 5 is followed by further instructions.

Are you...

man   woman

How old are you?

Are you cohabiting? (living with someone you have sex with)

yes   no

What is you marital status?

unmarried   married   separated   widow/widower

Have you ever had sexual intercourse?

yes   no

If you have answered *no* to question 5, proceed to question 101.

And that's where it kind of finishes for me. In fact, yesterday I spent the whole day gawping at my own form. I filled in the first four questions before ending up feeling as irritated and paranoid as before. I don't want to fill this form in before I've done it. And unlike Maria, I'd never contemplate sharing it with anyone.

Maybe, just maybe if I were to include Edel, then I could have continued beyond question five. But that doesn't count. In that first week after the party I almost got it out, but even then it didn't look impressive: I wrote *yes* to having had intercourse (thinking of Lara), but then for question six, **how old were you when you first had intercourse**, I'd have had to write thirty-four years old, and for question nine, **what method of contraception was used**, I couldn't come up with anything better than to tick the heading **other** and write *fell asleep* underneath.

I put the form down. It lay there with the back page turned up and the final questions staring up at me.

129. Thinking of your present situation, would you say you are mainly satisfied with life or dissatisfied?

completely satisfied   very satisfied

quite satisfied   neither satisfied nor dissatisfied

quite dissatisfied   extremely dissatisfied

Totally, unbelievably, fucking satisfied.

Typical

103. How many times have you masturbated in the last 30 days (satisfied yourself)? *Tell us about the last 30 days even if they have not been typical for you.*

Hmm, what shall I say: If I'm totally honest I reckon on it being about thirty-five or forty times. Once a day at least. Sometimes more. And that *is* typical.

Sometimes for more than five hours a day. I'm not sure that that can be described as normal. If I'd slept with someone that many times, that might perhaps be regarded as passably normal. It might even be something to boast about. But when I feel that same desire and I'm alone without anyone to share it with, and do it for myself, I'm mad.

Most people have answered that they masturbate on occasion, but that for the most part they keep to their partner. Some, or to be more precise, one person, has in fact answered that he masturbates more than thirty times a month, and then often for up to five hours at a time.

Maria has had no trouble moving beyond question six.

How old were you when you first had sexual intercourse?

Maria was fourteen. She slept with an old friend – a boy who was three years older than her – and they used coitus interruptus as the method of contraception. Since then she's had sex with both women and men, mainly men. But questions twelve and thirteen remain as yet unanswered.

How many men have you had sex with?

To the present date __ total number of men.
In the last five years __ men (*complete even if you have only had one partner*)

Or rather: she's filled the form in with pencil, but here and there she has rubbed things out. But from what I could see they were at least in double figures, but whether the first figure was a one or a two or a three or even a five was hard to know.

Still, she's most definitely done it.

Maria's not the least bit a virgin.

13. How many women have you had sex with?

'Have you had a form then?' asks Maria.

I'm not listening, but I feel a shiver down my spine. Maria *has* had sex with more women than me. Maria has had sex with women. Full stop.

The world wallows in sex, and I barely lick up the crumbs.

'OK! On second thought, perhaps you don't really have to read absolutely everything,' says Maria. I look up, she blushes. I've just read that Maria has masturbated fourteen times in the last thirty days (on account of her vow of chastity). I suspect that that was precisely what she hadn't wanted me to read.

'Have you had a form?' she repeats.

I shake my head and take my glasses off. Maria masturbating. Maria masturbating in the bathroom, sitting on the toilet with a toothbrush in her mouth, Maria masturbating with Lara when she visits, on the sofa, in front of the TV, in the kitchen, on the balcony, sitting, lying, standing, with her back against the wall to the room where I sleep. In my flat.

And all the time, I'm available.

Betty Dodson

And wanking is another of women's privileges: they can wank when they want. All the time. Without any feelings of shame. How many hours of women masturbating on video tape must there be? Estimated? Professionally and privately, both.

Endless.

While a naked man is almost always pathetic. Only women look powerful when they're naked. Apart from black men and American

Indians in wildlife programmes. On the internet there's this clip where Miss Venezuela loses her bikini bottoms in the Miss World Competition. It looks embarrassing. But she still looks gorgeous and sexy. No man would have done. Perhaps not even the world's most handsome man, for that matter.

I've read, and even seen TV programmes about courses in masturbation for women. But nobody would accept the same for men. And it would probably be women who'd object the most. Men who wank together are deviants. Or in conspiracy. And what would the other objections be? *Well, exactly what is there for men to learn? Men have it all hanging outside, don't they?* Women believe they're something superior and delicate, but they're not at all: they eat and drink and shit and they're as greedy as anyone else. It's only an illusion they're so sweet and lovely.

Masturbation courses for women are somehow a cut above. And it's titillating to think about: all those women lying with their hips in the air and passing the vibrators round. Taste a little here and touch a little there.

But picture five men in a room with pocket pussies or blow-up dolls – quite the opposite. On the hunt for that certain 'spot'.

That's not marketable.

Masturbation courses, my ass.

Man Know Your Body

Still, we read page after page in lifestyle magazines, a constant stream of articles complaining that women don't know enough about their bodies. And then men have to apologise the whole time for not knowing enough about women's bodies. If a woman doesn't get an orgasm, it's the man's fault. *From pornography, as a rule, boys learn that women have a 'hole', and that it's enough to just stick the penis in, without knowing more about the way her body works, and what's good for the girl.* Or about womb cancer. Blah blah blah.

I know more about female anatomy than I do my own. From school, magazines, books, wall charts, adverts. And if there's something you like, you've got to feel bad about it. *Often the girl finds it best with a position where she can have eye contact with the boy while the boy often prefers just to 'get down to it' without it being too personal.* Oh yeah, everything that's good for women is OK. We can take a closer look at that. Everything men like is abominable and degrading.

I don't think what I'm asking for is too much. I'm attentive, willing to learn and horny, but ugly. I don't need any courses to learn about my body, I know it: I'm fat, and I'm ugly. I orgasm when I wank. T-h-i-r t-y-f-i-v-e times per month.

If only I had Ron Jeremy's charisma, for example, perhaps I could live with it. I could have been a porn star, Captain Naff. I'd rather have a job where I could bathe in cunt than the job I have. If I was Ron Jeremy I could have been fat, repulsive and fabulous. But I'm too old to change my style. I am a virgin and nobody wants to love me. Nobody.

'Is something wrong?' asks Maria.

'What?'

'No, you just looked like you were ready to burst.'

'Oh, yeah...no...eh...I was just thinking.' I put my glasses on and drum my fingers against my thighs before getting up to open the fridge.

Maria tucks her questionnaire into her *Healthy Living* magazine, finishes her cup before putting on her outdoor clothes and saying she's off to Lara's.

Not

I want women to suffer. I want them to have a hard time with their appearance. I want them to begin slimming at age nine, to begin shaving their legs, their armpits and their pussies. I want to see young girls running around their neighbourhoods, taking themselves on long jogging trips far from Mummy and Daddy. They should shower in their swim-suits and get fungal infections. They should loathe themselves so badly they make themselves available for anyone. All women from age thirteen and upwards should lie in rows and beg for dick. Without really wanting it, they should never climax. The closest they should ever come is to suck dick, the *taste* of dick should be the closest they come to pleasure.

No, that's not what I want really.

I'm not really like that.

But I do *not* want to have an exclusively fat girlfriend either. That would be so bloody obvious. So superficial: why should I pair up with a girl just because the one thing we have in common is that we're fat? Are we going to sit there and be fat together? What do fat people talk about? Food?

Besides, I don't want to have a girlfriend out of need. I want a girlfriend because I want to give.

I want to love.

Finger Fucking

I've finger fucked. Masses. If that could count as sexual intercourse, I could have really upped my figures. That was what Eli, the girl I was engaged to at college, was particularly fond of: when she wasn't rubbing herself against my thighs, I finger fucked her.

Courage

After taking a shower I dial the number, then hang up after two ring tones, before trying again.

'Hi, it's Rino.'

'Hi,' says Lara.

'Would you like…to do something? I don't know…maybe find something to do one day?'

'Pardon?'

'No, I mean, if you want. I'll understand if you don't…but anyway, if you…perhaps you want to…perhaps it's not a good time.'

'Who is this? Sorry, but I can hardly hear with this music.'

'It's Rino.'

'Oh. Hi, Rino. How are you doing? Wait, I'll go and get Maria for you.'

Lara shouts out for Maria. I wave my hands into empty space as if to stop her, before running them through my hair.

Maria comes to the phone.

'So, what is it now, then?' she says sternly.

'Oh, nothing.'

She laughs.

'And so…' says Maria.

'Yeah, OK. Bye,' I say and hang up.

I stand there clutching the receiver, about to call Lara again, when suddenly it rings. It's Edel. She wants to meet up.

The Jacket

'Is there something special about that jacket since you wear it all the time?'

'No. What d'you mean?'

'I could easily take the sleeves up for you,' she says.

'What's wrong with them?'

'Oh, nothing, it's just that you clutch the sleeves in your hands some-times, mostly it looks kind of sweet, but I just thought, well, you know…' She smiles, her head tilted as she browses through a magazine.

'D'you think I can ring Lara?'

Maria laughs. 'Do you *want* to ring Lara?'

'Yeah.'

'Yeah, maybe you ought to ring her then. I don't know. You can always try, there's no harm.'

Edel

We've finished eating only to sit here without having anything to say, for what feels like hours. As soon as I arrived, Edel wanted to know all about Maria. And I've told her all there is to tell, from Håkon to the moving-in party. Consequently, she now refers to Maria as the 'sweet young thing', the 'kid' and the like. It's almost as if she's irritated with her. She stands up and then sits down again.

'You really ought to go soon,' says Edel.

'OK,' I say.

Lara

A few days later I ring Lara. It goes surprisingly smoothly. She says she'd thought about calling me and that it's probably best that we meet so we can get to talk a bit. I sigh with relief. It was that easy. And high time too, perhaps.

I'm standing there combing my hair when Maria appears in the doorway. She's munching a Snickers.

'You're so sweet when you comb your hair,' says Maria. 'You look like a little boy. Like you're about to line up for the school photo.'

I dip my comb in water and pat my hair with sausage fingers.

'Are you going out with Lara?'

I nod.

'Careful there,' smiles Maria and gives my lapels and collar a gentle tug. She holds the Snickers bar between her teeth and brushes my shoulders.

'How d'you mean?'

'Oh, nothing.' She disappears into the living room. 'You just have a nice time.'

With my hand on the door handle I stand there wondering whether to say goodbye or not, when Maria shouts from the living room, 'It's hot out, I'm not sure if you need that jacket, you know.'

After which I go to the loo twice. Take the jacket off, comb my hair, before putting it back on again. I'm already regretting it as I make my way down the stairs and out.

Hunger

Half an hour before our agreed time I turn up at Hunger. Each time I go to the toilet I check my hair, I can't help it, I have to get the comb out and comb it into place. And each time it feels equally peculiar. I straighten my jacket and try to stop myself hiding my hands up the sleeves.

As I emerge from the toilets one final time, she's sitting there. She rises halfway out of her chair and kisses me on both cheeks.

'Hi, Rino,' she says.

'Hi,' I say.

I ask if she'd like anything, she shakes her head, lifting her glass.

Then there's silence.

She lights a cigarette from a candle, then she flicks the ash from her very slim cigarette, and looks up.

'D'you drink everything with a straw?' she asks after a pause.

Dull

Lara unravels the cutlery from her napkin.

'So, Rino, tell me about yourself.'

'Like what?' I ask.

'I don't know; why you don't like seafood perhaps.'

'Oh, right.'

'Or have you spent time in jail?'

'What? No. How come, has someone said that?'

'No, it was nothing, just a bad joke.' She puts a mussel on her tongue. 'Well...?'

'Well, I don't know, I'm a pretty ordinary bloke, that's all, really.' I smile and cut a piece off my horse steak.

'Ah, well, that's rather dull,' she smiles and chews.

I wipe my clammy hands over the bend of my trouser knees before pressing the knife through the tough meat. I try to take it as a joke, it was just a joke, I can't tell, it must have been, I look up, push my glasses to the top of my nose and try to smile, to show I can handle it, I can handle it, I'm not daft, I've not been out-manoeuvred.

'Is everything all right?' asks the waiter.

I jump to and almost shout 'Perfect!', before realising almost instantly that he was addressing Lara.

I have to push my glasses back on my nose again.

Lara nods, takes a swig of wine and glances down at my plate. Where everything lies untouched. Virginal.

Go Boy Go

'Come on then, there must be something you can tell me?'

For a long time it streams out, just spills over; everything that doesn't bother me, things I put up with, my better qualities, the dog we had when I was a kid, the house, the road, the locality, a trip to the summer cottage when Dad lost his rag, the school I went to, my work, the dog that got run over later, every possible detail, more about work, strange dreams I've had, my appendix operation, the girlfriend I had at college. No sooner do I think something than it's said, and in the moment nothing seems either boring or stupid, nothing seems accidental, but then the stories begin to get muddled, I lose track or forget why I'm telling them, they feel totally meaningless. So I invent things to fit. Rattling on, until I'm completely on empty. Empty tank.

Boring

It is silent a while, and I'm about to say something else that comes to me, when I start to worry that what I'm saying is totally insignificant.

'Am I boring you?'

'No, no, you just carry on.' She pushes her plate aside and tries to get the waiter's attention, with an unlit cigarette at the ready.

For a while I carry on chatting. After all, it was her that got me going. The tough, chewy pieces of meat are cold as I place them in my mouth; I've totally forgotten to eat. My sentences grow gradually shorter and shorter, just words, almost, until I'm saying nothing and just chew. Not that it seems to bother her.

'I just wondered if we should go.'

Caught in the Act

Lara has paid. She had a company credit card she said she'd never managed to use. On the way down to town she's stopped off and looked in countless places, but none of them seems to be right. She meets plenty of people she knows and chats with briefly, but then she wants to leave again. I suggested the cinema, but we've discovered it's much too late, and she didn't really want to anyway.

We end up at Café con Bar. Lara sips from her glass as she sits in the red sofa, her face lit up by the lamp hanging from the ceiling. She never stops watching me, not even as she stumps out her cigarette or drinks from her glass. Not even when I look away. Her skin is smooth and clear. Firm. Her eyes clear, the whites white. It's unbelievable that we're sitting here.

'Why did you want to go out with me?'

'What?'

'I was just wondering why you rang me and wanted me to go out with you.'

'You seemed nice.'

'"Nice"? Was that all?'

'Well, yes.'

Lara looks at me without expression and twirls the glow of her cigarette down into the ashtray. I didn't mean to hurt her.

'No, I mean, you're attractive and exciting.'

I try to laugh. 'And nobody wants to be single.'

'Don't they?' She raises an eyebrow.

'No…' My shoulders rise questioningly before they lower again.

'So you're still single, are you?' she smiles.

'Yes.'

Caught in the Act II

We've scarcely spoken in the last half hour. Neither of us has really tried. Lara has been texting friends she'd hoped might come. Other than that she's either been inspecting the décor from top to bottom, or staring into space. It's as if she were waiting for something. Each time I've ordered myself a drink I've removed the straw.

In the toilets I think up more things to tell her, when it suddenly strikes me that I haven't asked her about her background or anything, shown any interest. Enough interest. I wash my hands and decide to sit in the sofa, rather than opposite her. After all, she has come out with me. We did kiss. And Maria did hint. There's got to be something.

Back down again, I sit in the sofa.

It seems a little awkward to begin with. Different. I've never done this before. At first Lara sits turned away, completing a text, then she straightens up and sits to face me with a newly lit cigarette. My jaws are locked tight. I struggle to open my mouth, only to close it a moment later.

'Why don't you tell me all about yourself,' I say, taking a sip of my drink.

'Rino, there's something I need to…' she begins.

I feel myself freeze all over, stiffen, then relax completely. Maybe it feels all right to be allowed to stop, to stop this chase, it wasn't going to lead anywhere anyway, and I can't understand how I could have been so daft as to believe that we might, yes, that we might perhaps have had something going. I breathe out, relax into the sofa. Everything's fine.

'Please, you don't need to.'

'Yes, but there really is something I have to say,' she continues.

'You don't have to, I know what I'm like, you know, dull. There's no need to say I'm not, because I know I am. I didn't mean to talk so much, I just thought it was all right, I'm just not used to this kind of thing, I'm no good at mingling, I'm not used to going out on dates.'

Lara looks over at me, her chin slightly raised.

'Because this is a date, isn't it? I thought so, anyway…I'm sorry if I've been pushy, but I thought since we'd kissed in the kitchen and stuff…well, you know…we can leave if you'd rather…do I seem totally weird? And it wasn't my intention to sit like this, on the sofa…I hope you don't think I've been totally weird.'

'Weird?'

'Yeah, crazy. I hope you don't think I'm *totally* pathetic, I mean.' I try to smile.

'I'm sorry. That wasn't what I wanted to talk about,' says Lara. 'But it's not important, why don't we sit here and finish our drinks. Perhaps some of my friends will come along. We'll see what happens, yeah?'

'Don't worry about me, I'll be fine, no problem.' I smile, straighten my back and try as discreetly as I can to wipe my brow with my napkin.

'Relax, Rino,' she laughs, resting her hand on my arm.

'I am relaxing, honestly,' I say, *'no worries.'* Still her touch feels like a giant, creeping insect, and it's not until she lets go that I can breathe again and sink back, relieved. She asks me what I'd like to drink. I don't know.

Five Centimetres

Lara returns with drinks and more cigarettes. For the next quarter of an hour, I let my upper body and hand gradually creep their way across the surface of the sofa until I'm almost touching her. I wonder if she'd take my hand in hers if it reached her. Or if she'd kiss me, if I came close enough. Or if she'd do neither. Perhaps there are too many people around, or perhaps she's not drunk enough, but most of all she probably doesn't want to.

She's sitting right next to me. *It* is right in front of me: I can smell her smell, and if only I had the touch, if I wasn't me, but someone else, I'd...he'd...have stretched his arm out and pulled her to him. Said all the right things. I can smell her, her perfume, her breath, her skin, her hair and her feet as she slips her shoes off at the heel to air them. And the warmth from her body, her hip and belly, streaming towards my arm.

Maybe she's just sitting here waiting. I *have* touched her before. Perhaps she's more patient and understanding than I thought. She wanted me to touch her at the party. She was the one to kiss me. She was the one to say she'd thought of calling me, and it was best we should meet up and talk. And she was the one to suggest we stay and finish our drinks, even when things got embarrassing. And she didn't have to come and sit in the sofa again when she got back from the bar: perhaps she really does want me to touch her, maybe all those things I said didn't have such an effect after all.

There's the teeniest-weeniest chance that that's how things are, and it's driving me to distraction. But I wish she'd take the initiative and not me. If only women knew how easy it was, to just do it, to take the initiative, everything would be so much simpler.

I forget to breathe. Now and again my lungs slip the air out in short, irregular bursts before sucking more in again, and my bloodstream lies strangulatingly hard in my throat.

My clammy hand slides across the last five centimetres of sofa and rushes to her thigh, just as a sudden little moan escapes my throat.

'Look, this really can't go on,' she says as she stubs her cigarette out in the ashtray. 'I have to get up early in the morning.'

I pull my hand back, clasp my hands.

'I should go home now.'

Lara clears her throat. I sit with my eyes closed and nod.

The Creep

I've found it impossible to pull myself together. All day I've let the phone ring on, from work, before getting up the next morning and calling them instead.

For the rest of the week I'm first at the office every morning, even if it's not necessary since I have an office at home. I sit there aimlessly throughout the day shuffling bits of paper, surfing the net, where I spend most of my time looking at porn websites, and drinking endless quantities of water from the dispenser in reception.

Water is slimming. It runs right through you. I run to the toilet with clammy hands.

My life has not changed. We had a party. But nothing came of it. Everything has just gone back to what it was, and I often catch myself inventing new ways and excuses for ending her tenancy. She's not planned any more parties. When she goes out, it's alone. Her friends have not become mine, even though she regularly passes best wishes on from people that were there, and tells me anecdotes about her friends as if I should know who she was talking about. *'You remember Anders. And Helge and Nikko?'* I shake my head. And that blows the entire build-up to her anecdote because she has to tell me how Helge's the one who worked in a bank, blah blah blah, etcetera, etcetera.

The only thing that gives me focus is running. I do my run almost every day. My shoes are grey and worn out now, but if I can extend the length of my circuit, I've promised myself a new pair.

Maria wants us to do something together again, and we go out. I take forever to get ready and in the end Maria's so fed up she stands at the front door stamping, keys at the ready. It's already late. We're not going to catch more than a couple of beers.

'I'm going to meet some friends.'

'There's some creep or other who's started phoning Lara,' says Maria as I put my shoes on. With a grim face Maria relates the constant abuse and obscenities to which Lara has been victim over the phone for the last week.

'Jesus, what a nutter!' I say, crouched over my shoes.

Maria nods and continues.

'Shit, how disgusting,' I manage to say eventually. 'What a…creep.'

The Creep II

'Hi there, Laura, it's Dave!' I shout down the line, trying to sound as American as I can.

'Dave? Dave who?' she asks.

'*Dave!*' I repeat.

'Dave, Dave,' she repeats to herself. 'Dave! Oh my god! How are you?'

'How's it going?' I ask. '*Laura.*'

'It's *La-ra*, stupid. No, I'm fine. So after all these years. How did you get my number?'

'Where are you?'

'At home.'

'What are you doing?'

'Absolutely nothing. Where are you?'

'Oh…I'm outside.'

'Europe?'

'No, outside.'

'Really…but why are you calling? After so many years. Jesus. I can't believe you could track my number down.'

'D'you wanna fuck?'

'(…)'

'I can fuck you, real hard. D'you know that? Deep in your cunt. In the ass. I'm fucking you right now. Can you feel my cock inside you?'

'Who is this?'

'I know what you are. You can suck cock. Suck daddy's cock.'

'Come on, your accent's not very convincing. Who is that? Is that Harald?' Lara laughs.

'This is Jesus. Is your pussy good and wet?'

'Harald, this isn't funny any more, stop it.'

I look down at my notes. I've run out of phrases.

She hangs up.

Revenge

'Well, she thinks she knows who it is, but he denies it. For a while she had a boyfriend from Yugoslavia, Mareck or something like that. The man that rang, well, his Norwegian was almost incomprehensible, just a load of deep breathing: *You hole! I fuck you! I 'ave you now on vee-di-o.*'

Maria's imitation sends shivers down my spine.

'But it's such a hassle to get records of everyone who's rung, so she's got herself a secret number. Have you tried to ring her again at all?'

'Once. Just a couple of times.'

'Yeah, well. I expect you'll be able to get the new number if you need it.'

'No, I don't suppose that'll be necessary.'

'Oh dear, are you nursing a broken heart?'

'No, not really. It's no big deal.'

Maria's friend is waiting for us, dressed in sandals and a pink skirt. She says hello briefly and tells me her name is Martine before she turns towards Maria with an irritable expression, and after a quick hug tells her how she's had to wait for over half an hour. She's one of the girls I've seen hundreds of times, around Grünerløkka, at the park café. One of the ones who often holds my gaze as I pass by the café windows.

Maria goes to the loo with Martine. It's Martine who comes out first. She nods in brief recognition without saying anything as her eyes rove around the entire venue, searching.

Spare Part

We only just manage to get ourselves a beer. Maria introduces me to a couple of friends who disappear into the crowd again, then Martine comes over and whispers something to her, eyeing me critically over Maria's shoulder. Maria shakes her head as if she can't understand or hear. I turn away.

As Maria turns back to me, Martine stops her abruptly and whispers something more. They exchange glances. Maria nods, then Martine goes back to the corner.

'What were you thinking of doing next?'

'What d'you mean?' I ask.

'Well, it's like this. Martine's been invited to a party.'

'Oh, right,' I say, trying not to reveal that I already understand what's going on.

Yet at the same time pleased for it to show a little, to prick her conscience just enough for her to speak up for me.

'And she doesn't know how many people she can take with her.'

I nod, looking down at the floor. I'm fucking well not going to let her think this is the first time I've been excluded like some bloody spare part.

'I understand,' I say.

'You're upset!' Maria laughs, looking sympathetic, tilting her head to one side, giving my arm a squeeze. She sighs.

'Course I'm not,' I laugh.

'Yes, you are.' Maria rocks up onto her toes before clasping her hands together in front of her. 'D'you know what? I'll go and tell her; either you come, or I won't bother.'

'No, don't…' I start, dismissing the idea with a wave.

'No, honestly. It's not an issue. Come on!' Maria takes my hand and pulls me after her to find Martine.

Seventeen

There are lots of people at the party. It's quite a small loft flat, but with several small rooms, yet somehow almost everyone seems to occupy the kitchen that's divided from the living room by only a central island built out of glass bricks. The island functions as a bar. It's stylish and gives me the urge to redecorate my flat. Do things up and organise some more parties. Without thinking, I've taken my shoes off as usual in the hall. Only afterwards do I notice nobody else has and that I'm the only one in socks.

But it's too late now.

'This is Alex,' says Maria. 'He lives here.'

I hate my feet.

'Hi there,' I say. 'Cool party.'

'Thanks, that's great, and what was your name again?'

When I do eventually manage to stutter my name out, he seems not to hear. A girl grabs his waist from behind and points in the direction of the sofa at the far end of the room.

Standing pressed up into the corner of the room between the window and the sofa is a guy wearing baggy jeans. He stands, head bowed bemeath the sloping ceiling, and a red-headed girl wearing an even redder velvet dress has her arms wrapped around his hips, her hands pushed up under his oversized sweater, hips swaying from side to side in rhythm to the music. He stands quite still, a hand laid awkwardly on her shoulder, as he turns and thrusts his head towards the glass from which he's drinking.

Alex slowly releases my hand.

'Oh, shh-i-t!' he says with a grimace and sticks a cigarette between his lips, not letting the couple slip from his sight.

Maria pulls me over to one side and points at the boy.

'That's Alex's cousin. He's visiting for work. He's only seventeen, apparently,' laughs Maria.

'Oh?'

'Which *she*, most definitely, is not. Shit, she is *crazy*.'

He's wearing white socks and a gold chain that hangs over his jumper and even when he drinks he stands stiff, his movements mechanical. He doesn't blink once, but just stares down at her. She's still standing there swaying, bowing her head and twisting a finger in his trouser waistband. Then leaning forwards she whispers something in the ear of a plump girl with dirty-blonde hair and cheap stonewashed jeans who's sitting squeezed up in the corner of the sofa, legs tucked under her. Looking bored.

Maria returns and hands me a glass.

'Mohito,' she says, and drinks.

'Wow,' I say and lean forwards, thanking Alex with a wave.

'He's a virgin,' laughs Maria.

'Pardon?' I ask, poking at the ice cubes with my straw.

'His cousin, Øyvind, he's a virgin.'

'A virgin?' I laugh.

'And *seventeen*,' laughs Maria.

'Oh, right, yes.' I take a sip of the drink she's brought me.

'It's about time to do something about it then, perhaps.' Maria smacks her lips and drinks as well.

I look across at the young man. The woman in the red dress has taken part of his gold chain in her mouth, as she stands there swaying. He seems unhappy about it. His hand has come up and his lips are moving, but I can't hear what he says over the music. He seems to be saying *that's expensive, that's bloody expensive.* Then she forces her hands deep under his shirt, the fabric forming folds, exposing his stomach, he has well-defined stomach muscles and the merest hint of a delicate line of hair up to his navel. She stops and stands still. She lets the chain fall from her mouth. He smiles. She kisses him.

For ages.

Then she steps back and traces her fingers over his chest and down to his stomach; he gives a start and then doubles up in laughter.

When I turn around, Maria's gone. Martine is standing there, but moves off before I have a chance to open my mouth to say anything.

Over in the corner the redhead has taken her handbag on her shoulder. Behind her the boy drains his glass in one, with his other hand resting on her back. She leans over to the plump girl in the sofa and points in my direction, then gives a little nod of the head. The girl gets up, straightening her trousers, with childlike movements: grabbing her waistband, tugging, front and back, to pull them up.

They make for a clumsy procession. There are people sitting all over the floor and CDs strewn everywhere. The girl leads the way, but turns back halfway between the living room and kitchen. The woman in red waves her on, picking her boots up from behind the sofa. The boots get dropped at least twice as she crosses the floor. And the girl stops, waiting nervously, index and middle fingers pressed to her lips as she watches them work their way through the crowd.

I stand aside so they can get past me more easily into the hall, but instead of taking the expected turn out of the room, the woman in red strides across the kitchen and opens a door, so small I'd assumed it was a larder. Instead, it turns out to be a kind of cubby hole, stretching out under the roof, and there's evidently a mattress on the floor inside. She must have been here before, or at least known about it; she just went straight over and opened it up. And then she proceeds to throw all her things in; the unco-operative boots, the handbag, a jacket, a pullover and at least two soft drink bottles. It all goes in.

'Don't forget me, then,' says the girl.

The boy has the palest blue eyes I've ever seen. They rove around the room for an instant. The woman in red, who's prettier perhaps from a distance, pulls herself up from the mattress and comes back through the doorway. She goes up to the girl with the trousers and leads her over to the boy.

'Can she come too, or what?' she says, indicating her friend.

He breaks into a grin. Indecisive, his head and back pressed against the wall.

Then he leans forward and whispers something in the ear of the woman in the red dress.

'So what's going on? Do I get to come, or not?' The girl, who's distanced herself a bit, steps forward again. She holds her hands in front of her, scratching the tips of her fingers together. She certainly isn't the prettiest.

Not that either of them are especially pretty.

I don't understand how she can dare say it so loud. People are gawping, some are laughing behind their hands, I'm not the only one whose ears are flapping. Still it's impossible to guess what's going on in *his* head. He's got the chance to have *two* women on his debut. And he refuses!

The redhead whispers something in the girl's ear, stroking her arm.

'Yeah, but why?' she asks a little irritably.

'I'm really sorry…' says the boy, shrugging his shoulders and stretching a hand out to the girl.

'Can you wait here a while though, yeah? I won't be long,' she says to the girl and creeps through the doorway.

The girl nods and saunters back into the living room. The young man is on his way through the little door when, leaving the group he was standing with, Alex steps out.

'And-what-are-you-up-to-now?' says Alex, putting his arm round the boy's shoulders. People are sniggering as they turn towards the drama in the corner of the kitchen.

'Have you got everything you need?'

'Yeah, don't be an asshole, I can take care of myself, thanks,' whispers the boy sourly, working himself free from Alex's grip.

'OK, it's your life…' says Alex, one hand leaned up against the door and making a demonstrative gesture into the little room. 'Get on in!'

The boy gives an irritated toss of the head, then bends down to get into the hidey hole.

Alex slams the door and laughs aloud as if washing his hands of everything: flicking them in the air and then wiping them down his chest.

When he laughs, it's like a great, huge roar.

I've forgotten my drink completely.

Breaking the Ice

It feels really peculiar after a while; here we all are, standing around, and everybody knows that right behind that wall they're lying there screwing. And apart from the odd titter around Alex to begin with, nobody takes a blind bit of notice. I try to exchange sympathetic glances with the girl in jeans to show that at least somebody understands, but she sits up in the corner of the sofa, staring out the window, biting her nails and spitting invisible specks on the floor with a faraway look in her eyes.

If the wall were glass, or we had X-ray vision, we would have seen them lying there.

I am standing just three metres away from two people screwing. It's impossible to get it out of my head. Three metres away someone's losing their virginity: a miracle!

And yet everybody looks bored.

Martine looks a bit lonely. She's drinking and looking around her. As if she were bored or waiting for something to happen. Then she gets up, moves over to the sink area where I'm standing, and rinses her glass. She fills it with water and drinks, warming her bare feet alternately on the backs of her knees. She is an even, golden brown from her toes to her bleached blonde hair. Her short, pink skirt sits soft and tight across her hips and thighs.

'I've seen you before,' I say out of the blue.

It just pops out. It's not that I'm trying to chat her up; it's just an attempt at making conversation. She just looked so bored.

'What d'you mean?' Martine asks.

'Oh, nothing,' I say. 'Just that I've seen you before. Out, I mean. At a café or somewhere round here.'

'And so?'

'Oh, nothing,' I say.

'Well, a lot of people see me around. Do I know you?'

'No...'

'And don't you think that's a really odd thing to say, just like that?'

'It's not a big deal,' I say.

She turns towards Maria, who has come into view amongst Alex's group.

'Do you know this guy well, or what?'

Presumably Maria can't hear anything over the music, but she also seems pretty drunk and just waves back, smiling. Martine looks down, irritated.

'It really wasn't a big deal,' I repeat, 'I just saw you out in town earlier, and so I thought I'd say so.'

'Yeah, so where was that then, eh? Have we been introduced?'

'Well, I don't know…'

'So d'you know lots of people here, then? Anyway, how d'you know Maria? Where do you fit in the picture?'

I open my mouth to answer, but end up with my shoulders raised and hands waving defensively.

'Are you flirting with my girl?' a guy behind me asks.

'No, I just…'

'Hey, Mathias! You're here! Have you only just arrived?' Her face brightens and she turns away from the CD rack.

'Sorry, I didn't know you had a boyfriend,' I say. It just pops out. I've no idea why, it just does, without me even thinking.

'What the fuck's that supposed to mean? Is that somehow relevant?'

'Who's this, eh?' asks the guy, putting his arm around Martine.

'Haven't the faintest, some guy Maria's dragged along again.'

People say all kinds of things: but what makes the difference is who says them. I'm the kind girls like to take revenge on.

It seems I'm the kind of man some women find useful when they want 'revenge'. When they want to get back at the world. I recognise the signs, I've seen it all before: they use me like a test dummy to see how far they can push things. They zoom in on me, I'll say something out of place, try to buy them a drink, and then they can start to bully me, preferably with an audience.

If things just hadn't been so superficial, and if the same women didn't just melt the moment some good-looking guy suddenly paid them attention.

Like now.

Martine drops me totally, and without my having a moment to explain, she slinks off with this new guy. I'm left standing there. And perhaps what rankles me the most is that she's so disinterested I don't even have a chance to explain myself. Just let me talk, and I will. But she says I'm a weirdo, and I don't have the chance to prove otherwise and say I'm not mad. That it was a stupid slip, a misunderstanding. But hey, I can be the buffoon, see if I care. Just see if I care. Though I should be furious, really. Fucking furious.

Limbo

At first, the party starts to empty, and people leave, but then the intercom starts buzzing and without even troubling to ask who they are, Alex is letting people in. In fact I'm about to go, and I've already been in the hall and put my shoes on. Getting my shoes back on makes things better somehow. Not having to stand around in my socks any more. And I'm still harbouring a hope: perhaps somebody might come along. Somebody who wants to talk to me. Perhaps it'll happen. Right here. Somebody might come back home with me. Or maybe it'll happen. As easily as for the seventeen-year-old.

And I thought I'd wait and see if Maria's making moves to go as well. I might score some points with Martine, if she sees Maria doesn't think I'm mad. But Martine's been ignoring me. Apart from some time sitting like a fixture in one of the armchairs browsing through CD covers, I've spent the entire time in silence, standing next to the kitchen island.

A couple of times, when Martine's come over for some water, or passed me on her way to the toilet, I've tried to catch her attention. Given her little nods that she hasn't returned. I'm not sure I'll bother next time. It's beginning to look rather daft.

'Sorry about earlier,' I ventured.

'Forget it. It's fine.'

'Yes, but I...'

'It's fine,' she repeated, turning the palm of her hand to me before lifting her glass to her lips.

It was a short affair, that's for certain: the woman in red is dancing alone in the middle of the room. Not long after the incident with Martine, I caught sight of her creeping out from the little room, adjusting her clothes.

Soon after, the girl in the baggy jeans said she'd had enough and was going home. To begin with the redhead talked her into staying a little longer. They danced together. But the instant she stopped giving her attention, the girl was flopped out again and seemed as distant as ever.

'Are things all right?' I asked once.

She didn't answer.

The cousin lay in the room for ages, yelling out for Alex. Then after talking with him Alex went as go-between in an attempt to get the redhead to talk to the youngster. But as soon as Alex put a hand on her shoulder, she just pulled her shoulder away with a jerk and tossed her head.

'I can't be assed,' was all she said, continuing to dance on her own. '*Nah, I can't be assed.*'

That started Alex laughing again. From the kitchen cupboard he fetched a bird warbler and leaned into the little room, releasing a duck-quacking burst of laughter at his newly plucked cousin. After which the boy wandered round the flat semi-comatose and still naked from the waist up, as he made a few vain attempts at talking to her on the dance floor.

And now he's seeking comfort from some of Alex's friends in another room.

I stand leaning against the kitchen island in my own thoughts, pissed as anything from mixing such a variety of dregs. Maria only pops her head round occasionally, to give me more to drink.

Then, all of a sudden, the woman in red is standing in front of me.

She stretches a hand out.

And traces her index finger across my stomach; from my chest all the way down to my navel.

'You've gotta dance,' she says, head inclined. She beckons and moves coquettishly into the centre of the room.

'Teh-heh,' I say, '*Teh-heh.*' Nothing more. A daft, neighing little laugh.

Since she's stroked me on my stomach I imagine I might be in with a chance here. But if I were to sleep with her now, I'd prefer to have been on a desert island. I mean: no witnesses.

So I decide I'll hang around and see. If she and I are the last ones left at the after-party, then that's fine. And since it's already light out, there may not be that long to wait.

Then it suddenly occurs to me that it might seem too obvious. I might look desperate. If she's as bloody horny as it seems, why can't she take the initiative?

I decide to drop a hint.

Invisible

I signal that I'm about to leave, to see whether she'll notice. That I'm going. I open the door and adjust a shoe.

She's milling around in the kitchen in front of me.

I crouch down, untie then retie my laces, trying all the while to measure the time lapse since she stroked me on my stomach.

I cough.

The seventeen-year-old has livened up, and seems to have a show going in the next room, I hear him rapping: *I've had more bitches than all ya mother fuckers have had hot meals*, or something similar.

He gets applause.

I close the door to the party.

'Bye,' I say.

But nobody answers.

Then I wonder if she might leave too, now I've gone, and whether my best option is to stand here and wait a while.

Perhaps we'll bump into each other in the hallway. Then perhaps I'll start to talk to her.

I picture her coming out of the door. Neither of us needs to say a word, we start to snog: she comes out, she strokes my stomach, and we snog.

I could have taken her right here.

She could have come out, and stroked my stomach again, and asked where I live. Not my name or anything like that, just whether I lived nearby.

And I do.

I reckon it's too obvious to stand right outside the front door waiting, so I decide to place myself a bit further down the hallway.

Further down the hallway, I think it might be better to wait outside, perhaps standing in the hallway's a bit odd, too.

Outside I get the hiccups. I've been standing there for I don't know how many minutes with my arms hanging limply before me, just staring blindly at the door. As if I'd had a black-out.

Slowly I make my way towards the 7-Eleven.

And from 7-Eleven I slowly make my way home.

She doesn't follow me.

The Mark

'I think I'll ring that woman Martine, and apologise for yesterday.'

'Per-lease, give it a break!' says Maria. 'She can be such a bitch.'

'Yes, but I just thought I should apologise and get it over with.'

'Give over, Rino, you shouldn't give her a second thought. She was probably pre-menstrual, if that's any comfort. Anyway, Lara thinks you're a perfect specimen.'

'I see.'

'At least, that's what she thought *before*. She said you were the perfect breeding specimen. She wants kids so much, you see. But take care, that's probably all she does want.'

'Oh?'

'I certainly don't think she's after a boyfriend.'

Maria is standing in the hallway on her way out. She's put her shoes on and now she twists her shoulder bag into place. She smiles. And before I've had time to think, she steps forward and plants a kiss on my cheek before rushing out.

'Bye,' I say as the door shuts.

Her smell hangs on the air. She was just out of the shower. There's a smell of shampoo, body lotion and perfume, and when I go in the bathroom, I discover she's left a big, squishy lipstick mark where she kissed me.

I'd intended to take a shower as well, really. But instead I comb my hair, change my clothes and go out.

But before I leave, I take one of Maria's Kleenexes and soften the lipstick mark just enough, so it won't seem too obvious.

So that's how it is. That's how it feels. To have someone. I walk down the street, looking every single person in the eye. I have nothing to be ashamed of. Absolutely nothing to be ashamed of. I exist too. I am. Someone is waiting for me at home, someone has kissed me on the cheek and sent me out into the world, perhaps someone is lying there and waiting, blissfully satisfied, in bed, waiting for something nice to eat, something I'm going to buy, and prepare. Because I'm kind and caring. Someone is waiting. Someone loves me.

I pick out some vegetables at Sultan, pull at the transparent plastic bags, and watch the stream of people as they pass up and down the pavement. People catch sight of it, either standing at the vegetable stand or passing by: they glance over at me, scrutinise me and throw a swift glance at the mark on my cheek. The grocer with his square glasses smiles at me, I pay and smile back.

Instead of going straight home, I stroll down to 7-Eleven on Olaf Rye's Square to buy a newspaper and a cup of coffee. Then for a while, I stand there outside holding my coffee before drifting slowly past Fru Hagen, stirring it gently.

Gry isn't in Mucho Mas. I stick my head in the door and count the waitresses. One of them peers up from her newspaper with lazy eyes while the other wipes the tables.

Then it hits me. The video store. If there was one person I'd want to see this mark, it's the man at the video store. After going in and out of there for years, *alone*, snooping nervously amongst his shelves, it would be great to balance the books a little.

And the best thing of all is that he is indeed sitting there. He sits hunched over the counter, nodding lazily as I trudge through the open door.

I make straight for the new releases, careful to study the covers with my cheek turned towards him as I gradually work my way towards the counter.

On his way back as he puts the video in its cover, he looks up at me and smiles before raising his eyebrows twice as if in acknowledgement. He's seen it.

I pay and leave.

For a while I stand on the corner, having gone back and forth a couple of times, before I gather the courage to go into Bar Boca.

The waitress is as tiny as a little doll with two red flecks for cheeks. She dries her hands on her apron and asks what I want. I'll have a quick glass.

While she's pulling the beer, she glances quickly up at me.

I hoist myself up onto the stool.

'You've got lipstick on your cheek,' she smiles.

'Oh?' I say.

Quiet

Later that day I ring: I'm going to talk to her this time, I'm going to present myself for who I am. I'm going to ask her if she'd like to come out with me again. I want to explain, perhaps she'll understand.

'I've got friends who work for the phone company,' she says.

Totally Quiet

I say nothing. I try to open my mouth.

I hang up.

Best Intentions

I buy a box of chocolates. The biggest box I can find, and find a card with a drawing of a little dog with big sorrowful eyes and the words 'Sorry' printed on it. *Sorry for everything*, I write in spidery letters, not mine. Halfway through I change hands so as to disguise my writing even more.

I sign it 'Dave', in inverted commas.

Holiday

'Hey, listen, I'm disappearing soon for a couple of weeks. Taking a trip down to Spain with Lara.'

'Right,' I say. 'But wasn't that meant to be in the autumn?'

'Yeah, yeah, but we're only going to Spain. Everybody goes to the Med at least once a year, it's like taking the ferry to Denmark.'

'Oh, right... So *everybody* does it.'

'You'll never guess,' she shouts from the kitchen and coming in with a glass of drinking yoghurt. 'Can you believe Lara got a parcel from that creep?'

'Oh?' I say.

'Yeah, he sent her chocolates.'

'Right, well, that was...'

'Can you believe it? Chocolates. Some nerve or what.'

'What d'you mean?'

'Well, would you have eaten those chocolates? And with a card, and everything, with something written in this sick, sick handwriting, *hope you forgive me* or something like that. Christ almighty. And to top it all, "hugs", can you believe it, best wishes this and that.'

'Jesus, is he a total weirdo or what?' I add. I crack my knuckles.

'Don't you think?'

'Yes, mad.'

'Yes, she's totally stressed out, more than ever now, because it means he knows where she *lives* too, doesn't it.'

'That's interesting,' I add.

'She can't handle it any more. She's taking time off work. This psychologist she knows thinks it must be somebody she knows doing it. It could be somebody from work, but Christ almighty, she even thought it was you for a while.' Maria laughs without looking over towards me.

'Still, we're going away now. That'll be fun,' she says.

'Couldn't you get it checked for fingerprints?' I say.

'What?'

'The King Haakon chocolates.'

'I expect she's chucked them ages ago.' Maria finishes her drinking yoghurt in one gulp and with a raised eyebrow she looks at me.

Stupid

I am so stupid, stupid, stupid. More than anything I want to kill myself. I lie in my room all night, my index finger pressed to my temple. *Stupid, stupid, stupid.* Whatever I do, it's wrong. I can't get anything right. Nothing.

Nothing.

But what I'll do, next time I see her, is tell her I like her, that I think it's a shame we didn't get the chance to get to know each other better.

'You know what? I think you're really...nice.'

Just like that.

Straight out.

Apartment Groupies

It's baking hot. All I want is to sit out on the balcony in the shade, have a cold drink and eat the tub of low-calorie ice cream I've got in my bag.

That's before I arrive home to find Maria and Lara sunning themselves out there.

Naked.

Of course.

I assume the flat's empty at first: lately Maria's been out most of the time, either at the café or in the park, so I piss with the door open and pad about in my underpants before noticing the low, droning sound of a radio drifting through the half-open balcony door.

Clearly this is the day to do battle with those bikini lines.

And strewn around them are travel brochures, magazines, glasses of juice and sun cream. It looks as if she's asleep, an orange and blue book covering her face. Maria's drawn an anchor on the chest of the girl on the cover. Her pubes are smooth-shaven with a little stripe of hair. From above, looking down, it looks like a little heart.

Lara's lying on her stomach.

It's just so bloody typical: now I'll be banished to the inside of the flat until they feel like going out or putting their clothes on. I am certainly *not* going to sit out there. I'm bloody well not going to sit there and be caught peeping. I try to think of a hundred ways around it, but nothing seems viable.

Instead I sneak into my room and swing the bedroom window open. Then I tiptoe carefully through the living room, out into the kitchen, fetch a spoon and sit with my back to the little darlings out on the balcony and begin filling my face with my ice cream. Shovelling a spoonful down and spying in the window.

To begin with not much happens. I put another spoonful in my mouth, cross my arms stubbornly and just stare. Maria looks ridiculous with a square head, hair that sticks out and a spiky fanny. Lara has two creases and spare tyres across her hips. Her bum sags a little at the top of her thighs.

And here I sit: this is my flat, really. But if I so much as step out there, I'll just be a slimy little toe-rag on the lookout for an eyeful of pussy.

Maria mumbles something or other.

Lara answers.

Rino, I hear her say. *Rino*, something or other.

Then something happens. Maria lifts the book off her face.

'Did you hear that?'

Lara mumbles something in reply.

I squash the soft ice cream against the roof of my mouth.

Suddenly Maria gets up and dashes across the balcony.

Lara rises on all fours, ass in the air.

I swallow, pressing the cream down my gullet, and pull some trousers on.

Fuck you. Fuck you both. Pussies.

The spectacle from the park reaches all the way up here.

Attractive

'What's happening?' I ask from the balcony door. They stand naked at the balustrade. Lara crumples slightly, making a dive for something to cover herself, while Maria just waves me across without turning.

'There's a fight in the park, quick.'

Birkelunden Park is buzzing. People are getting up from their blankets, most standing frozen. Some are packing up as the kids tug at their trouser legs: a dark-skinned youth with smooth-shaven head and jeans is holding a redheaded man with tracksuit bottoms and a beard by the collar of an oversized green T-shirt as he tries to get a punch in.

'What happened?' I ask.

'No idea,' says Maria.

The man in the tracksuit bottoms hangs exhausted from the youth's singlet, head sinking down between his arms. It's obvious the younger man's got style. And the redhead has none.

Maria skips on her toes, chews her fingers.

'But I *think* the guy with the beard started...'

Half-turning, I see Lara wriggling into a pair of knickers before coming to stand next to us with her arms folded.

Two full-on punches later and the man in tracksuit bottoms is on all fours. Then the youth lets rip and kicks him in the face. There's a slamming sound from his shoe. The blows they've exchanged until now have been soundless, but that single kick is audible all the way up here.

A thud, a ghastly sound.

'Did you see that?' says Maria, clinging onto my arm. Her cheeks and her throat are completely red. She shakes her head with open mouth and wide eyes before peering over the edge again.

A girl steps between the youth and the man. Shaking an outstretched fist threateningly, the youth sticks two fingers up before allowing himself to be led from the park and out into Toftes Street. The girl is pushing a pram in front of her. The youth nurses his right hand as he tosses his head and breaks into a grimace.

A moment later the man in tracksuit bottoms staggers up the path, circling his own axis twice before continuing and finally coming to the drinking fountain. The park calms a little. He splashes water on his face from the fountain. He's bleeding from a cut over his eyebrow. He fills his mouth with water and spits it out again.

Attractive II

Seconds later a toddler, in just its nappies, comes whizzing out on wobbly legs, out of the park and onto Thorvald Meyer's Street, before being rescued by a man in cut-off jeans who sprints after. He lifts the child from in front of a ringing tram.

But there's no one to watch that.

Behind us Lara pulls a dress on, stretches her knicker elastic over her ass and then gathers her things together. I fetch my tub of ice cream and sit down at the balcony door.

'How are things going?' I ask. '*How are you?*'

Lara shades her eyes and squints over at me.

'All right.'

Not a single readable expression crosses her face. She just looks at me.

I stand there and nod, my spoon stuck down into the tub.

You're really nice, d'you know that? I like you.

'Well, well,' is all I eventually succeed in getting out.

Masturbation

Shortly after Lara has left, Maria tidies everything in from the balcony. The book, the portable radio, the thermos of squash. Then she vanishes into her room.

She's in there for ages.

There's total silence.

She can't be sleeping, and she doesn't exactly do much these days.

She emerges smiling and with flushed cheeks, a towel around her waist, and takes a quick shower before dressing and dashing out.

'What's the matter?' she asks. 'Is something wrong?'

I'd lay a wager she's masturbated, and it was triggered by the fight in the park.

Housemates

The day starts with my getting out of bed to be confronted with a sheet of paper Maria gives to me before I've even managed to go to the toilet, or have a wash or even get something down me, wet or dry.

At the top of the sheet, it says *Cleaning Rota.*

So, the little wretch has sat down, in her corner, with her cute little pen and those luxurious magazines of hers to lean on, and drawn up an ever so dinky schedule for how the cleaning should be done in the flat. How generous. How fantastically thoughtful.

'Do we need to make it so formal?' I ask.

'It hasn't worked up to now.'

'No, it certainly hasn't.'

But it's not my damned fault. I've been cleaning. A lot. After both her and me.

'Well. Actually, I've done a lot of cleaning,' I begin.

'So have I,' snaps Maria.

'Yes, well, but perhaps I've done rather more cleaning than you, then.'

'Rino,' she sighs. 'That's how it feels for everyone. It's subjective.' Maria leans across the table, peering up into my face as she twiddles her pen between her fingers.

I sit there chewing the end of my thumb for a while before running my fingers through my hair.

'No, it is *objective*,' I say, meeting her eyes.

Irritated, she clicks her tongue against the roof of her mouth, one eyebrow raised.

We sit like that for some time. Maria stares down at the sheet of paper, sipping her tea. There's a deadly silence. I can't believe I'm letting this get to me.

'OK,' I say after some time in which neither of us has said anything. 'We'll have to try it.'

'Great!' Maria smiles and adds, 'I'm going down to the shop, d'you want anything?'

Does she really think I'll fall for that?

I shake my head.

Suck my bottom lip in.

Slam

Damned if I'm going to jump to attention. For the rest of the day I try to hold the mask and stay mainly in my room, which seems to irritate the life out of her. She comes into my room several times on the pretexts of wanting answers to the most trivial and banal questions, and each time she ends up standing in my doorway studying her nails, utterly self-absorbed. And nearly every time she ends up reminding me about the cleaning.

I answer that I've got the point, but that I need to get some work done first.

When she's finished, I tell her to close the door.

Once, she even comes in to read her e-mail, which I grudgingly allow, and as she sits there at my computer, she suggests I might as well use the spare time to get started on the cleaning.

With a smile, admittedly.

I've made up my mind to get her, that's it, there can be no more doubt, I'm merely waiting for the right moment to explode.

Although things don't come to a head until the evening: I tidy round the flat a bit, dust and throw away some old newspapers and pizza boxes. It looks a sight in here, that's for certain. Maria's lying on the sofa under a blanket with a book lying open and travel brochures flung on the floor in front of the sofa.

She's fallen asleep. Snoring lightly, a corner of her mouth moist.

I poke her in the shoulder.

'Hey! Maria,' I say.

She doesn't react.

'Oi, you!' I continue.

She seems to jump. She breathes hard through her nose and presses herself up into the corner of the sofa, blinded by the reading lamp.

'What? What?' she says, screwing her face up into a grimace so as to regain her vision.

'Could you help me move the coffee table so I can get the carpet out onto the balcony?' I ask.

'Yeah, sure, you needn't poke me to death for that!'

'Huh?'

'You poked me. It hurt. You needn't be so rough.'

Rubbing her arm, Maria slowly gets up, and, doubled over, she hobbles around the table. Meanwhile I've managed to be standing there, bent over the table, hands holding both sides, ready to lift, for a good while.

'Get going, then,' I say.

'Oh, for heaven's sake! Wait a couple of seconds, can't you, my foot's gone to sleep.'

'Come on. You've been nagging all day.'

'Yes, but you could have started with the washing up maybe, instead of tidying up just where I'm lying.'

'Washing up?' I ask, straightening up.

'Oh, I see. Of course you haven't done any of the washing up, have you.'

'Truth be told, I haven't! I don't make very much of the washing up. If you'd managed to get your head out from those magazines of yours for two seconds, or that blasted book of yours, then you would have seen that I do the washing up every time. I do *my* washing up, but I don't always do *yours*. It isn't so complicated to put the rest in the dishwasher either, is it? I can't be fucking arsed to go around cleaning up after you and your friends. It looks bloody disgusting every time you've had people round. How d'you think it is for me to bring anyone home?'

'Oh sorry, forgive me for having a social life.'

'You're so bloody naïve.'

'What, me? Naïve? What are you on about?' says Maria, tapping herself on the chest hard with her fingertips.

'You come here with your little piece of paper and somehow that sorts everything out. Like some spoiled little girl. What I'm saying is that I live here. You rent my flat, and if you can't behave properly, I'll have to look round for another flatmate.'

She just looks at me.

'OK. Point one. You said you didn't have a boyfriend. But the first thing you drag back is some nutter who goes off with my video player and sneaks around here and eats what he wants from the fridge, and who sits and sits the *whole* fucking day playing TV games in the living room and never goes out unless it's to get something to eat. You don't respect anything, not the bathroom, nothing. You take things without asking. You piss about, sunning yourself naked on the balcony, coming home late at night and screwing around and keeping me awake. It's as if nobody else lived here except you. You've washed the floor twice, tops. And tidied round here twice. Tops! The only thing I've seen you wash up or put in the dishwasher is your fucking teacup. You all sit around smoking. And apart from stinking the place out with smoke, you use the cups and glasses as ashtrays. Then you come with your pathetic list that's somehow going to straighten everything out. You come in and use my computer when you feel like it. And why is it that every time you check your e-mail on my computer, I have to spend two hours fixing a pile of system failures, eh?'

'What the fuck are you on about? At least I don't spend half the day in some bastard chat room discussing whores with the other sickos.'

She crosses her arms and tilts her head.

'What the fuck are *you* on about?' My voice fades, as if I'm whispering or gone hoarse. There's a tingling sensation in my hands, like ants, my fingers have gone limp.

'I've seen that paedo-sado-cumshot stuff you sit there gawping at. Perhaps it would do you some good to stop looking at spunked-out crack whores, and live some more instead.'

'When did you see that on my computer?' A feeling of nausea rises in my throat.

'When I've checked my mail of course, d'you think I'm totally soft, or what? It's not that difficult to find out where people have been. Schoolgirls websites. Christ, how pathetic can you get?'

'What d'you mean?' I can't control my voice.

'It's hardly surprising you're not getting any of the real thing, sitting in front of that computer all day.'

'What d'you mean?' My hands are shaking, my mouth is dry.

She just stands there staring at me, arms crossed.

'What I said.'

'Have you been reading my questionnaire?' I yell.

She blinks, drops of spit going in her face.

After a pause she eventually answers, 'So what if I have? You read mine, for Christ's sake.'

Her face reddens, she blinks.

'It was secret!'

'So why d'you leave it lying around in front of the computer, then?' She shakes her head as she talks, her eyes shut.

'It's my room. You shouldn't sneak around in my room.'

'Pfff, it was just lying there.'

'It isn't like that for me!'

Maria uncrosses her arms and leans towards me with her mouth open and cheeks flushed red. And there she stands, her arms out to the side and a mute, open mouth, before suddenly screaming, 'I don't give a shit! I'm not staying here past the autumn anyway, and if it's going to be anything like it has so far, I, for one, can't be bothered. I'll move out *before* I go travelling.'

'Travelling? Where to, eh?' I laugh. 'The way you're going, it'll be a wonder if you have two pennies to rub together after the summer. How about paying your rent, *then* you can buy your air tickets. Perhaps you should get your ass off of that sofa and work a bit, now, while you have a summer holiday, instead of staring at the TV and lying in the park all day!'

'I'll go to Lara's and stay there till we leave. Then I'll move out when I come back from Spain. Fucking psycho!'

'Psycho?' I exclaim.

She turns as if to leave.

'Whore!' I scream.

And then suddenly I watch myself doing it: I grab the remote control and smash it so hard into the wall that plastic pieces and microchips rain down over the entire room.

She breathes heavily, just looking at me.

I stand motionless and watch her run into her room.

In under a minute Maria runs out of the flat.

Slamming the door.

Repulsive

It's all over. She doesn't want to live here any more. Maria's moving out. It's that simple. I sigh with relief. It's over. It's over. Now I'll have it all to myself again.

Alternatively: I could get a new flatmate, someone I can get on with. I can start fresh and count this as a useful experience. Perhaps this'll lead to better things. Perhaps the next woman to move in will be my age, or perhaps even younger and easier to, well, you know, easier to control than Maria. Someone I can boss around a bit. Or even someone who likes me that way.

My shoulders ease. I laugh quietly to myself at the thought of how I've let her have it. I got her! I fucking got her! My body begins to relax. I open all the doors in the flat. Into the living room, the bathroom, the bedroom, Maria's room. Then I fetch a tub of ice cream and walk around the rooms before sitting out on the balcony and stuffing myself with it. Great spoonfuls. It's either so cold in my throat that it's sticking in my gullet, or I'm about to cry. There's nothing to be sad about. I don't want to cry. I shift my feet, go on eating.

And if I do start to blub, I've no idea why: whether it's because Maria's seen all that stuff, because she's moving out, because I yelled at her and because she's sad, or because I've not quarrelled with anyone for ten years.

I want to wank.

I want to call a prostitute.

Or someone who might just hold me.

I drag the armchair close up to the TV and use my foot to flick through the channels, and eat until there's almost no ice cream left.

In the end the ice cream's melted.

I try to surf the net, but instead I find myself sitting thinking about how Maria's been sitting here too, and seen everything. I end up looking at the funny pages. Cars spinning off the road. Bloopers. Daft animals and kids. Sports people making tossers of themselves. People dying with their trousers down. The telephone rings. I look at my watch. Lift the receiver. It's Lara.

'Hi, Rino.' She breathes deep, her voice is soft and subdued.

'Hi,' I say.

'It's Lara. Er…Maria's wondering if she can come home?'

'Of course she can,' I answer.

'Good, then she'll be there soon.'

I am anything but calm in the next quarter of an hour. I'm ready to pick up where we left off. I want to grab hold of her and shake her hard. And long. Like in an old movie: I imagine slapping her. With the flat of my hand. 1-2-3. Smack-smack-smack.

I stand by EVERYTHING I said! EVERYTHING! And she hasn't any right to go looking through my things. This is my flat. What I do in my room is my business.

She opens the door and I slap her down: thwack! So her body falls back, legs sprawling to the side.

She opens the door and I immediately start scolding her. *Look at me!* I shout. *Look at me!*

She looks at me, neither of us saying a thing. And then she lowers her gaze.

She walks in. I bend her over the kitchen table.

I slap her. She sinks down with a swollen, bleeding lip and gives me a blow job.

'This is real, Rino,' she says.

Demanding nothing in return.

Instead, she lets herself in almost noiselessly, into the hallway. No footsteps on the stairs. Nothing. Almost as if she's been standing there all the time. She lets herself in, slips her shoes off and takes her jacket off, walks straight across the room where she stands next to me.

And the instant the door opens, I walk straight into the living room, where, of all things, I start picking up the pieces of the remote control.

Then I stop.

She's tugging at my sleeve.

I can't move. I want to open my mouth, but I have nothing to say, and everything I want to say, I dare not say. Everything has come to a complete stop. Like a rusty bit of iron. All I can do is push my glasses into place.

I stare hard at a single point on the floor until she tugs at my sleeve again.

Maria's face is rigid as if she's angry; with flushed cheeks, tight lips and narrowed nostrils.

I look away again, realising I've got to leave.

Then Maria turns me around and puts her arms round me.

'That was really horrible,' she whispers.

Maria sobs against my chest. I pat her gently on the back.

'You've been so strange for ages, you have to say when something's bothering you. You mustn't get so cross again.'

She puts her arms around my neck and pulls my head down. Maria sobs. My neck's soaking. And slippery. And this doesn't look like stopping.

Fillip

'Are you up?' Fillip shouts into the intercom. I've slept just a few short hours. The flat's unbearably hot. There's a thin whistling sound coming from Fillip's breathing, down there in the street below.

'You got anything to drink?' is the first thing he says as he stands there with his wrinkly knock-knees, his chopped-off jeans and his T-shirt with a map of Spain on the front. White socks. Worn-out trainers.

'You've gotta come into town with me. It's a real lark down there.' Fillip gulps some water down and breathes deeply through his nose.

'You gotta bring your camera,' Fillip adds. 'I promised me mum some pickies.'

Summer Carnival

The square outside Central Station is full of people who have begun to assemble for the parade. We sit on the steps. My stomach's rumbling, I still haven't eaten much today. Sitting below us are some girls wearing suits of fluorescent pastel-coloured fun fur. The legs of their boots are covered in the same fluorescent fur and go all the way up to their knees. Earlier they were tramping round the square, and now they sit, pouring Evian into their boots as they shake their feet and flick cigarette ends around them.

Fillip's sweating like a pig. His fringe is black. We've decided to walk down to town rather than take the tram. I'm regretting it. Not on my own account, but his. But then for my sake too, in that I'll be associated with him.

'So how come you're not out of breath, eh?' he asks.

'I don't know...I go training,' I answer.

'But you're not exactly a featherweight, either, are you?'

I shrug my shoulders.

Fillip opens a can of beer. I have no idea where he's got them hidden. Apart from his T-shirt and shorts he's only got a thin coat with him.

'Run out of water,' he says, stretching his neck towards the can.

A short man in a cotton vest walks across to take the microphone on the float, a decorated lorry over on the other side of the parade: *Welcome, everybody, to the Summer Carnival! Everybody has come today in celebration of electronic music and dance.* Applause. *But is that all? We can dance all year. Today we're dancing for more than just ourselves, we're dancing to celebrate a colourful richness of diversity. Take a look around you, and see how different we all are. And each one of us knows that we are many, many more, here and at home, each with their own personality and their own will to do…*

Next to me I hear the sound of Fillip belching, followed by yet another can being opened and a finger poked in and sucked clean of beer.

Let's show the world that we stand together. However we may look, however we feel, wherever we come from or wherever we wish we were! Happy Carnival!

And with that we hear behind us: '*Move along there, this is a public place. Don't let's see you drinking here, please.*'

We turn around.

'But there's hundreds of people drinking here now, so why d'you have to stop me, eh?' Fillip points at all the girls in their fluorescent furs, who are pouring a half litre can down them. Compared to Fillip's 0.33 can.

'We'll be talking to them later.'

'Yeah, sure!' says Fillip and throws a glance at me.

'Excuse me?' asks the policewoman.

'What?' asks Fillip.

'Did you say something?'

'Me? Nope. Nothing.'

'Are you going to get rid of that can then, or what?'

'Yeah, yeah, yeah.'

'Are you being difficult?'

'Nah. But aren't you gonna go down and tell them girls as well, then?'

'You do know I could fine you?'

'I've had a fine from you before.'

'From me? I don't remember that.'

'Well, not exactly you, but, well, you know.'

'Really? So are you going to stop drinking, and go to a pub? There's plenty of good places with outside tables too, you know.'

'Nobody's drinking here.'

'Didn't you have a can of beer just this minute?'

'Nope. No cans of beer here. He went and chucked it,' says Fillip, pointing at me.

The policewoman looks at me.

'Eh…it's true,' I say and nod my head. It's impossible to conceive how he's managed it, but the can has vanished without a trace. The policewoman surveys us, shakes her head, before saying goodbye with a salute-like flick of her finger.

And less than two seconds after their backs are turned, Fillip's sitting there, can in hand, taking one long swig.

He laughs.

'Pedants. Worse than the commies when they were down in the Grand Canaries.'

'*Communists?*'

'Yup.'

And with that he snaps open another can. 'Want some?'

I shake my head. 'I'm hungry,' I say.

'Only gotta ask,' says Fillip, waving the can. In other words there are *more* in the larder.

He points in the direction of the parade. 'What was that I said? She's never gonna say a thing to those girls. Lady-cops. They're the worst. Look at her, walking right past them. And it's just to annoy me. Typical.'

Fillip laughs. 'You see that?' he says, giving his nose a squeeze and starting to tell the story of how he broke his nose.

'Policeman in Sandefjord. I was quarrelling with my girl, right. I didn't hit her or anything. I don't hit ladies. You can give a little correction, perhaps, but I only hit with a flat hand, I don't *hit*, know what I mean?'

I nod.

'Know what I mean?'

'Yeah, sure,' I say and look up.

Fillip sits, eyes roving around him.

'Now, where was I?' he asks.

'No idea. Haven't the faintest,' I say.

' "I'm arguing with her," I says to them, "not you." There's two of them holding me down with the baton from behind, like. "Look," I says. "Am I resisting? Am I?" Then he grins, know what I mean? You shoulda seen that smirk on his face as he smashed me over my nose.'

'I'm hungry,' I repeat after a while.

At McDonald's I get myself a McFeast menu. Fillip wants the quarter pounder. Extra large.

'You seen any action then?' Fillip stuffs a bunch of fries in his mouth, getting mayonnaise on his moustache, and hunches over his burger again with both hands.

'What d'you mean?'

'You know…you had your way with that flatmate of yours?'

'Hm…' I smile, assemble my burger and shift my feet under the table.

Fillip laughs. Not loudly, but it sounds really imbecilic: a couple of girls in leopard print miniskirts and bikini tops at the next table raise their eyebrows and exchange glances over their milkshakes. Crossed legs swinging.

When it doesn't feel like we're being spied on any longer, I tell him about the party. About Lara. And Maria.

'Yeah, yeah, better beware, now.'

'What d'you mean?' I ask.

'Watch they don't get their claws in you.' Fillip chews.

'Oh?'

'Well, once you're onto a good thing, likely there's a lot more where it came from, if you get my drift. Mustn't lose hold, once you've got it.'

'I've got what?'

'*It*.' Fillip grins, wiping his mouth with his screwed-up napkin between his hands.

'Right.'

'Get it?'

I sit, staring at his moustache, waiting for him to get the hint.

It.

Wendy Shalit

Carnival float after carnival float glides down Karl Johan Street, filled with people dressed in next to nothing. I dash up to Grensen to buy a pair of earplugs at the chemists. On my return, Fillip's standing there biting the end off a double frankfurter with a bottle of water stuck in his back pocket.

'See that one there? What d'you reckon on her?' Fillip points at a rather tall, slender woman dancing in the middle of the cavalcade.

'Not bad...' I begin.

'Ha! Got you fooled there!' laughs Fillip. 'That's not a woman, look.'

'Oh?'

'That's a bloke, can't you see? It's hard to tell sometimes.' He drinks from the bottle before pointing with it. 'Look, here come the rest of the trannies. Imagine, going to feel pussy and finding a bloody great lunch-box down there instead.'

There are people pushing from behind and both Fillip and I, and others too, lose our balance, stumbling forwards. Fillip only just saves himself from falling to the ground by grabbing a lamppost. Crimson with anger, he turns, fingers grasped tight around his bottle.

'Can you fucking well stop pushing so bloody hard?'

'Yeah, yeah,' a young boy's voice sniggers behind us.

'Did you say something, eh?' Fillip turns again.

'We don't want any trouble,' says a small brunette.

'I'm not making trouble. I just want people to stop bloody pushing so hard.'

A short, plump girl with a large nose is swirling something round her that looks like a glow-in-the-dark plastic ribbon.

'Fucking hell. She's a bit of a porky, isn't she,' Fillip chortles, pointing up at the float before turning away to squeeze the last dribble of water from his bottle. Then he almost sends himself cross-eyed staring down its neck to check there's nothing left.

A chap in tight cycling shorts and a black singlet pushes a fat lady with short, crippled legs and large sunglasses in a wheelchair up Karl Johan Street. She's waving a little flag. I've no idea what it stands for.

Fillip is laughing raucously.

To begin with I want to go because it's so embarrassing. Fillip's laughing. But then I notice all the people round us, gossiping, laughing, pointing. I loosen my earplugs discreetly and begin listening to what people are saying all round. Up until this moment everything seemed like a seamless hum amidst the music, but now it's as if I can use my head like a radio to tune into various frequencies: *Why is she standing there shaking her ass? She's got nothing worth showing! How does she have the nerve to dress like that when she hasn't got anything worth showing? Blimey! She's not even cute, so why is she standing there making a display of herself? Yuckee! Shit, that is so repulsive. Fucking hell, man, check out that Asian chick there. Asian? Where? Which one? Oh, definitely! Drop-dead gorgeous.*

After a while it's as if I can't separate these voices from the ones inside my head, the ones I sometimes think I can hear saying, *Jesus! Look at those two fatsos standing there gawping. And d'you see that one there, you'd never think he'd ever...*

'I can't bear any more,' I say.

Fillip nods.

Edel

We've moved back and we're standing in Parliament Square deciding what to do when I hear her voice behind me.

'I thought you'd be here, Rino.'

She tilts her head and smiles falsely. Then she pushes her pram the final metre towards us. Her daughter squirms in the pram, kicking her feet against the footrest. Tied to the handle of the pram is a helium balloon that twirls and bounces in Edel's face. Edel pulls back with closed eyes, reaching out blindly to catch the balloon.

'Now, will you just sit still!' shouts Edel. Grasping the cord of the balloon, she leans forward and presses the girl down into her seat before fumbling in the bag that hangs from the handle and pulling out a bottle of Coke.

Rolling her eyes and fanning herself with a hand, she takes a mouthful. Then she gives the bottle to the kid.

'Here, drink your Coke.'

Edel straightens up and smiles.

'So! What have you done with that little friend of yours, eh?'

Fillip belches. His gaze alternates expectantly between Edel and me, grinning.

'Isn't she too big to be sitting in that pram?' asks Fillip.

Edel flashes a glance at him before continuing in the same tone.

'Perhaps she's off displaying herself in the cavalcade...?' Edel tilts her head again.

I still haven't opened my mouth.

'No, she...' I begin.

The little girl scrambles out of her pram. Edel reaches forward to make her sit down again, before gathering herself and turning to me.

'Hey. You know what? You couldn't take her over to the cavalcade, so she can see, could you? Then I can go over to Sara's tent and have a beer? Oh, please! You'd be an angel.'

Edel smiles.

'D'you want to go over there with the man to watch? Do you remember Rino?' Edel crouches down next to her. She looks up at me, then down at Edel. She shakes her head.

She doesn't want to come at first. She shakes her head and turns away. Edel wipes some ice cream from her mouth. Licking a napkin, she rubs the corners of her mouth and her cheeks. Then she pushes her over to me, takes the pram and kicks the brakes off.

Fillip laughs.

The little girl squints up at me. She turns to look back at her mother, then takes my hand.

Edel waves. I open my mouth, only to shut it again. Fillip clears a path through the crowd and we almost get to the curb before our path is blocked.

She cranes her neck. I peer down into those wide open, shining eyes. A surge goes through the crowd and frightened that she might disappear amongst so many people, I lift her up.

I hold her up to see the parade.

Fillip turns against the pressure from behind, his fringe mussed up.

And thus I'm forced to remember this day for the rest of my life. A frozen moment: lifting a small girl who gazes, wide-eyed, down Karl Johan Street with a finger in her mouth.

'I want Mummy,' she says.

I nod and turn.

The Creep III

Maria has been away for nearly two weeks now, first to her parents' house before going to Spain with Lara, and now I have almost another two weeks to myself. I think I'll at least be able to get some work done now before I take a holiday too. But the day after the cavalcade I am woken, at some ungodly hour, of course, by Håkon, who rings on the door asking for Maria. Fillip shakes me awake to tell me there's *a bloke at the door who wants to come in.*

'She's gone abroad,' I say in the intercom.

'Shit. Can I come up and fetch a couple of things? I was going to borrow the PlayStation.'

'No.'

And with that I put the receiver down. He just manages to get it in that I'm a rotten bastard and that I'd better be careful if I see him again. But *my* last word is: 'No.'

Fillip puts his shoes on behind me as Håkon keeps pressing like a maniac on the intercom. After a quick briefing Fillip trundles down, and I stand listening in to their conversation.

Fillip: Yeah, what are you after?

Håkon: Huh?

Fillip: Yeah, you keep buzzing.

Håkon: Yeah, but for another bloke.

Fillip: Nah, it's my door you're ringing on, mate. What are you after?

Håkon: Sorry, honestly, but...

Fillip: Go home, we haven't got any computer games here.

Håkon: Huh? Yeah, but – fucking hell.

Fillip: The lady's moved out. So you can forget ringing here and making a nuisance of yerself.

Håkon: Huh?

Fillip: You got muck in your ears?

Håkon: No.

Fillip: Right. Well, shove off, then.

Håkon: OK.

Fillip: Hey, Rino mate. Ta ta. We'll talk later this week!

I pad around the flat for a while wondering what to do with myself. I want to go for a run, but I should really do some work. I shower, put clean clothes on, eat two apples and some watermelon. Look at my watch, and in doing so spill drinking yoghurt all over my chest and stomach.

I stand there and wipe myself with the rancid washing up cloth, when suddenly it wells up inside me.

'FUCK,' I bawl, flinging the cloth from me and swiping out at the milk carton. I smash the cupboard door and slam my fists into the bench.

Fuck It

That dumb jacket of yours. Those dumb glasses. Those pathetic, clammy fingers on those fat paws you never know what to do with.

That repulsive, flabby belly and those deep-creased wrinkles over your ugly knock knees.

Town

I rip off my clothes, put my grey hooded jacket on and set off for town. I'm in a raging fury, but it feels good. It wants out, out of my body, out of my system.

Twenty minutes later I'm standing in the opticians.

'It's been some time since I've come across any like this,' says the salesman, holding my glasses up before him.

'I want lenses,' I say, and half an hour later I text Maria from inside H&M. *Name two good aftershaves*, I write. In less than two minutes she's answered.

She's lying on the beach, she texts me, and after a trip to the wine merchants I leave the perfume counter, put myself straight in a taxi home, where I absolutely must have a shower before I put my new clothes on.

Hairdressers

She's wearing a slightly manly shirt with a wide collar, open at the neck, tanned skin over her cleavage and breasts. She tells me that she has time available and that all I have to do is sit in the chair. As she runs her fingers through my hair, she asks somewhat pointedly whether it's been a long time since I had a cut perhaps. 'About a month, isn't it?'

I nod. My eyes grow heavy. The way she lets her nails scrape my scalp sends tiny shivers down my neck and back. Spreading in ripples across my chest.

She wedges the back of my head between her breasts as she places her fingers on my ears to measure. She asks if I'm satisfied.

'Pardon?' I ask.

'Are you satisfied with it?' she asks.

I nod.

I look at her skin. And half an hour later I'm lying on a sun bed two blocks away. Afterwards I shower, trim the hairs on my stomach and crotch before shaving my balls and the insides of my thighs.

The Flat

I sit on the balcony with my wine, salad and a lit candle. My entire body itches from the sun bed, but it's OK, it doesn't bother me. There's already a line under my watchstrap. My smooth, new-shaven skin nicks.

I make the decision to at least consider calling one of those clinics that advertise plastic surgery. The food's good. The wine's good. In a moment of insanity I almost call Edel, but catch myself in time. After a while, I feel very alone somehow, in a way I've never felt before: I feel like going out. Not like sitting indoors, but going out. To just go and sit somewhere, to be surrounded by people.

Nothing spectacular.

I'm not expecting the whole world to change in a day.

Mucho Mas II

'Wow, you look so different today, I hardly recognised you,' says Gry. 'Oh, you're not wearing any glasses, that's what it is.'

Gry offers the menu.

'I think I'll just have a beer,' I say and sit at the bar.

'What have you been up to?' she asks.

'Oh, not a lot, been pretty quiet,' I answer.

'D'you know Gry well, then?' asks a guy next to me.

'What? Me? No…'

'Sorry, it was just that it looked that way, you know.' He twirls the ash off his cigarette along the rim of the ashtray.

'No, I suppose I'm just a secret admirer,' I smile as Gry puts the beer down.

Gry looks quizzically at me. It looks as though she's blushing. I just smile and feel like the bravest man in the world.

Practice

The flat lies in darkness behind me. I stand out on the balcony, watching the people below and smelling the unfamiliar scent of my new aftershave, not quite believing that it's me. A soft wind blows through my new-cut hair.

A strange feeling that everything's going to turn out all right comes over me.

I walk through the flat without turning the light on, into Maria's room, where I lie down in her bed. It's completely different from last time: her tops are hanging from the wardrobe door, the cupboard's full of clothes, pictures on the walls, a pair of forgotten socks, plants, bedclothes, everything seems so cosy and safe, as if I were packed in air and cotton wool, a delicate perfume, her pillow, the duvet.

I lie down with my clothes on, roll the duvet into a bundle at my side.

It can all turn out all right, I don't need to be me if I don't want to be, there's nothing to force me. There's another me lying there, waiting.

I must buy some flowers and plants.

Rhinoceros

In the night I have this dream that has haunted me since I was a child: a rhinoceros stands in an empty room with broken windows, grey, peeling walls and plaster on the floors.

Suddenly the rhinoceros crashes through the floor into the room below.

On the next floor down, the rhinoceros crashes through once more.

Then again the rhinoceros crashes through the floorboards, like sheets of paper.

The rhinoceros thunders through the floors.

Again and again.

Ad infinitum.

Trust

'Goodness, it's stuffy in here. Is it all right if I open the window a bit?' Maria's dad has white hair, a square body with bony, rectangular fingers and bears not the least resemblance to his daughter. He could have been my father, but my dad's thin. Maria's father puts a bag of clothes down which she probably left behind at home.

'Well. We just wanted to see how she's getting on, how she's living, you know.'

He fiddles with the latch on the window before sitting at the foot of the bed, hands folded. He gazes round, looking up at the wardrobe door. Nods. I'm about to wander off to the kitchen when he opens his mouth as if to say something, but then closes it again.

'Is she doing all right?' he asks as I turn.

'Sure,' I answer and shrug my shoulders.

'Is she good around the house as well? She tidies up after herself and isn't more of a nuisance than necessary?'

'No, no. No problem at all.'

'So she seems reasonably well organised. She comes home in the evenings and sleeps well and seems healthy and happy?'

'Yes.'

'Right, well, that's good.' He nods, lifting his gaze from the floor and out into the backyard. 'We've had some difficult years, you see. Maria's always been a wild one, she does what she wants on the whole, but we're pleased about the way she's been developing lately. Her mother's a bit worried, you know.'

He gets up and claps his hands against his thighs.

'Well, well,' he says. 'Well, well.'

He shuts the window, takes a couple of steps towards the door, but changing his mind he grabs the duvet, shakes it a couple of times, then spreads it smoothly and neatens the sheet. He sighs through his nose once, inspects the room: the bedside table, the clothes on the floor, a pile of papers, body lotion and massage oil.

Ikea

I ring Dad and ask if he can drive me out to Ikea. When we arrive he walks in front of me with the trolley, talking into his mobile, while I go back to leaf through the catalogue. Dad's wife, who on paper is my step-mother, if you ignore the fact that she's barely three years older than me, has been sitting out in the car for ages, waiting.

Dad refers to me as *Junior* on the mobile. But it's at the tills things get really embarrassing when he calls me his sprog and it gets rubbed in that he's paying for the whole shebang. Otherwise everything's perfect.

He *is* in fact the one paying.

Dad wants the Swedish meatballs and rings his wife in the car, who says she'll survive.

It's only eleven o'clock.

'I think I'll just have an ice cream,' I say.

Dad stares across at me as if I had finally confessed to being gay and that this was something he'd always known deep down, but had nonetheless refused to confront. Without further ado he orders meatballs and an ice cream. He holds his wallet open in front of him and pulls out a 200 kroner note.

When the assistant asks if he wants chocolate sprinkles on his ice cream, Dad grabs the tray, snorts dismissively a couple of times and motions in my direction.

'Sprinkles?' she asks.

'No, thanks,' I answer.

Garden Centre

I have to shout in the car. My stepmother insists on playing the same Celine Dion album we played on the way out. At first Dad grunts that he's got to pay excess on the trailer rental, and that it'll take forever to carry all these things up, but eventually he pulls over and I dash into the garden centre.

When I get back with my plants and I'm finally sitting in the back seat, my stepmother suddenly dashes out, promising it'll only take five minutes. Dad throws his head down, with both hands grabbing hard around the wheel, chewing violently on his gum, and looks at me in the rear view mirror before giving the car stereo a smack, causing it to spit Celine Dion out.

Two seconds later he's in a good mood again. He looks at me in the rear view mirror.

We laugh.

The Return

Back home we empty the trailer of Ikea things and carry them up to the flat. As my stepmother follows me up with the plants, she asks if I've found myself a girlfriend. I shake my head. Dad takes a look around Maria's room. The back of his shirt's wet. He nods to himself. He thinks it smells stuffy.

I must stop sleeping in there.

'Your hair looks nice,' she manages to say before scooting after Dad. Now and again she tries to be considerate. But I generally find it nauseating. And when it's not nauseating, it's plain weird.

First I take everything down and clear the old furniture away. Put the coffee table, the cupboard and shelves down in the cellar. Roll up the carpet.

Maria's Return

It's evening when Maria finally returns home at the end of the week. She rings the bell and I run down to help her carry her luggage up. She doesn't notice anything at first. She goes into the kitchen and drinks a large glass of water as she gazes around her, eyebrows raised.

'It's all new,' she exclaims and fills her glass again. 'And how about you? You look so different.'

'Nah, I don't know, I...' I hold back at first, but eventually hint at the hair and the missing glasses.

She can't take it all in straight away, but shakes her head and screws her eyes up before finally opening them wide in amazement.

'That's what it is! Good god! But you look so good!'

'It's not too outrageous, is it?' I grin.

'What's that smell?' asks Maria.

'It's not too outrageous, is it?' I ask again, pointing at my hair.

'No, no. It's great,' she laughs and gives me a hug.

'*Hello,*' she says when she hugs me, 'hello!'

'Hello, hello,' I say and pat her carefully on the back. My fingers melt into the furrow that runs down the centre of her back.

She asks what the smell is again, instantly answering her own question by saying she can see I've been painting and that it's great.

The Gift

'Oh, I've got a present for you,' says Maria suddenly, as I'm about to take her through to show her the living room. She starts rummaging in her bag. And I experience a moment of pure rapture: nobody, as far as I can remember, for many years, has bought a present for me. Nobody apart from family, that is.

And I've never had a woman to show a newly done up flat to, either.

I stand there hopping behind her in the doorway.

Small hops of anticipation. A parcel. It's all so unexpected.

Maria tells me to close my eyes.

And when I open them again, I have to choose which hand.

I choose the left.

But it's two sizes too small. A T-shirt.

'Nice,' I say and try to smile.

'That was just a fun present, really, I've got another one too.'

Maria lifts her bag and staggers into the living room with it dangling between her legs, then dumps it down again and gazes all round.

'This is so amazingly brilliant! Wow, you've really been at it.'

I stand there with my T-shirt.

'Did you have a good time?'

'Nah, it's been dead boring, but all right, I suppose. The first few days I just lay there puking and hardly managed to drag myself out onto the terrace. Lara did loads, travelled round and got to see a bit of the island, she met a bloke. I lay on the beach mainly and I only went to the disco two or three evenings.'

I stretch the T-shirt out in front of me and study the print.

Maria gets up and stretches her back before holding up a bottle of Jameson's.

'Got any ice cubes?'

Printed: *Sex Instructor. First lesson free!*

I wouldn't be seen dead in it.

Weight

Next day I get home from my run and weigh myself. I have lost a whole three kilos. I can't even be bothered to remove my pyjamas to cheat off another couple of grams. Three kilos, at least, and that's after drinking almost two litres of water when I got back from running.

Maria's speaking to me, but I haven't got the least idea what she's saying. Her lips are moving, but I'm just holding my breath, waiting for the moment when I can interrupt and announce my sensational news.

She tucks her legs under her, changing channels with the remote.

'Is it okay if I flick channels?' Maria asks.

'Sure!' I almost shout and just as I think my moment has arrived, her mobile goes off. She peers at the display with an irritated expression, half rolling her eyes, before blinking wearily and turning her gaze towards the television again.

I take a deep breath.

I position myself to the centre of the room, right of the TV, and stand there, arms almost girlishly out to the sides, hands clenched and probably wearing an insane grin.

The phone goes again. I sigh. This time Maria answers it, gets up and starts clearing things off the table, her cup, plate, ashtray, all the time talking in clipped sentences with the phone wedged between her cheek and shoulder.

Sweat has begun to gather in the small of my back. I move over to the window. It feels as though all the tension in my body has somehow accumulated in my rear, and for a moment I'm worried I might have a dark sweat mark on my ass. Though when I touch my pyjamas they're dry, but then before I know it I've released a really loud fart into the room. Maria's still in the kitchen and it's not certain she's heard. To cover up, I drum my fingers on the window. As if deep in thought.

Maria comes in. I turn and smile. She bursts out laughing and wafts her hand in front of her face. *'Fucking hell, Rino,'* she says, turning from the phone, her robe simultaneously falling open as she stretches out for a glass on the table.

Maria sends me a you-got-that-for-nothing glance.

I spend the next hour just messing about, really; putting CDs on and running round after Maria, who's either calling people or being called, and in truth I'm not having such a bad time. I make coffee and then using only gestures ask if she wants some too, and when she raises a hand in answer, I understand she doesn't, and when eventually she changes her mind, I understand that too, and even the amount she wants, filling a cup halfway before placing it before her. I realise I'm enjoying myself.

In barely twenty minutes I've done more work than I have in the last three weeks. And when I log on, I see I haven't surfed porn for almost four days.

When Maria has taken her position on the sofa once more, I rush into the room, arms outstretched, opening and closing my fists.

'GUESS WHAT!' I shout.

She peers up at me with curiosity.

'What?' she says hesitantly.

'I HAVE LOST THREE KILOS!'

Maria nods her head approvingly, as if to say, good for you.

I'm about to add a little fanfare, and go TA-DA! to underline how pleased I am, but instead I yell, 'THREE KILOS!'

'Christ, it doesn't show,' she says after a pause. 'I mean it probably does, sort of, but...' She turns her gaze to the TV and can't be bothered, or doesn't dare to follow up on this sensitive subject.

My mouth tightens and twists. I struggle to arrive at a smile I can hold until I get to my room. Then, as if to just rub it in, and this is so fucking typical, things like that only ever make it worse and people only ever say these things to fat people so they won't get a complex about being fat, and I've heard her saying it to her friends when they're discussing their weight, then she says it: 'Oh, are you slimming? You don't need to, you're not fat. I like big men, myself.'

She really doesn't need to lie. I know I'm fat, and that I'm less fat now than I've been in ages.

But then: three kilos isn't much to lose. I am, after all, still *fat*.

Swimming Trunks

'I don't have any swimming trunks anyway,' I say.

Suddenly I'm scared again. Even with my progress and weight loss the idea of venturing onto the beach hadn't entered my head. Like so many things, it's been years since the last time. And besides, I've an appointment with Dad for him to come over and install a new kitchen worktop. And I haven't even been to the loo yet, anyway.

'Oh, for heaven's sake, we can get that sorted, just as long as we catch the boat with the others.'

Maria rolls her towel and shoves it into her bag. She's wearing sandals, shorts and just a white bikini top.

'It's going to be excellent, we're going to have a barbecue and go swimming. There'll be a whole gang of us. And there'll be people you've already met, Helge, Anders and Niklas.'

I shake my head determinedly. I need a shit.

'Come on!'

Stress

'So, where d'you want to buy your trunks?' asks Maria on the tram.

'I don't know,' I answer.

'Well, where did you last buy trunks, then?'

'I've never really bought trunks.'

'You've *never* bought trunks?'

Not since college.

Maria decides that if we nip into H&M in Oslo City and find some-thing quickly, we'll just manage it. But presented with the racks of swimwear I chicken out, begging her to choose something while I go and look at other things. I eventually return with a pair of khaki shorts.

'You're not thinking of swimming in khakis, are you?' She presses some chewing gum between her front teeth and gives me a quizzical look before showing me a pair of Bermuda shorts and some rather more tight-fitting trunks.

'No, of course not.'

Finally I decide on the Bermuda shorts, pay, put the khaki shorts on in the changing rooms and meet Maria outside.

'We're not going to get the boat on time,' says Maria, 'but it's OK. No point stressing.'

At the supermarket we buy a disposable barbecue and some food, and buy an ice cream and a soft drink each. Then we wander slowly down in what I assume is the direction of the quay, and as time passes I wonder whether some of the passers-by might not mistake us for a couple: we're suddenly so similarly dressed. And doing the same things.

And if Maria's had the same thought, I wonder whether it bothers her.

But not much.

Mum

The queue's much longer than I imagined. Maria swears aloud.

'Hi there, I don't think we've met properly,' says Martine, putting her bag down and stretching a hand out to me.

Dad phones. He's fuming, asking me why I'm not at home as arranged. It takes time before he understands what I'm up to. But when he eventually does, he's fine about it. In fact, he approves. It's good I'm getting out. He'll just drive home and fetch the spare key, and I mustn't give it another thought. I must enjoy myself and send his regards to Maria.

When I hang up, Maria asks me who it was.

'Why doesn't your mother ever call?'

'She's dead,' I answer.

'Oh, that's very sad.'

'Hmm,' I say.

'My mother's dead too,' Martine says a moment later.

'That's great!' I very nearly say. It almost slips out from sheer excitement. We have something in common!

Cold Crust

'Aren't you going to take some things off? You'll melt. Come for a dip, at least...'

'Nah, I don't know.'

'What? You don't know? Have we got to drag you in, or what?'

Maria kicks her sandals off. The boys call up to her from the water's edge, and with a smile she wriggles out of her shorts, thumbs in her waistband and ass against the beach. She smiles. Turns.

Then Maria runs out into the water.

I'm left behind, sitting with Martine, who's taking her clothes off slowly. She folds them in a pile. Twists her skirt around and undoes her zip. She casts a glance in my direction. I'm watching.

'Hey, watch out!' I whisper. But before she has time to react Helge comes hurtling across, chucking water all over her from a little plastic bucket before running off again.

'You lousy shit,' she hisses.

I try to send her a look that says I agree that it was rather unnecessary. But she pretends not to have noticed and smiles as she leans forward, squeezing her hair.

Then she takes me completely off guard. With her hands held behind her back, Martine gazes at me impassively. It's the last thing I'm expecting. I think she's going to say something and I hold her gaze, when her breasts tumble out.

They're large. And as her bra slips away, they swing from side to side.

A stabbing in my chest, I feel myself blush uncontrollably and my lungs constrict. I'd thought she was shy at first, since she was undressing so slowly. She bends back down to place her bra on her beach towel, gets up, tosses her hair back, and looks at me with lazy eyes.

'Aren't you coming too, then?'

Rather than get changed, I decide to swim in my khakis. My dick is swelling and it would be such a hassle. I take my sweat-soaked shirt off, empty my pockets and lumber after her, trying all the while not to stare too long or too hard at her ass. She's all goose-pimply from the bucket of water. Delicate, blonde hairs on the small of her back.

'Is it warm?' she shouts, tugging at her thong with her finger. Then she turns.

As if she had eyes in the back of her head: 'Come on, get in, then.'

I mumble, sneak up so as to be level with Martine rather than hovering behind her. I dip one foot in the water. I look over at her, up the length of those long legs with stubbly hairs around her bikini line, her breasts with their erect nipples.

She flashes me a glance.

My dick stirs and I start to run out into the sea.

The Change

'Hello, there,' says Helge. I actually recognise him from the party. And the people I take to be Niklas and Anders raise their chins from the surface of the water by way of greeting. I wave.

'Water's bloody brilliant,' says Nikko after introducing himself.

Afterwards, it's as if the icy water had filled my body, invigorating me. I feel like a compacted snowball with a hard crust of ice. I peer across at Nikko; somehow his body seems to spill over, he has skinny legs and spare tyres that hang over his shorts. And without it appearing to bother him in the least, he chats away with everybody as he squirms about on his towel, smoking and sipping his Coke.

I don't know. I feel I've changed: I can run for three-quarters of an hour non-stop now if I want, I can do a hundred and fifty sit-ups and at least forty push-ups.

That's not bad, really. I've got a belly, my fat's there, but it's a firm fat. At least I haven't got any spare tyres.

I get up.

'Are you going to the sweet shop?'

'No,' I answer, 'I think I'll go for another swim.'

Bikini

I swim, play cards with Helge and Nikko. Who drink tons of Coke, allegedly to cure their hangovers. Eventually I manage to smuggle the bathing trunks on as well. I change in the beach toilets, emerge into the bright sunlight, then practically change my mind and walk halfway back to the toilets before gritting my teeth and forcing myself to go back to the others, where I slap the wet khakis down on the ground and stand bewildered. It's done. The sweat runs off me. If I sit down now I'll only be restless. I take another dip instead. Anders and Helge have enviably nice, even tans. Helge's teeth glint every time he smiles. He's the more reserved. Nikko's the one I find it easiest to compare myself to, but on the other hand he's also the most energetic and bubbly. Anders is more laid back: he has uneven beard growth, but it seems not to trouble him. He even sat for a while in the sun wearing a black woolly hat. On his tanned chest he has a tattoo of a paw mark. Claw marks. He's the tallest as well.

When I get back from the kiosk, Maria looks up at me, her hand shading her eyes.

'You're going to look like a lobster if you don't get some cream on soon,' says Maria.

Sun cream. When did I sunbathe last? Outside? Not for as long as I remember. As a kid, perhaps. I've thought about it often, but never dared. Anyway, I'm counting on the preparation I've done on the sun bed being enough.

'You're just like a big kid,' laughs Martine.

I look at her. Then away.

'Yes. Your lips'll go blue soon.'

I look at her again.

'You're in the water all the time.'

'Oh, right,' I say.

Maria asks if I can rub cream on her back. Lying on her stomach, she passes me the orange bottle. Martine's breasts are still troubling me. She has no stripes from her bikini, and half sits, half lies with her arms stretched behind her as her gaze follows Helge and Anders on their return from the water. I'm chuffed that with the trust that Maria puts in me, Martine's getting the chance to see I'm not a total loser.

'You'll have to undo my bikini strap,' says Maria.

'Oh, right,' I reply.

With the palms of my hands already filled with sun cream, I pick at her straps carefully with the tips of my fingers. Maria pushes her hair from her neck. She's lying with her head propped in her hands. The straps slip in my sticky, knotted fingers, but as I try to avoid the cream running from my hands, I have to work with them turned up the wrong way. It's useless. Finally I stand up, hands stuck out in front of me. Maria turns, wondering.

'Can I have something to wipe my hands on?' I ask. 'I can't hold anything properly.'

'Oh, for heaven's sake, can't you just rub the cream off onto *me*, then?'

'Are you sure?' I ask.

'Yeah, course,' she laughs.

I kneel down next to her. For a split second it's as if I don't dare, but then suddenly I force my hands down onto her back, placing a dab on each shoulder and on the small of her back before twisting her bikini top undone.

'Who's a lucky man then?' smiles Anders. He pulls the ring off a can of beer and crosses his legs. Nikko lifts his gaze quietly from the backgammon board. Twiddles his toes.

I'm undressing her.

That's what I'm doing.

'Sorry,' I say suddenly.

Ego Massage

A single moment betrays her. Martine is watching. Impassive. Chewing on some gum. She stops chewing, raises her eyebrows, and seems to be turning something in her imagination. Then she squints up at me from an angle, but averts her gaze with flushed cheeks before she catches my eye, stares down at her stomach and blows a bubble. The bubble bursts with a little smack. Her breasts sway as she throws the dice on the backgammon board.

To begin with it's almost as if I'm trying to rub sun cream on *without* actually touching Maria, and instead letting the cream lie in a layer *between* my hands and her back. Her skin. But after Maria comments that she's never in the world going to get brown that way, I allow myself to touch her more firmly: I rub her so I can feel her shoulder blades and each vertebra in her spine. I let my fingers glide, pushing a wave of skin before them, up and down her spine. Follow the soft muscles from the armpit, down over the ribs, notch by notch, down the centre and then out over the soft sides above her bikini, the curve between her back and ass.

Then, as I sit with Maria behind me, rubbing cream on my back, I look up to find Martine's gaze: she's examining my swimming trunks.

Chewing on her gum.

Mastering

'We'll have to do the barbecue soon,' shouts Anders. Nikko and Helge have spent the entire day discussing their bowel movements vociferously and chatting on their mobiles with the girls they met yesterday. They are a whirl of text messages and telephone conversations.

'Can't you be boss, then?' asks Nikko.

'Of what?' I ask.

'The barbecuing. Sausages and stuff.'

During the barbecue Nikko and Anders make sure to keep me supplied in beers. Anders makes himself most at home, eating whatever sausages he wants. The others wait until I say they're ready. It feels a bit awkward touching other people's food. At first, I felt sure some of them wouldn't want any, without giving any reason, because they'd think it was disgusting that I'd touched the food. But everybody's eaten. So everything's relatively fine.

'Sausages are so damned underrated,' laughs Nikko, leaning forward on his toes to avoid his sausage and relish sliding down and landing on his clothes.

Fillip

'Your phone's ringing,' says Helge and gets up, sausage in one hand and my droning mobile in the other. For a moment I think it might be work, or that it might be Dad. Something to lend me the appearance of being normal and interesting. That the world needs me.

Instead it's Fillip.

'Why aren't you picking up? D'you wanna go for a couple of beers?' There's a snapping sound and a bottle cap clatters on the concrete of a terrace at the other end.

'Eh, can't,' I mumble.

'What you up to, mate? Where are you?'

'I'm out having a barbecue.'

'Oh right, where's that then?'

'Out.'

'Out with the ladies then, are you?' asks Fillip.

'Yeah, they're here too,' I say as quietly as I can.

'Where are you, then? Over in the park?'

'I don't really know,' I reply.

'Come on, d'you think I'm thick?' says Fillip.

'No, of course not.'

'I'm not that thick, you know.' Fillip takes another slug. 'Why can't you just tell me where you are, and I can come down. Got some bangers in the freezer.'

'Hang on there,' I tell him.

I press my thumb over the receiver and count to twenty in my head, then lift the phone to my ear and say, 'We're leaving soon, can't I ring you later?'

Fillip laughs and says, '*Yeah, mate. Sure.*'

We hang up.

Clothes

Maria sits with her hands tucked up the sleeves of her hooded jacket. Having eaten her fill from the barbecue, she readjusts her towel and asks me to come and sit in front of her. Anders rolls what I assume to be a joint, with the excited assistance of Nikko. Maria pushes her feet in under me. Martine's put a cotton polo neck jumper on. I've switched my mobile to silent. Fillip has tried to call twice. And left messages both times.

'So why aren't I permitted to warm your feet then, eh?' asks Anders.

'Because,' answers Maria in a light tone that verges on the flirtatious.

Not pursuing it, Anders turns away instead to sneeze. He gives a contented chuckle and blows his nose before getting a nasal spray and inhaling. He continues rolling the joint, poking at its edges with long, elegant fingers. Straight nails. Smooth skin between his knuckles. Silver rings.

'It's great here,' says Nikko.

'You're fucking cool, man,' I say suddenly.

There's complete silence.

Nikko looks up at me, a bottle of beer held to his lips, then stares down.

'I think Rino said something to you, Anders,' Maria says after a while.

'Huh? What was that?' asks Anders and lights up his joint.

'Er…no…I was just saying how hip you are.'

It's just as quiet.

'Kind of…' I add. I shrug my shoulders.

Leaning forward, Martine turns the portable radio on. She smiles awkwardly. Nikko scratches his leg with his foot. 'Fucking cosy here, man,' he mumbles, giving an encouraging nod of the head. Maria sits motionless behind me. As if holding her breath.

'Oh, right. You reckon so, eh? That's great.' Anders sits up and crosses his legs. 'Cool, man.' He nods in my direction, passing me the joint. Then he places his free hand on Martine's bare feet. They've hardly talked, but Martine has gradually edged her way around the blanket, and resting her head on my bag, she has her knees crooked and feet stretched out towards him. It all appears entirely without effort on his side.

Without looking at her even. He closes his hands over the arches of her feet.

I feel I've spoiled things for Maria. That he's choosing Martine because Maria's sitting with me. And it's not even that it means that much to me. Perhaps she's only done it to give him a hint.

'You've got to pass it on,' Maria whispers, coaxing the joint from my fingers and taking a drag before passing it to Martine, who lifts her head from my bag.

When they've finished their smoke, Nikko and Helge get up. Helge scoops up the Frisbee and lumbers off towards the lawn beyond the volleyball net. I'm feeling a bit dizzy. I'm getting restless from sitting still, it feels as if my body's itching all over and the barbecue keeps coming up in little gulps every time I burp. Added to which I'm getting nervous on Maria's behalf. I don't want to come between them.

'Can I come and join you?' I shout after them.

'*Sure,*' answers Helge.

Wild

My clothes are warm and light. Practical. And as I send the Frisbee flying, there's no resistance. The soft, light cotton feels like a gentle electricity against my sunburned skin. I'm warm and focused: my only concern is with throwing the Frisbee. And then a certain something happens: this Frisbee becomes the most beautiful thing I have ever seen. Ever. As it glides away. Slicing soundlessly through the air. This feels like one of the best things I have ever done. That somehow this is what it's all about: keeping the Frisbee in the air!

Now and then I scream. With my hands on my head. Running my fingers through my hair as the Frisbee flies through the air. I jump restlessly up and down, beside myself with excitement as it goes from Helge to Nikko, or when they fail to catch it and the disk lies fallen to the ground. *This is what matters*, I think to myself. The three of us together. Standing in a triangle and throwing, with the peach-coloured sunset behind us.

That's how life should be, and right now that's how it is, I think to myself. I'm exultant. I stretch my arms out in the air and shout to Nikko, who laughs back.

'This is cool!' shouts Nikko.

'Cool!' I shout, my voice shrill in my head.

I get a prick of bad conscience when the thought of Fillip suddenly comes to me. I think how he, more than anybody, ought to have been here now. But if he'd been here, he'd have just thought this was daft. He'd have just sat there on the blanket and interpreted it as disloyalty when I disappeared with the others. He'd have cracked jokes about me. He'd have said how this wasn't the real me. That I wasn't really spontaneous. If Fillip had been here I'd have had to go home on an earlier ferry because he was bored. Fillip would have insisted we go to a pub. That served cheap beer. Where people were themselves. Or if not, everybody would have gone early anyway, because things would have been awkward. Tiresome.

The solution comes to me suddenly. I have to stop seeing Fillip. We can't be friends. As much as the thought sends shivers through me, I also feel a kind of pride. A freedom. It's the first time I've dumped anybody. But if things are to continue, we've *got* to split. This is my new life. I can do anything at all. I can crack this.

Helge throws the Frisbee way off course and it lands over by the lawn. Maria takes no notice of it. She's staring straight ahead of her, arms wrapped around bent knees. Staring at something out on the fjord. I wave at Helge, running towards the Frisbee and picking it up. As I reach it I skid, coming to my knees before Maria.

'My life is wild!' I whisper.

She smiles awkwardly.

'It's all so beautiful. I mean, my life has gone wild since you moved in, the last few weeks; the parties, the people, going out, Spain, your present, this barbecue, swimming, I mean everything, all together, the way people say hello to me when I go out and stuff, it's crazy to think about.'

I sit there and catch my breath.

'It's just so…'

'Wild?' concludes Maria.

'Yes!' I shout and fling my arms in the air. 'I am so happy you moved in with me, it's so wonderful… It's just so amazing…'

The boys are yelling from behind me, wanting to get on with the game. 'Stop flirting with the girls,' they shout.

Suddenly I lean over and give her a hug.

'I'm sorry,' I say and have to look down. I fidget with the Frisbee. This was all a little sudden for her perhaps.

But I just had to.

'It's fine,' she says.

I throw a glance towards Martine to see if she's been taking notice of any of this. But she's fiddling with a mobile in the crook of Anders's arm, who gets up and walks over to Helge and Nikko.

'Are you in love, or what?' shouts Nikko.

I'm on the point of saying *I like you so much* but realise it'll be a bit too stupid, a bit too much at once. I run over and throw the Frisbee as hard as I can.

'You can go and fetch that one,' says Helge to Nikko. But Nikko's already on his way over to the bonfire, with a can of beer to his lips. He slings himself down.

'Okay, okay, okay,' I say, panting, bent forwards and resting against my knees, then standing up I shout aloud, 'Woo-hoo-oo!' with my head thrown back and face turned to the sky.

Then, I run.

Like a Ghost

I couldn't ask for more: everything's perfect. I'm not checking anyone out, really; this is more than enough in one go. Sun. Water. Bonfire. Warmth. I don't have more expectations, at least not now. This is more than enough in one go. After all, I've got to begin somewhere. If this continues, I'm bound to find someone.

We are standing in a large circle, with twenty to thirty metres between us, the disk floating further and further. Then somebody prods my shoulder. It's Fillip. He staggers back a couple of steps. Fumbles after a can of beer from his pocket. Opens it with a ripping sound.

'So this is where you are. Where are the ladies?'

Nikko stands there in bewilderment and picks the Frisbee up.

But this is only the workings of my imagination. A ceaseless niggling down my spine.

Again and again.

Friends

'Maria?' I ask.

'Yes?' answers Maria.

'You are my friend, aren't you?'

'Yes,' answers Maria.

Then after a short pause she asks, 'Why?'

'Oh, nothing,'

It's fine.

The Lunch Party

A couple of days after the beach trip the city is seething with people. There's not a hint of a breeze. I saunter along the streets with my bottle of water and aching muscles, looking around as I crunch on an apple. It seems the weather's going to hold over the weekend, despite the forecast promising rain. As I spring up the stairs and let myself in, my body feels light.

Indoors, the kitchen table is covered with shopping bags, food and vegetables.

Lara kisses me on both cheeks.

'Jesus! What's happened to you then?' she asks. She has a lovely, even tan.

I shrug my shoulders and take a final munch on my apple.

'I've stopped wearing glasses.' I feel flushed just saying it and don't want to seem too full of myself. 'I've started wearing contact lenses.'

'You've got so thin! But we'll soon get you fattened up.' She cuts the plastic off a bottle of wine and passes it for me to open.

'You've got a lovely flat,' says Martine.

'Thanks,' I say and pull the cork from the bottle.

Out Just Out

We've no vanilla sauce for dessert, I'm short of beer and I feel like cigarettes and offer to run down to the shop. But when I get back, something doesn't seem right. Maria comes towards me with hurried steps and Lara stands in the living room leaning against the wall with the telephone to her ear, staring out onto the balcony. She scratches the back of her leg with the other foot nervously, then hangs up and peers over at me.

'I'm so sorry...we thought you'd locked yourself out...so Lara just opened the door.'

Then I hear that shrill, drunken voice out on the balcony.

'Who is she?' asks Maria.

It's totally silent on the balcony apart from the sound of the traffic that drifts in through the doors.

'We had to pay for her cab. She didn't have any money,' Maria whispers and half turns in towards the living room.

'Who hasn't put the toilet lid down?' the drunken voice yells. 'Didn't anyone teach you that? That it's rude not to put the seat back down? Especially with so many nice ladies around. Has Rino come?' Lara nods in the direction of the balcony and I see her bring her hand to her cheek. I close my eyes, and feel Maria relieve me of the bag and stroke my arm before going into the kitchen.

Here we go, I think to myself as I hear the stumbling footsteps crossing the doorstep on their way into the living room.

'Ri-noo!' She has bits of prawn in the corners of her mouth and blue teeth. 'I thought I'd surprise you with a bottle of wine. But you've got a house full of friends. They're going to make food for us.'

She walks bent forwards. Shoes clacking.

'What a gorgeous flat you've got! And there was me thinking you lived in some miserable bachelor bed-sit.'

She rests a hand on my arm, forcing herself into my field of vision.

'Aren't you pleased?'

I could have died.

Or killed.

The Child

Edel sits at the corner of the table and eats, acting ever-so-humble, alternating between fingers and fork. No, of course not, nobody must trouble themselves on her account. She could drink a little glass of wine, but she didn't really need any food. Although, perhaps she could be *persuaded* to eat a little. That would be lovely. But only a little, of course, and nobody should lay a place for her, if she could just have a little bit of food on a plate, so she could taste.

Edel doesn't touch the vegetables. She makes straight for the fillets.

And even before this she'd had Helge peeling prawns for her. They'd just got so difficult, you know. And between mouthfuls she chain smokes; crams a piece of food in her mouth and then immediately lights up. And the whole time she scowls at Lara, who stares grimly back at her.

Lara has asked her several times to stop smoking while everyone's eating. Edel has either failed to answer or she's mumbled, 'Yes, yes, but we are sitting outside, aren't we?'

Any attempts at conversation are stopped dead in their tracks.

'Exceptionally good lunch, I'd say.' Nikko chews and smiles, his enthusiasm following yet another uncomfortable and long silence.

'Cheers!' he adds.

Everyone lifts their glasses.

Out

I try to eat, without feeling much appetite, as I attempt to turn a deaf ear to Edel's embarrassing antics.

'Tequila!' she'd shouted suddenly, just before lunch, in the direction of the living room where Nikko and Helge were standing and talking about something.

'What?' Helge shouted back.

She rose and went over to the balcony door.

'Were you talking about tequila?'

'Huh? Tequila? No,' Helge answered.

'I just thought I heard someone mention tequila. Wouldn't say no to a glass.'

'No, I'm sure you wouldn't,' mumbled Helge in the living room.

I caught sight of Nikko slapping him on the shoulder.

Then later, when everyone was finally sitting down, she began to tell the story of some supposed girlfriend of hers, who'd come up with an appalling drinking game at company parties.

'It's not just you lads who can drink tequila, you know,' she laughed, slapping Nikko on the shoulder.

And she went on with the story about her friend and how she'd commanded all her male colleagues to lie on the floor, washed their belly buttons and then poured tequila in them.

'She what? Where?' Nikko asked. 'At the party?'

'Yes, of course. And then she climbs all over them and licks up all the tequila.'

Then Edel laughed so heartily her hair fell in front of her face, occasionally getting coughing fits before starting to laugh again.

Nikko and Helge were peeling prawns, their arms held stiffly and pulling faces.

'Licking it all up…tequila. From these blokes' navels!' Edel laughed.

And for a while it passed tolerably, or at least I succeeded in not listening. Maria chatted with Lara and I, and Edel sat on her own with Nikko and Helge.

'Have any of you girls read the paper today, then?' she asked.

'No. What about?' asked Maria.

I'd read the paper. I felt like kicking Maria's shin, but didn't. One of the headline stories was about the increase in sales of sex toys. Dildos. Edel sniggered.

But since nobody took her up on the subject, and nobody wanted to know more, she let it pass. No point talking openly about dildos, then.

'You lot don't need that, anyway, do you, you're all such pretty girls.' She drank from her glass, lit a cigarette.

'Can you wait with smoking until after we've eaten?' Lara asked.

'Aren't they pretty, Rino?' said Edel, ignoring Lara.

I nodded.

'You're all so pretty. And you,' she said, turning to Martine suddenly, 'have just such fabulous boobs!' Martine wiped her hands, smiled awkwardly and thanked her, as politely as she could.

'Really nice. Men adore boobs. I don't know why, just sacks of fat, really, aren't they. An ass on your bosom. Men just love fondling boobs. Don't ask me why. *Wow, look at that...it's a boob!'* Edel groped the air as if weighing a pair of boobs, before leaning back and staring out into thin air, across the park.

'You're awfully quiet, Rino, is something the matter?'

'No, I'm fine.'

'Were any of you at the carnival, then?' I hear Edel ask.

'What carnival?' Lara asks.

'You could have been in it, you're so pretty,' laughs Edel, placing her hand on Lara's forearm for an instant. Lara stares down at the hand. Edel almost falls off her chair as she leans back and lifts her glass to drink.

'What carnival?' repeats Lara, carefully guiding her fork into her mouth in an almost mechanical motion, her other hand resting in her lap.

'The one with all the naked people dancing.'

Martine coughs. She brings her hand up to her mouth and twists around in her chair, leaning towards the edge of the balcony. I presume she's trying to hide that she's laughing.

'Ask Rino, he was there, he'll remember what it was called.'

'I know the one. But I wasn't there,' Lara says quietly. She's stopped eating. She sits with her hands in her lap. Lifts her napkin to wipe her mouth. Takes a careful sip of wine.

Then nobody says anything for some time. Nikko and Helge start to clear the plates. Edel pushes herself even further out from the table, and ends up sitting completely alone, practically up in the corner, blinking. Sitting with one leg crossed over the other and her body bent forwards over her knees. Edel's tongue works frenetically at getting a little piece of meat from between her teeth.

'They're lovely girls you've got here,' she says without anyone seeming to pay any attention.

Edel sits as if she's in a trance, her head bobbing, body slumped forwards.

'Shall we order you a cab?' Martine asks after a while.

'No, no.' Edel sits up straight, her eyes wandering wildly and taking a deep swig from her glass.

Helge comes out of the kitchen with oven gloves and puts an ovenproof dish on the table, followed by Nikko, who leans over with a tablemat for it.

'Do you want us to order you a cab?' Nikko asks.

'She hasn't got any money anyway,' Martine whispers.

'Lissen, I'm not gaun in no fikken cab!' Edel barks, knocking back the last of her red wine.

Everybody exchanges looks. Shivers descend my spine. Either she's possessed or else Edel's managed to keep that accent under wraps: I've never actually asked her where she comes from. Martine stands leaning over the edge of balcony, her back quivering.

Nikko and Helge stick a spoon into the pie-like dessert and announce that it's served. The smell of apples wafts across the balcony. Edel comes to. She drags her chair back up to the table again.

'Dessert?' she asks.

Edel eats like a little child. With the excuse of the pie being so crumbly, she eats with her fingers, and she has sauce on her face. When she tries to wipe it off with the back of her hand, she merely spreads it further across her face.

'So yummy,' she mumbles.

More than anything I feel like crying. Maria has patted me on the thigh a couple of times and squeezed my hand. 'If you want, you can just chuck her out,' she said. And while Edel was in the toilet, Lara stroked my back and told me I mustn't be too kind.

'Hoo's choried me wine?' Edel hissed when she got back to find the bottle empty. Instead of waiting for a reply, she helped herself from Maria's bottle.

But on my return from the toilet, Edel's sitting as if she was short sighted, her plate right up to her face, guiding the crumbs to her mouth in her fingertips. It's quieter than ever, sounds rising from the street below. And everybody sits round the table, all synchronised with their faces turned away from her. Martine leans her cheek in her hand, her face hidden behind her fingers. Lara barely picks at her food, while

Nikko has simply decided to wolf his down and is sitting, leaning back, smoking. I allow my gaze to travel over them without making eye contact with anyone. Maria's sitting on her hands, staring into her plate.

'We might have had a child together. Has he told you that?' slurs Edel as she smacks her lips gleefully with a mouthful of cake and vanilla sauce.

Like a great wave through my body, it vibrates, starting in my ankles and moving up through my legs. I stand up with my mouth open wide: 'GET OUT!' I scream. And as I get up the table comes with me. Glasses overturn and there's a clatter of cutlery.

'I'm asking you, please, just go!'

At first it appears Edel doesn't understand that the request is directed at her. She stares straight ahead, as if she's waiting for some peripheral row amongst her hosts to settle. It has nothing to do with her. She takes another gulp of wine with heavy eyelids, then glares up at me.

'Well, isn't he the charming one, suddenly.'

'We never had a relationship. She's lying. She's lying!' I repeat.

'Do you all find Rino charming, too?'

Nobody says a thing. Lara rubs the tips of her fingers against her thumb on one hand, before finally putting it under the table to join the other. She views Edel with an irritated raised eyebrow, then stares down into the table. Nikko rests his chin on *one* index finger, drumming on his wineglass.

'I think you should stop, now,' says Lara sternly.

'You'd never have lived here if it wasn't such a smart flat.' Edel looks sternly back at Lara.

'Actually, it's me who...' Maria begins.

'I've no idea what you're talking about. I'm just a guest here. Like *you*,' says Lara, folding her arms.

'Easy for you to say, when you're so pretty. I'll leave you in peace, Rino, with your lovely ladies. No one's exactly friendly round here anyway. I know when I'm not welcome.'

Her handbag opens as she goes to a grab it, and out of it tumble her make-up, sanitary towels, notebooks, her address book, banknotes. She kneels down and scoops them all up.

Edel has money.

For a cab.

Intercom

At first it seems that the flat is in total silence. I stand leaning against the front door, my eyes closed. Edel's footsteps have long since vanished from the stairwell. Everyone's out on the balcony. I stand here. And nobody says anything. It seems everything is silent, but then the sound of the Stina Nordenstam CD fills the room.

And just as I open my eyes and think that it's over at last, the intercom buzzes abruptly right next to my head.

For a while I stand holding my hands over the bell. When it doesn't appear to let up, but rather transforms into one long endless wailing, I shut the door into the living room. Maria just manages to poke her head round to see, but turns without expression and walks towards the balcony as the door swings to.

'Yes?' I say.

'You're a rat, Rino, you are so fucking low, d'you know that? And I'll be having words with a few people, just so you know.'

'Just go,' I whisper.

She hangs up.

'Men are so fucking gullible,' she says when she calls up again. 'D'you know why? Because you are so fucking vain.'

'I'll call the police,' I say.

'Yeah, go ahead. Then I can tell them a few things.' She gasps for air. 'How does it feel to be a rapist, Rino?'

'What?'

'Huh? Just send them down here, go on, and I'll tell them what you've done to me. Use and dispose.' She hisses scornfully into the intercom.

I clamp my hand over the speaker till the blood vanishes from the edges of my fingers.

Some Things Last for Ages

The flat is calm. I've been lying on my stomach in bed, only getting up for something to drink, listening to Lara and Maria's voices as they move around the flat, tidying, chatting and eating. Martine, Nikko and Helge have eventually taken a trip down to town.

There's a knock on the door.

Lara comes in first. She sits down on the edge of the bed with one leg tucked under her. She gives my neck a rub.

'How's it going?' she asks.

I sigh heavily and raise my hand as if about to say something, but there's nothing to say.

'Hey, Rino, wouldn't you like to sit together with me and Maria before we go out? D'you want to come with us? You can come too, if you feel like it. If you want. And you feel up to it.'

Maria comes in, but says nothing.

'Everything's fine,' I say. 'It doesn't bother me that much, you know. I'm not exactly going to top myself,' I laugh.

But they don't laugh.

'You've got to stop that now,' Lara says with firmness. 'Now come with me.'

She takes my hand and leads me into the living room. I'm reluctant at first, I feel it's kind of important to make it clear I'm not completely helpless.

'Sit down,' she says. 'What'll you have to drink?'

Lara's warm body under my head. Her fingers in my hair, and my feet tucked into the crooks of Maria's knees. So many sounds, from outside and inside: Lara's breathing, her stomach rumbling, the soft, warm fabric against my ear, slow stroking of her hand back and forth over my cheek; fingertips, back of hand, fingertips. Then she stops and drinks a little, before starting over again.

'Are you asleep?' asks Maria.

I don't answer.

'His hair's nice. It suits him with his hair combed back,' says Lara. 'It smells nice.' She sniffs me. It tickles.

'Come on,' says Maria, 'or it'll end up like last time.' She laughs. I feel soft fingers stroking my hair, the lights are turned off, the CD plays itself to the end in the player. I lie there, feeling the warmth vanish from the cushion. Laughter in the stairwell.

A last sigh, and I am far away.

Rohypnol

My head's reeling. It takes effort to hold it up. I don't know how long I've been asleep on the sofa, my T-shirt and underpants are soaked through with sweat. It trickles down over my back as I sit up.

I pick up the phone.

'Can you come and fetch me?' she asks.

'Where are you' I ask.

'In the toilet.'

'Yes, but *where?*'

'I tried to phone Lara, but she's not answering. I think he put something in my drink, but I puked it up.'

'Just tell me *where* you are, and I'll come and get you,' I say.

The Doorman

I'm nauseous, everything's spinning as I tie my shoelaces, I have to go into the kitchen to splash cold water on my face. I cup my hands and gulp down as much water as I can before staggering down the stairs and out into the street, where I run so fast that now and again my upper body lurches ahead. I run non-stop down the road, straight to the queue that I squeeze past to get to the doorman. The sweat pours off me. 'I've got to get in, it's an emergency,' I try to say as quietly and calmly as I can.

'You got a stamp, mate?' the doorman asks.

'What d'you mean, stamp?' I ask.

'You'll have to queue up like the others.' He steps out onto the pavement.

A sporadic laughter ripples through the queue.

'Please,' I say, 'it's an emergency.'

'You look in a bit of a sweat, mate, perhaps you should take a walk round the block.' He presses four fingers against my ribcage.

'But I know…what's his name…' I try to remember the name of the guy who's always handing me leaflets.

'Look, mate. It's no good. You get to the back of the queue or come another day. But to be honest, I can't see you gettin' in 'ere tonight.' He looks at his watch. 'It's closin' time soon, anyway.'

The giggling in the queue gives way to an expectant, tense silence.

The doorman shoves me two steps out onto the pavement.

He beckons another doorman over. He's not my size either.

'Okay!' I bark. 'My little sister's in there, she's half-cut and underage, and if you don't call the police, I will. Whatever happens, I'm going in there in one minute.' A bloke shouts towards us from the queue. 'YEAH!' he shouts, clapping his hands together: '*Action!*' A pair of giggling friends try to hush him.

The doorman spits a lump of chewing gum into his hand, rolls it in his palm for a few seconds before tossing it behind him.

With my heart pounding I prepare to plough straight through him.

He looks pensively down the street, avoiding my gaze.

'OK, this way,' he says quietly.

Inside

It's over in a minute, seconds: with the doorman behind me I squeeze through the smoke-filled venue. 'Can you see her anywhere?' the doorman repeats every ten seconds. It's crammed, I plough through the crowds, then I see her with her back against the wall at the furthest end of the venue, handbag in front of her and Håkon leaning in next to her. 'We're going back to my place,' he keeps telling her. I grab Maria's arm and drag her after me. 'Oh, come on!' says Håkon behind me.

'I have to go home,' says Maria without looking up.

'Well, well, well, it's Maria!' laughs the doorman. We're out.

'Can you walk?' I ask when we've got further up the street.

'Course I can,' she answers, and I let go of her.

'I was just thinking we could get a cab,' I say.

'Oh, right,' she answers, 'no, it's nice to get a bit of fresh air.'

She gives a quick glance behind her, takes two steps. And with something that sounds like a fit of coughing she starts to cry, snuggling close to me and pressing her forehead against my chest.

I catch her handbag just before it meets the ground.

Sleep

The sweat pours off me. In the bathroom I wrench my sticky clothes off and turn the shower on. Only now do I begin to feel the effects of the ordeal on my legs and throat, my hot, swollen feet stinging against the tiles. A horrible, faint nausea tingling in my throat like shockwaves from the tension.

As the shampoo runs out of my hair, I hear Maria come in. She sits on the toilet, gets up and washes her hands before removing her make-up.

'Are you finished?' she asks, squeezing water out of a ball of cotton wool.

'Almost,' I answer.

Maria unhooks her bra and pulls her knickers down over her thighs, steps out of them and puts them on the washing machine. She leans over the sink to take her lenses out. I stand there and wait for her to put something on as I let the warm water run onto the back of my neck, peering out into the room from under my arm. She's slow and slightly clumsy in her movements. Strokes herself under her breasts as she brushes her teeth, takes a hairgrip out of her hair.

Almost simultaneously to my taking a step back with my towel to dry myself, Maria pulls the curtain aside and slides in front of me with her head bowed. Her stomach brushes against my arm, she turns the shower back on.

Maria smoothes her wet hair back with her hands. Broad cascades of water tumble down her back, following the furrow down the length of her spine, out to each side where the water seems to liberate itself over her goose-pimply skin. She presses her shoulder blades back, and lowers them.

Maria lifts a foot up behind her and, supporting herself against the wall, cleans between her toes with her fingers. She lowers her foot again and then repeats the action with her other foot. As she puts her foot down, she slips back and her smooth, wet ass brushes against my dick. My dick is standing straight out.

'Oops,' she laughs, stepping back under the spray, cupping her hands in front of her face.

'Was it nice having a shower?' she asks.

'Yes.'

'Are you going to stay up a while?'

'I don't know.'

'OK.'

On my way out of the shower I bump into her again. Her wet body slides in front of me as I bend down.

Her back.

Her ass.

Her thigh.

Against my chest. Dick. Thigh.

Virginity's Got a Twisted Mind

In my bedroom I change into my pyjamas, put some deodorant and aftershave on. Then I eat a slice of bread with some cheese and turkey slices. Maria comes in, holding a glass of drinking yoghurt. She sits in the chair and for a moment it looks as if she might fall asleep. Head nodding. She straightens herself and squints round.

'Everything all right?' I ask.

'Fine,' she answers, opening her eyes again and getting up to rinse her glass. On her way out of the room she switches the light off, and for a couple of seconds I sit there in darkness until she returns and flicks the switch back on.

'Whoops,' she says.

I brush the crumbs from my plate, put it in the dishwasher and go to bed. Her mobile rings in the living room. I lie there listening for her steps to see if she'll answer. It rings to the end.

A text bleeps.

Then it rings again.

I lie there fiddling with the flex of my bedside lamp. I am tranquil. The whole experience has left me feeling tranquil in some way, yet at the same time uneasy, maybe at the sight of Maria. I savour the memory of her in the shower, it feels somehow real, pure. I could look at her, it was allowed, it didn't feel stolen, like usual. And not like looking at a film either, where it's been bought.

I feel no shame.

But my body's itching, as if the bedclothes are strangling me. I get up. I scratch. Take off my pyjamas. I don't want to sleep. I don't want to wank. Perhaps I'll read a book. Or something. I go back to bed with a comic book and the duvet half covering me.

Maria gets up again. Her steps wander through the flat to the bathroom, to the kitchen, then she appears in my doorway, her duvet round her.

'Are you awake?' she asks.

'Yes,' I answer.

'Can I sleep in here?'

'Sure,' I clear my throat.

'I'd rather not sleep alone,' she whispers. 'I've no idea what I've had down me.'

'That's no problem,' I say, turning a page in my comic magazine.

Maria throws her duvet in and goes back to fetch a pillow. I make room in the bed, moving to one side of the mattress, tucking my duvet closer. Shoving her pillow ahead of her, she glides onto the bed. She lets out a sigh. She shudders and cries some more.

'I am so incredibly tired,' she says. 'Wake me if I breathe too heavily, or if I stop.' She turns her head towards me. 'And, listen…thank you so-so-so much for coming to rescue me.'

'You're nice,' she whispers. 'You're great.'

I read further into the series, with little concentration, turn, and then ask, 'Shall I turn the light off?'

Then it occurs to me: 'Do you want me to put some clothes on?'

She doesn't answer.

'Maria,' I ask, 'are you asleep?'

She doesn't answer.

Fat Sparrows Don't Fly

After a while I turn the lights off. Maria is breathing deeply, but evenly. So as not to fall out when I'm asleep, I nudge myself a little further into the bed; I think I've exaggerated the distance somewhat. I wrench the pillow into place under my head and turn onto my stomach.

My dick swells beneath me, squeezed between mattress and body.

I bend my knee up under me and feel a pocket of warmth, warm bedclothes. At first I think my knee's slipped under her duvet, but it's her who has pushed her legs under mine.

I'm lying there, Maria's shins close against my knees.

I've got a lump in my throat. I've never lain like this before. Not like this. It feels as though I'm about to cry. And I stretch my hand out to stroke her hair, only to pull it back quickly. It feels like the briefest moment, when I just nod off and wake again with an aching dick beneath me. The sun's risen and the flat is drenched in heat. Maria is still lying there sleeping on her side, tangled in her duvet, half in and half out.

My dick brushes against warm, soft skin. When I lift my head I see that Maria's nightgown lies crumpled around her naked hips.

She doesn't answer when I say her name.

I breathe out, try to breathe in, but it's as though my chest is locked. I open the window, twist and turn in my sheets. My dick reminds me of an overripe fruit, as if the delicate skin on its head is about to burst from the pressure within, like a fermented plum.

It's like I'm on remote control. Blood, chemistry, everything surging through my body, pumping and pressing against throat and temples, my hands vibrating and my thighs trembling.

First, I think I might just wank. I push myself right over to the edge of the mattress, and a little bit down so as to get the best view I can, and put my hand out to catch my load. But something in me stops.

I heave my way over. Lay the duvet over me and her, lie right up close. First I let my dick rest in the cleft between her buttocks, then bending it, I guide it up between her legs.

I am inside her.

I slip right in, without resistance. She is moist and warm.

I stay like this, completely silent, breathing, listening for Maria's breathing, with the head of my dick just inside her opening.

At the same time I realise that this isn't going to work.

And yet, I try: I lay my hands on her soft hips, squeezing my hand in beneath her, I grab her and pull her onto me, shoving against her ass and force myself deep inside.

Only two or three more thrusts, and I'd cum; there's nothing in the whole world that I want more (everyone else gets to cum, apart from me, I've been denied it my whole life, it feels so unfair, and now it is right there, in front of me, a little more, and it's done). Still, I pull out, put everything in place, and lift the duvet back over her.

Cunt

If I have to explain my actions tomorrow, I don't know if she'll understand. It smells of her, from my dick and up to my stomach there's a moist, smooth stripe from her. And it tastes of her when I put my fingers in my mouth: I stand in the bathroom with my dick pointed at the plughole in the sink, and all I'm really thinking is that I've got cunt on my dick, cunt on my dick, cunt on my dick, *cunt on my dick.*

Love

Recently, I've been pretty content, actually. I have some difficulty looking people in the eye, it's always there, the depths have been reached. But I'm on my way up again now. In fact, I have a notion that my experience with Maria might represent some sort of move forwards.

I fluctuate from not having any conscience and giving it not the slightest thought, to my conscience suddenly pricking again. I don't know how I'll live with it: it's an insane thing to have done. Even if she were to forgive me, there's no certainty she'd want to continue living here.

Yet it's clear she suspects nothing. She's not suffering as a result. She'll have no lasting effects, so long as nobody says anything. And that's what makes it possible to carry on. Sometimes I'm about to say it. For a split second I'll almost believe that she'd forgive me if I did.

But the fact is that it was, perhaps, in a technical sense, rape.

And there is no way I can justify that. What I did to Maria that night is the most insane, desperate thing I've done. It's one thing to fantasise about it. Another to try.

It's like beginning over again. Everything's been overturned. My first reaction was to chuck her out, terminate the contract, be done with it, without explanation and without considering what she might do. Whether she's going to travel or going to stay. But the last few weeks have been the best since she moved in. I've understood that there's something fundamentally wrong with me, and that the things that are wrong are quite different to what I once thought they were.

It's as if something inside me has been woken. Like getting a pair of glasses, new eyes: I see people, I see myself. And I'm not boring, either.

Not in the least. I've been a ticking bomb. And it's not that it was love. I'm not even in love with Maria. Not with Lara either, for that matter. How it would have turned out if I'd been in love, I dare not think.

I'm just lonely. I've missed out so much on life.

If she had the slightest suspicion, if she were to ask, I'd be ready to tell her everything, I'd admit everything, I'd just have to. If, for example, I'd given her a sexually transmitted disease.

Which isn't very likely.

Another thing may be that *she* could have infected me with something.

For now, I say nothing.

Because there's no way of me putting everything to rights.

So I don't try to put everything to rights.

The following day, things continued as normal. She got up, made a few calls which hopefully might lead to consequences for Håkon, and spent the day relaxing.

'Yeah, I know, but perhaps you didn't really need to be *so* dramatic,' was Maria's commentary on the way I'd gone in to fetch her. And then she apologised that perhaps she'd *invaded* me in the shower.

'But I was so out of it, and I do know you, kind of, it just felt so natural, *in the moment,* you know…'

And it wasn't the first time she'd shared a shower with a friend, anyway.

'I'm actually really used to it, with other people, but you really have to say something next time if it bothers you, I can take it, you know.'

And she dashed out.

The Funeral

Oddly enough, it's Dad who tells me. He rings to invite me to his annual barbecue, and by chance, before he hangs up, he asks me if I remember Fillip who used to work for him. Without bothering to tell him about the contact we've had recently, I just answer that I do. Then Dad tells me that Fillip has been found dead in his flat.

Even then I don't open my mouth.

Dad explains they think Fillip had been lying there a while. He was found lying on his stomach in the sofa. It was his heart or maybe a stroke. And the funeral's already been.

A few days later I stand at his grave with a bouquet of flowers in one hand and a plastic bag with food for Dad's barbecue in the other. The grave looks fresh. What's most eye catching are all the wreaths: it's clear that in one way or another, Fillip has managed to achieve what I have not. I push my bouquet in amongst the wreaths and the flowers.

Dearest son.

My good friend.

Dad.

Fillip has, if nothing else, been loved. By many. People have cared about him. Perhaps I'm a little jealous. And a bit relieved. Apart from that, I feel almost nothing. Here lies perhaps the only friend I ever had, and all I can do is feel pity for myself. I have no friends. I had one friend, but I couldn't go on being his friend. Because it held me back from making friends.

It doesn't give me a bad conscience.

Not at all.

It's just sad.

Life

At the barbecue, Dad's friends make a fantastic flap and fuss about why my new girlfriend isn't with me. At first I don't understand what they're going on about, but then I realise that they're talking about Maria. And once I've dashed everyone's expectations by revealing that there is no girlfriend, hardly anybody bothers asking me about anything more. I feel dopey from all the meat and cheap beer, and end up sitting alone imagining all these people at my funeral.

They'd have to talk about everything else but me.

I doze off. Dad suggests I lie down in my old room, but I can't stand being here, so he drives me to the train station.

I sleep and am woken by my head bumping against the compartment window. I'm sitting facing the wrong direction, and being dragged backwards through the landscape, and everything I see, all the little snippets of the lives outside, shake me almost to the core: a father with his son and daughter tidying their sailboat, a bloke in sandals standing on a stool, a screwdriver in hand and nails stuck in his mouth, fastening some contraption onto the house wall while his wife props him up by leaning her back against his backside. About to lose balance herself, she hides her laughing face by looking down, when she spots us on the train below looking at her. Two teenagers snog at the back of my carriage. A red barn at the top of the hill behind the field, a tractor, a new Volvo driving in under the railway bridge and gliding further and further into the distance.

Like an infinite commercial for all the things I really want for myself.

Life.

Blue

'I don't understand fucking shit,' begins Maria just as I take a large gulp of coffee. Even though the coffee's scalding, I try hard to maintain a passive, yet at the same time suitably interested expression. It's too hot to swallow and too difficult to spit out: I feel my gums blister.

I *have* seen the pregnancy test.

And the previous ones she's thrown in the bin over the past few days.

I know what she is about to say.

'How the hell is it possible?' she carries on. And then, 'I can't go through yet another abortion!'

Then she gets up from the kitchen chair and darts across the room to the bin, and lifts out the test, just as I did ten minutes ago when I heard her puking in the bathroom, checking one last time that it's positive. She shakes it twice and taps it with a gloomy expression before flinging the test back into the bin.

'I haven't slept with a living soul since I had my last period! I really don't understand shit.'

'Oh?'

'Yeah, I haven't had my period for ages, half the time they're so light anyway, sometimes non-existent, and since I haven't had much sex, I really haven't thought about it.'

Maria gets up from the table and brushes the crumbs off her plate. She starts to put the food away, but changes her mind, cuts three huge hunks of bread and goes back to the fridge and begins taking all the food out again.

There's a card from Edel on the fridge door that Maria put there when I showed it to her.

You've got some big problems, little man. I am so deeply offended I never want to see you again.

And on the front: 'Get well soon!'

'You're a cheap, cheap lady,' Maria whistles to herself.

Then she stands there in silence, paralysed, the milk carton held hori-
zontally in front of her for some twenty seconds before she dashes into
the bathroom to throw up.

I am going to be a dad.

I just don't quite know how I'll break the wonderful news.

Plump

Later that afternoon I hear the doorbell ring, and not long after Maria
opens the door of my room to tell me she's ordered a set meal from
China Express, and I should help myself. She sits in her underwear
with a blanket round her waist, shovelling her food down with chop-
sticks, her cheeks flushed, and complaining incessantly about the heat.

After the food we sit on the sofa in front of the TV with not much to say
when suddenly she starts laughing. 'Ah, I get it now...' is all she says before
she goes quiet again. Then she bursts into laughter and waves her hand in
front of her face, leading me to conclude that my feet pong or something.

'What is it?' I venture.

'Oh, nothing,' she laughs.

'Really?'

'No, I can't say. You'd be so pissed off.'

Now I'm certain I pong. That it's something about me.

'Well, I've just realised how… No, it's nothing.'

I shift my feet.

'You know, Lara?'

Yeahyeahyeahyeahyeah.

'Yeah, sure,' I say.

'You know what?' she asks, eyes wide.

'Well?'

'Well, I couldn't understand till now, because I've only had sex with girls lately.' Maria pauses and smiles as she tries not to look too smug about saying such a thing. I wish it were me.

'Apart from this guy *I sucked off*, of course. But otherwise I've kept my vow of celibacy. But Lara told me she tried telling you this when you went out. That was the main reason she went out with you, probably. Well, not *just* that, obviously, don't get me wrong.' Maria laughs and rests her hand on my knee.

The hairs rise on the back of my neck.

'OK, this is going to be a touch tricky…' Maria's twists her mouth and makes a smacking sound. She half-sits, tucking a foot under one knee.

'Lara was going to stay over with me after the party, when you were snogging each other. You *were* snogging each other, weren't you? So it didn't come totally out of the blue. Did it? That does show there was something going on before we found you in the shower.' Maria leans forward and locks my gaze, her eyebrows arched. 'So when we got you into your bedroom and started taking your clothes off, she couldn't help herself, you see. Well, she seems really proper perhaps, but… Well, we lie you on your bed and take all the rest of your clothes off, because you're soaking wet. She's totally off the wall, so she grabs hold of your willy. She says she's *got* to have a feel. She's never seen such a huge willy before. And she's pissed, isn't she, so she kind of kneads it…and says something or other. But then…'

Maria scratches her nose and laughs.

'Then all of a sudden you sit up, and you grab her by the shoulder and mumble something totally incomprehensible. Lara's in shock, sort of, but instead of letting go, she holds on even tighter. Maybe because she's scared. And then it just cums. Masses of it.'

I say nothing. Maria presses her face into a cushion. She rocks her body back and forth.

'But does that mean…?'

'I don't know, but it was *everywhere*… Over her arms. Her dress. I hardly knew it was possible for there to be so much. And Lara panicked and went stumbling about.' Maria sits with one hand tucked under her armpit as she rests her head, hiding her face with the other. 'And there was so much. There just seemed to be no end to it.'

'But does that mean, do you really think I'm responsible?'

Her laughter trails off.

'Well, yeah. And it must have run down on the toilet seat when we were in the bathroom, 'cause Lara had to change afterwards and I nearly pissed myself with laughing so much. And then she fell on top of me, and she had it all over her, on her dress and her hands when she tried to get up, and it was just *totally* out of control, because she just lay there laughing, completely hysterical. But I remember that it was sticky when I sat down on the toilet seat, and that we thought it could look like, well, you know, like *sperm*. But then I just forgot about it.'

'Do you really believe that?' I ask.

'Yeah, maybe, what do you think? It *might* have happened. At least you've got another one to add to your questionnaire.'

'You what?'

'Oh, nothing.'

'Some *monster* you've got down there,' I hear her say quietly to herself. 'Lara's suggested she could adopt the baby. She's dead jealous, she doesn't talk about anything else except having a baby; it'd be completely perfect for her. Just not for me. Anyhow, my tits'll be really nice.'

'Oh, yeah?'

'I think so. But then after a bit I'll probably end up getting really fat too.'

Maria tucks her feet under her. Sighs.

The Jacket

In the evening I tidy around the flat, throw away old newspapers and magazines. There are some cardboard boxes in the hall cupboard I think Maria might want for packing. I pull them out, noticing a slightly musty, penetrating odour. Old. The worn out, coarse fibres of my old jacket, as it hangs there limply on its hanger. It annoys me that I've not noticed it before. That it took me so long.

It smells strange. So this is what I've smelled like to other people. I laugh quietly to myself, suddenly realising the impression we must have made. The jacket. And I.

But this isn't me. This isn't me any longer.

So long as I never need to return to the old me.

I stand for a moment stroking the sleeve between my thumb and index finger. Then I kick the cardboard box out into the hallway.

It isn't me.

Lara

The phone rings. I take it. It is completely silent at the other end.

'Hello?' I repeat.

'Hi, Rino,' she says after a while.

Shivers descend my spine

'Oh, hi,' I say.

'How are you doing?' she asks.

'So so,' I say. 'A friend of mine died.'

I feel a stab inside me, it's a pretty low-down card to play. Whether it helps or not, I know what's coming anyway.

'I know,' she says, 'condolences. But, Rino...'

'Yes,' I say.

'Don't do it again.

'(...)'

'I understand you must have felt hurt and hard done by, you've had good enough reason for that.'

'Oh?'

'But just don't do it again. Do you understand?'

'Yes.'

'Good. Anyway, we'll talk later in the week and forget all about this. All right?'

'Yes,' I say.

'Great,' she says.

Quasimodo

I hear Maria throwing up in the bathroom. And perhaps some people might think I ought to be dead chuffed: after all, I've succeeded in spreading my genes, fulfilled my biological function, the true meaning of all existence, the thing which is, after all, the reason for our being equipped with these urges. But if I'm entirely meaningless, that somehow makes whoever, he or she, that might perhaps be making their way into this world, entirely meaningless too.

Perhaps it would have felt better if I'd been in love. Really in love. Like Beauty and the Beast. If I were obsessed with her. Really in love. As if everything around us were a test, and the only way to have her would be to *take* her: and I'd bear her on my shoulders as a whole village looked on, carrying lit torches. Like sleeping in each others' arms. Something more than mere release.

But that's not how it is.

If that's how it had been, she'd have wanted me too. That would have been a love beyond all bounds. And all I've been concerned with is just to do *it*. To go to bed with someone. To finally jab it in. Screw somebody.

I am superficial. Maria's sweet. But she's superficial too.

Thus far I've never felt love. Not for anyone. Not even for myself. Perhaps I won't ever feel love. Just this sick, sick desire.

I want to love.

Not just be some old mongrel that gets to jab it in. If I'm in love with anybody, it has to be Gry from Mucho Mas. But how the hell would I know, I don't even know her.

Maria's going to move out. And with that, all the things that are hers: the friends, the trips to the beach, all the things that have suddenly been opened up for me over the last months.

And I'll be left here.

Everything will be like it was before.

And it's my own fault.

It Happens

I lie half asleep most of the day without the will to get out of bed, listening to the phone ring. Incessantly. It might have been work, and then I wouldn't have answered anyway. But it isn't.

Only after a long shower, coffee and breakfast do I finally dare to pick it up.

'Hello. It's Maria's father. Is Maria there?'

'Oh, hi there,' I answer.

'Is Maria there?'

'I don't know. I've just got back,' I lie in a high-pitched tone. 'Hang on a bit, I'll have a look.'

I walk across to the living room wall and knock twice.

'Maria...?' I shout. 'Maria?'

After waiting suitably long, I lift the receiver.

'I'm sorry, she's not at home. Can I take a message?'

'Maria is pregnant,' says Maria's father.

'(...)'

'She might not dare answer the phone.'

'(...)'

'Could you ask Maria to phone her mother?'

'(...)'

'Tell her that her mother's very worried, but that everything will work out fine.'

Before I get to say anything, he's hung up.

Home

I am still standing with the phone in my hand when Maria lets herself in. She pushes the front door open with her foot and staggers in carrying two overfilled plastic bags. Her shoulder bag slips down her arm, she struggles to keep balance, and then she lets everything drop and sinks down onto the bench in the hallway.

'F-u-c-k,' she moans, head bowed and eyes closed.

She's looking bloated, I can see it now: she's put weight on, her boobs have grown and she's got a double chin. When she lies on an angle she gets two dimples on her bosom, and the underside of her chin lies in a little roll of fat over the point of her chin.

Not knowing what else to do, I go out into the kitchen to get a glass of water.

'I'm so stupid,' she wails. 'It's only just hit me now.'

'What has?' It's all going to come out now, I think, she's finally made the connection.

'I even went to the doctor today.'

'And...?'

'But I am so fucking stupid. I went to the doctor and she tells me that I'm not that far gone at all, and I've even bought new clothes because the ones I've got now aren't going to fit much longer. And then I go to the travel agency to pick up the tickets, and everything's going fine until I'm about to pay. Then it hits me.'

'What?' I crouch down with the glass of water in front of me.

'That I'm pregnant.'

'Oh, I see.'

'I was about to swipe my card and everything, and I haven't told the girl I'm travelling with or anything, then it suddenly hit me, and I had to cancel. I suddenly realised that I couldn't travel, and then the guy at the travel agency said that I still had to pay the deposit, and then I got incredibly pissed off and made a scene, and then they said I'd have to take it up with the insurance company, and so I just walked out.' She looks up.

'I've bought loads of food.'

She takes the glass of water at last.

'I need someone to hold me. Can you please hold me?' Maria looks up at me with big, moist eyes. She's got threads of spit between her lips, and I have never been closer to telling her the truth.

Maria puts her glass down on the chest of drawers, I lurch forward and she puts her arms around me.

'This is such a cliché: just when I finally move away from home.' She sobs into my neck. 'You are so good,' she says. She stretches herself, and presses me between her breasts.

'Your father called,' I say after a pause and notice my knees are starting to ache.

'I know,' she sobs, 'we think it's best I move back home.'

We.

Then she cries even more.

I have to get out.

Run.

Love

After finishing my run, I weigh myself and see I've lost another two kilos. And I'm not deluding myself either; I measure my progress at the same time and after the same sessions each time. It's not just sweat. When I stood here last, following a similar session, I weighed roughly two kilos more.

Maria, on the other hand, is lying in front of the TV, with cake crumbs on her stomach and a tub of Häagen Dazs on the table with a spoon in it. It's as if she's swelling by the hour, growing rounder and rounder.

'Is everything OK?' I ask, holding my arms behind my back to stretch my triceps.

'Listen, I won't be moving out straight away, you know,' she says, indicating the cardboard boxes I've put in front of her bedroom door. She grins, with food stuck between her front teeth.

'Oh right, I just thought…' I say vaguely.

Maria smiles wryly, looks at me and shoves the spoon into her mouth. And I feel a sense of unbelievable happiness bubbling up inside. I march across the room and gather the boxes up.

'Can't you come and sit here for a bit?' she asks. 'I don't want to be alone now, I need some warmth, I need to be held…have some physical contact.'

'Of course,' I answer, suddenly not quite knowing where to put the boxes. I almost put them straight down, but then I decide to go out and throw them back into the cupboard, and fetch myself a glass of apple juice. Maria shouts from the living room that I'll need to bring a bowl if I want some ice cream.

'What are you watching?' I ask and sit down.

'*Copland.*' Maria tucks her feet under my thighs.

After a while I notice Maria drift closer and closer. As I shove big spoonfuls of ice cream into my mouth, I feel her feet move around me, her calves against the small of my back, her fingers circling my vertebrae playfully.

'Lie down on your side,' she whispers, shifting me onto my side, my head lying in her lap.

'What kind of ice cream is this?' I ask.

'Look on the tub,' she answers.

I look on the tub. Strawberry Cheesecake.

'Oh, right,' I say.

'You dumbo,' she laughs.

Then Maria turns my face towards her, bends down and kisses me. I just manage to swallow the ice cream in my mouth. Her lips are soft and cold. As she sits up again, I close my eyes.

The television hums in the background. Apart from that, it's amazingly peaceful in the flat. Maria opens her robe and twines her legs about me. We go on lying there, kissing as she strokes my hair, neck, chest and waist, strokes her cheek against mine.

After a while she gets up and goes into the bathroom. When she comes back, she stands in front of me and takes my hand. She wants me to follow. But I remain lying there, my arm covering my face, blood pumping and pumping through my body.

'Is there something wrong?' she asks.

I don't know what to do. I've never done this before, not like this.

'No, nothing,' I whisper, trying to gather myself.

'Come on,' she says, smiling, 'it's only sex.'